D0955594

STYX

BAVO DHOOGE
with Josh Pachter

SIMON451

New York London Toronto Sydney New Delhi

 **SIMON**451

An Imprint of Simon & Schuster
1230 Avenue of the Americas
New York, NY 10020

This book is a work of fiction. Any references to historical events,
real people, or real places are used fictitiously. Other names, characters,
places, and events are products of the authors' imaginations, and any resemblance
to actual events or places or persons, living or dead, is entirely coincidental.

Copyright © 2014 by Houtekiet and Bavo Dhooge
English language translation copyright © 2015 by Bavo Dhooge and Josh Pachter.
Originally published in 2014 in Flemish/Dutch by VBK Houtekiet of Antwerp,
Belgium, as *Styx* by Bavo Dhooge. Published by agreement with the authors and
VBK Houtekiet.

All rights reserved, including the right to reproduce this book or
portions thereof in any form whatsoever. For information address
Simon & Schuster Subsidiary Rights Department,
1230 Avenue of the Americas, New York, NY 10020.

First Simon451 hardcover edition November 2015

SIMON & SCHUSTER and colophon are registered trademarks of
Simon & Schuster, Inc.

For information about special discounts for bulk purchases,
please contact Simon & Schuster Special Sales at 1-866-506-1949
or business@simonandschuster.com

The Simon & Schuster Speakers Bureau can bring authors to your
live event. For more information or to book an event contact the
Simon & Schuster Speakers Bureau at 1-866-248-3049 or visit
our website at www.simonspeakers.com

Interior design by Lewelin Polanco

Manufactured in the United States of America

10 9 8 7 6 5 4 3 2 1

Library of Congress Cataloging-in-Publication Data is available.

ISBN 978-1-4767-8464-9
ISBN 978-1-4767-8466-3 (ebook)

The dead might as well try to speak to the living as the old to the young.

—WILLA CATHER (1873–1947)

I had a dream, which was not all a dream.
The bright sun was extinguish'd, and the stars
Did wander darkling in the eternal space,
Rayless, and pathless, and the icy earth
Swung blind and blackening in the moonless air;
Morn came and went—and came, and brought no day.

—LORD BYRON, "DARKNESS"

STYX

CHAPTER 1

At three AM it was quiet on the beach. The greedy gulls would come later. Lovers would stroll hand in hand beside the sea. But now the empty sand stretched out like an infinite desert, its surface stippled by a chill drizzle. Curtains of mist turned the scene into an apocalyptic postcard of ancient times, a dark river without beginning or end that flowed between two incompatible worlds.

No lights burned in the apartments that lined the dike. No one standing on a balcony at that moment would have spotted the man bent over beside the breakwater. Only if you stood right beside him would you have heard him grunt with the effort of his digging. He worked quickly, although it would be at least two hours before anyone else arrived at the beach. The local fishermen, on most mornings the earliest of early birds, were at this hour still fast asleep in their beds, dreaming of perfect storms. The season's first tourists would wait until the sun was high in the sky before settling into their rented chaise lounges and slathering themselves with coconut oil.

At this hour, the digger might have been the only living soul in all of Ostend, the sole inhabitant of a Sunday painter's landscape. An observer—had there been one—might have expected to see him sweeping a metal detector across the sand, searching for buried watches, rings, or coins. Instead, his hands gripped a shovel, and, with short, jerky movements, he was digging a hole.

From time to time he paused, resettled the yellow sou'wester hat that matched his oilskin slicker, and rested for three beats as the rain kept time. All around him were traces of yesterday's fun: collapsed sand castles, half washed away by the tide, a deflated beach ball, an abandoned pair of water wings, a kite's ragged tail.

It would all be so desolate, so pitiable, were the man not doing his best to give the beach a bit more class.

The rain intensified. The hole was three feet deep now, an almost precise circle three feet in diameter, and only the top half of the digger's body was visible above its lip. Another three—no, two—shovelfuls, and he would be finished.

Un, deux, et voilà.

He leaned on his shovel, considered what he had done, and saw that it was good. Turning around, he found himself eye to eye with the young woman lying stretched out on the beach beside the hole. Her naked body had been washed almost clean by the rain.

The man bent forward and rested his arms nonchalantly on the edge of the pit, as if awaiting his turn at a drugstore counter. From that position, he could look her in the eye one last time.

"I don't know where I get the inspiration," he told her. "But no artist can ever answer that question. Inspiration seeks him out, brings out the best he has to offer the world."

When he felt recovered from his labor, he hoisted himself out of the hole. The rain drummed against his hat and slicker, danced off the plastic mask that lay near the body.

Between mask and body stood an overflowing plastic bucket. It was a standard sand bucket, decorated with cartoon images of Casper the Friendly Ghost, the sort of toy a child would fill with starfish and shells, crabs and jellyfish.

But this bucket held no such childish treasures. It was full of human organs, and sticking up from the slurry, like the stem of an amaryllis growing from a flowerpot, was the haft of his *sica*, a reproduction of an ancient Illyrian dagger.

He knelt beside the body and pulled the sica free. Its long curved blade, decorated with incised circles, was razor sharp, and he carefully excised the pièce de résistance: the heart. It was slippery, thanks not only to the blood but the rain, and he almost dropped it.

"My heart is in my work," he said aloud. "Maybe you think what I do is not art, but it is, truly. Of course, it's also a craft, a métier, and it can only be practiced by men of honor."

He tossed the heart into the bucket with the rest of the organs: the liver, the stomach, the kidneys, the lungs. In the dark, it was impossible to distinguish one from the other. The rain had turned it all to bouillabaisse.

The man swiped at the blood on his pants and clapped the wet, bloody sand from his hands. The woman's body was almost completely flat, like an empty air mattress. The sight stimulated him to hunker down beside her and fill his hands, not with organs this time, but with sand. He scooped up a double handful and let the wet grains trickle through his fingers.

He'd chosen this spot carefully, close to the third breakwater, far from the dike, knowing the tide here would leave behind a hard surface as it withdrew. The sand stuck to itself like potter's clay.

"Some say that what I do is not a métier. The same fools who say that the matador denies the bull a noble death. But I say both arts are honorable. I give my women a second chance at life. I immortalize them, capturing the most important moment of each sad existence in its most aesthetically elegant form."

As he spoke, he began to pack the hollowed-out corpse with fistfuls of sand. This part of the job required no finesse and progressed quickly. Removing the organs was always more difficult, more complicated, than refilling the empty container.

"The challenge is to find that one perfect pose. The ideal position. But I say it again: in killing them, I gift them with eternal life. What greater gift could any man offer them? If I die—and I say 'if,' not 'when'—I want the exact same treatment. No wax Madame Tussaud replica for me."

And once again voilà. He patted down the surface of the packed sand with the blade of his shovel, then glanced at his watch. He was pleased to find himself ahead of schedule. There was still plenty of time.

He sat with his legs in the lotus position and took the old leather cigar case from his pocket. He was about to unpack his tools when he heard voices waft across the sand. He rolled silently into the pit and froze. The voices came no closer. He waited a long minute, then carefully peeked out over the lip of his hole. There was no one there. It must have been a pair of night owls, taking the long way home from some late revel.

The man allowed a few more seconds to pass, then got to his feet. With his hat tented helmet-like over his head, he looked like a WWI soldier contemplating the Ypres battlefield from the shelter of a front-line trench.

He slid the cigar case open and pulled out his spool of fishing line.

In the beginning, the first time, he'd tried to use ordinary sewing thread, but of course that proved far too thin to get the job done right. For his second victim, he'd switched to fishing line, which was much stronger. It was more difficult to manage, but he'd quickly gotten the hang of it.

He launched the stopwatch on his iPhone. Last time, it had taken him twelve minutes and twenty-four seconds to sew the body closed. This time, he hoped to break that record.

"I think I can do it, Carl," he said, as if being interviewed by an imaginary sports reporter. "I feel good. My fingers are ready. If the wind's with me, anything can happen. I don't really know *how* fast I can go."

He tapped Start and set to work. Anyone watching from the dike would have thought he was baiting a hook and preparing for a day of fishing.

He broke the record, finishing up in less than ten minutes, and he could tell right away that this would be—so far, at least—the master-piece of the collection. His chef d'oeuvre. A piece that belonged in the Mu.ZEE, Ostend's preeminent art museum.

"Let's sit you up nice and straight, my girl," he said.

He moved behind the body, grabbed its head, and hauled it to a half-sitting position, propping it up against the bucket of organs.

"Nice," he said.

He examined her closely, like an artist positioning a painting in the place of honor on a gallery wall. He'd come up with the idea of mounting a public display nine years ago, during Ostend's Beaufort 2006 open-air exhibition: all around town, statues had been erected, a bronze knight here, a wooden horse there.

"A revelation!" the critics had enthused. "Art for the man in the street!"

Well, now it was his turn.

And here it stood.

Or sat, actually.

His latest contribution to the city's art scene.

But of course he wasn't quite finished, not yet.

Again he reached for his sica, and, with the graceful economy of movement of a samurai, he sliced the four limbs from the body, then the head. What remained was a woman's torso, planted in the sand, its breasts its sole distinctive feature.

He was carried away by the beauty of it, completely overwhelmed.

He set the head carefully off to one side, posed it so it was gazing up at its own dismembered body.

He nodded approvingly and took from his pocket the greeting card he'd bought in a gift shop on the dike several weeks ago, already preparing for this moment. On it he had carefully printed a legend:

#3 IN A SERIES: A GIFT TO ALL THE TOURISTS HEADING OFF FOR A FUN DAY AT THE BEACH.

He propped the card beside the torso. The finishing touch.

The man stepped back and admired his handiwork. The body was more alive now than it had ever been. If you looked at her, sitting there on the sand, headless and helpless and hopeless, she seemed to be a natural part of the environment, a sculpted piece of flotsam washed up by the tide from the other side of the Channel.

One more little chore, and he would be finished.

He picked up his shovel, planted his feet in the sand, bent his knees slightly, and lined up the putt. He drew the shovel's blade back a few inches, then tapped the severed head neatly into the cup. Inside his own head, the gallery that ringed the green murmured appreciatively.

"It's all in the wrists, Carl," he said, smiling shyly.

Almost as an afterthought, he kicked the arms and legs and the plastic shopping bag that held the girl's clothing and cheap clutch into the hole and quickly filled it in, leaving the naked body standing proudly on the beach, facing—if you could call it that—the shore.

Then he clambered up onto the breakwater, stripped off his clothing, and dove into the ice-cold vastness of the North Sea, half to cleanse himself of the blood and sand but also half simple ritual. Every artist has his routine.

He spent five minutes in the water, freed at last from the stress, from the pressure to perform. Swimming in the rain was a unique experience. He felt part of two worlds at once: above him the summer shower descending from the heavens, below him the roiling sea that seemed eager to suck him down into hell.

He emerged from his swim, muscles taut, and quickly dressed in clean clothing from his gym bag. He packed his bloody work clothes, his shovel, his plastic mask, and his dagger in the bag and carried it across the hard-packed sand toward the dike, where he'd left his black Hyundai Santa Fe and its trailer, retracing the path he'd taken an hour before, when he'd dragged the body from the trailer down to the breakwater.

Never in his life had he felt so vibrant, so full of energy.

But he knew that he would be dead again in the morning. And that would mean it wasn't over, there was still work to be done. He would have to go on, to keep reinventing himself, time after time after time.

He slid behind the wheel, rolled down his window, and took one last lingering look back. From this vantage point, his latest triumph was hidden from the eye. All he could see was the sky, the sea, and the sand.

"Death and rebirth," he murmured softly. "Forever and ever, amen."

And then he put the car in gear and drove away.

CHAPTER 2

For months now, Raphael Styx had stretched out each night on the hardwood floor beside the bed and wrestled his way toward dreamland without much success. The pains in his back and especially his hip refused to grant him the relief of slumber.

Recently, when he turned forty, he began swallowing 5 mg of Mogadon every other night. The pills allowed him at least a few hours of rest, and he was sleeping now, despite the inflammation in his wrists, despite the corn on his right big toe, despite his hemorrhoids.

And then the phone rang.

"Sleeping, goddammit," he muttered.

He fumbled for his iPhone, hoping to silence it before the ringtone—"Get Up, Stand Up"—woke Isabelle, but all he accomplished was to knock it from the night table to the floor, where Bob Marley ordered him to stand up for his rights. He rolled over to grab it, and a lightning bolt lanced through his hip.

"God *damn* it," he exploded.

Above him, in the bed, Isabelle stirred.

"Rafe, can you get that, please!"

He found the phone and answered it.

"Styx," he rumbled.

He recognized the caller's voice immediately. It was John Crevits.

"What's up, John?"

Crevits spoke softly, punctuating his sentences with sighs that wafted through the iPhone's little speaker like gentle sea breezes.

"Where?"

Styx sat up and reached over the New York guidebook on his nightstand to switch on the bedside lamp. The guidebook had been sitting there for half a year, but he hadn't yet gotten around to opening it.

"All right, I'm on my way."

He ended the call and struggled to his feet. The days when he could sleep spooned up against his wife and jump out of bed at the crack of dawn were over. Now, even walking took effort. Shit, forty years old and it was like he was eighty.

"Who was it?" Isabelle yawned, pulling the comforter over her head.

"Crevits," said Styx. "Go back to sleep."

"John? In the middle of the night?"

Styx checked his watch and saw that it was six AM.

"Night's almost over. It's morning."

"It's an ungodly hour for a phone call," she complained.

"What do you want me to say? I'm the one who has to get up."

Beneath her blankets, she stretched herself like a cat. Styx sat on the edge of the bed and reached for his trousers. Picking up the pants was bad enough. Getting into them was worse.

"Fuck," he said.

There was no response.

"I'm falling apart here."

"What else is new?"

"Thanks for your support."

"You haven't called for another appointment, have you?" asked Isabelle, her head still hidden from view, her voice muffled.

"An appointment with who?"

"You know who. That doctor. For your hip."

"No, I've already seen him twice, don't want to see him again."

"Suit yourself."

"Go back to sleep," he said.

"It's your own fault, Rafe."

"I'll deal with it."

It had started with his socks. Putting them on had become an obstacle course. And, since a guy's got to put on a pair of socks every morning, that was a problem. Was it some sort of muscle strain? No, according to their family physician, who'd referred him to Dr. S. Vrancken, an orthopedist.

Vrancken had begun with an ultrasound. As he traced Styx's body with the smooth head of his gel-smeared instrument, Styx watched his own innards scroll by on the computer screen, an assortment of black and gray surfaces that the specialist had identified as his vital organs.

The orthopedist informed Styx that he definitely didn't have a hernia. Vrancken—in his early fifties with short gray hair, his short-sleeved golf shirts revealing surprisingly muscular bronzed arms—had presented his conclusions carefully, as if he were a military officer informing a father that his son had died in some distant war zone.

Styx's pain wasn't the result of an injury, he'd explained. It was a symptom of arthritis.

"I thought only old people got arthritis," Styx said.

"In layman's terms, your hip is kaput," the specialist had told him. "It's worn out. Happens to around nine to eleven percent of people over the age of thirty-five. You can probably make it through a couple of months on painkillers, and if it gets much worse I can give you a shot of cortisone, but there's no way around it: within a year, you're going to need a hip replacement."

"A prosthetic?"

"We call it an artificial joint. I see people in their late thirties who need this surgery."

"I just turned forty."

"Well, then," said Dr. Vrancken, "I don't need to sugarcoat it for you. You get to forty and wake up pain-free, you're probably dead. That'll be fifty euros, but you'll get most of it back from your health insurance."

After that visit, the pain in his hip got worse, so Styx saw Vrancken a second time. The doctor ordered X-rays, just to make sure, and the cop had dutifully reported to the hospital a couple of days ago. All he could do now was wait for the results.

And that was where things stood.

On his way out of the bedroom, he heard Isabelle mutter, "Try to keep it down, Rafe. Victor needs his sleep. He's got an art history test today."

Styx closed the door, but otherwise ignored her instructions. This was *his* house, *he* brought home the lion's share of the bacon, so *he* got to make the rules. She had nothing to complain about.

He headed for the stairs, but paused to look in on Victor. The boy lay sprawled across his rumpled bedclothes, fully dressed and sound asleep. His art history textbook lay open beside him, and his desk lamp still burned. Styx gazed down at the thirteen-year-old, his little boy, no longer little. Once upon a time, he would have pulled the covers over him and kissed his forehead, but those days were long gone.

Over the last couple of years, their relationship had become difficult, pricklish, a minefield. It got harder and harder for the two of them to get along, especially since Victor's grandfather—Isabelle's father—had suddenly died just a few weeks ago. Victor and his grandfather, Marc Gerard, were cut from the same cloth, and, since Marc's death, Styx had been kept busy with the funeral, with visits to and from the surviving family members, with writing an obituary and the reading of the will.

"How can you be so cold?" Victor had demanded, more than once. "Don't you have any feelings?"

He had feelings. And the pain of his son's accusations hurt him even more than the pain of losing his father-in-law.

Now Raphael Styx tore his eyes away from his sleeping son and switched off the lamp. Downstairs, he had to fight with his shoes. Bending over was torture, so he kicked his way into them without using his hands. Before leaving the house, he took his badge and his gun—a Glock 19 semiautomatic—down from the top shelf of the hall closet. He put them where they belonged, opened the door, and inhaled the fresh sea air of Ostend.

It took Styx less than ten minutes to reach the address he'd been given. He parked his Fiat on the Albert I Promenade, between the Toi Moi & La Mer restaurant and the dike. Out on the horizon, dawn was breaking. In the past, this sight had always moved him. Today, though, it seemed somehow fake. Sunsets are always vulgar, a Flemish writer had once quipped, but sunrises in Ostend were somehow both vulgar and poetic.

He stood on the dike and saw the lighthouse blink on and off in the distance. His cell phone rang.

"Chief Inspector Styx?"

"Yeah. Where are you?"

"Third breakwater to the left."

"I see you."

"It's no picnic, I'm warning you."

"I'll be right there."

He ended the call and headed down the wooden staircase to the beach. He set off as briskly as he could across the sand, past a line of rental cabanas, heading straight for the group of figures barely visible in the distance.

The sand was sloshy from last night's rain and difficult to walk on. After a hundred feet, though, he crossed an invisible tidal line, and the harder surface was a blessing to his knees and calves. When he reached the third breakwater, he found a knot of men milling around, chatting among themselves, doing nothing. A man in civilian clothes was taking pictures, and another was lifting fingerprints.

"Somebody bring me up to speed," said Styx, not wasting time on a greeting. An elegantly dressed young detective named Joachim Delacroix was the first to react. Styx knew Delacroix by name and reputation. He was a self-satisfied immigrant from the Congo, only a year on the force and recently transferred to the coast from Brussels. No one seemed to know where he found the money to pay for his obviously expensive wardrobe. Styx hated him, though he didn't really know him. He hated a lot of people. It wasn't the color of Delacroix's skin or the fancy dress that bothered him. It was what the rookie represented: Delacroix was a prime example of the new breed of cop, heavy on ambition but light on empathy, the type who started every day by dropping to the floor and counting off fifty push-ups—unlike Styx, who had to count off fifty seconds before he could get *up* from the floor beside his bed in the morning.

"Chief Inspector," the rookie said, his accent French. "I'd say good morning, but that doesn't seem appropriate under these circumstances."

"And what circumstances are they?"

"See for yourself."

Delacroix stepped aside, revealing something perched on the sand beside the breakwater—a shape, a figure, a doll. A thing that had once been human and alive, now without limbs or a head. A hole had been dug in the sand beside it, and, when Styx stepped over to it and looked down, his stomach flipped and he had to fight back the urge to vomit.

"Jesus Christ."

He turned away quickly, and looked back at the nude torso propped into a semi-standing position on the beach. A long dotted line ran from throat to hip. On closer inspection, the dotted line revealed itself to be some kind of stitching, either a thick plastic thread or possibly ordinary fishing line.

"When did the report come in?"

"Half an hour ago," Delacroix replied. "Victim's name is Madeleine Bohy. She's thirty-four years old and employed at a nursing home here in the area."

"Quick work," said Styx. "How did you get all that so fast?"

"Her purse is in the hole," said Delacroix, "complete with identity card."

Styx stared through the spot where Madeleine Bohy's head ought to be, focusing on the sea twenty yards behind her.

"The Stuffer?"

"Certainly looks like it," said Delacroix. He came up beside Styx and nodded at the naked body. "Third victim, third woman, and the third time the vic's been put on display in a public place."

"First time she's been stripped naked and cut into pieces, though."

"Yes, he really did a number on this one."

Styx bent over and tried to ignore the pain in his hip. He ran a palm across his mouth as if he were deep in thought, but in fact was hiding a grimace. He examined the card that had been left propped against the torso.

"Another sick pun," he said.

"Too bad he doesn't sign them," Delacroix said, and waved over the fingerprint tech, Dirk Niemegeers.

Barely glancing up from his clipboard, Niemegeers said, "It's useless. There's nothing on the card and you can't get prints off sand. At least he left the last one out on the street."

"You didn't come up with anything then," said Styx.

"He's a careful bastard. We haven't found a thing. The body was washed clean of any traces. The bucket's full of DNA, but it's the victim's."

Styx moved around behind the dead woman and peered into the bucket that helped hold her upright: a dense mass of dark-red and brown gunk that stank to holy hell.

"Her organs," Niemegeers said.

"I take it he used his shovel again?"

"We haven't had time to check it yet, but we're assuming that this one's also been scooped out and refilled with sand."

"Shit," said Styx. "How much fucking sand does it take to fill up a human body?"

Niemegeers looked up at last. "We haven't weighed it," he said. "We do, you'll be the first person I tell."

And with that, he wandered off. Styx nodded at one of the other officers, and the man brought over a thin bedsheet. It fluttered like a white flag in the early morning, until two men draped it over the body and tucked in the ends. Now, shrouded in white, Madeleine Bohy looked even more like a statue—the Venus of Ostend—ready to be unveiled by the mayor in a public ceremony.

"How'd we get the word?" Styx asked.

"Tip was phoned in," said Delacroix. "This time *not* by some tourist who thought it was a real artwork and took a picture of it."

Delacroix was referring to the murder of Elisa Wouters, the Stuffer's second victim. That time, the serial killer had left the body intact, in the middle of the night and the middle of the Kapellestraat, Ostend's busiest shopping street. He'd posed the dead woman on the steps to the dike, as if she were begging for spare change, with a hand-printed note on an otherwise innocuous greeting card in the pocket of her skirt reading #2 IN A SERIES: TAKING STEPS TO CREATE A MORE BEAUTIFUL OSTEND.

It had taken until midmorning before any of the passing tourists or locals realized that something wasn't quite right about the picture. How many people had walked past her, on their way to a little sun and fun, a little casual shopping?

Styx hadn't gotten much sleep that night, not from the pain in his hip or even the memory of the horrible thing on the steps, but from simple bewilderment. How could dozens, probably hundreds of people have marched up and down those steps past a dead body without noticing it?

"Details?" asked Styx.

"I told you: she's—"

"Not the victim. The guy who called it in. *Was* it a guy? Did you get a name? A phone number? An address?"

Delacroix took out his notebook. In this day of iPhones and tablets, he was apparently a traditionalist, probably did it to make himself seem more serious and reliable.

"The call came in at five twenty-four. A male voice. He said his name was Spilliaert."

"Spilliaert," Styx repeated. The name seemed familiar, but he wasn't sure why.

"He said he goes out for a swim early every morning."

"And?"

"And he found her here on the beach. The number he was calling from turns out to be a landline. We were able to identify the location. It's right here in Ostend."

"Excellent," said Styx. "The address?"

"Hofstraat 24. It's a side street off the Promenade. The call came from an apartment on the fifth floor."

"And where is this early swimmer now? Halfway across the Channel?"

Delacroix ignored the chief inspector's attempt at humor. "No, he said he's working an early shift this week and didn't want to be late."

"Jesus," said Styx, "the guy finds a decapitated body on the beach, calls it in, and then just heads off to work?"

"We tried to keep him on the line, but he hung up."

"So what? You had his number."

"We called back, but he didn't pick up."

"And you don't know where he works?"

"He didn't give us a chance to ask," said Delacroix. "I sent two men to talk with the neighbors, but nobody seems to know anything about him."

"So this is either a guy who loves his job and doesn't want to miss a minute, or else he's fucking with us. How could you let him just hang up on you?"

"How was I supposed to stop him? All we can do now is pick him up when he gets home from work."

"*I'll* decide what we can do now," Styx snarled.

STYX

He wanted to smack the rookie in his smug face. But he knew Delacroix hadn't really done anything wrong. It was lucky the murder had been called in so early. Still, it was weird: man goes out for an early swim, sees a dead body next to the breakwater, calls the cops . . . and then just takes off.

"Any footprints?"

"Lots," said Delacroix. "Too many. Look around: half of Ostend must have been out here yesterday."

"Anything else?"

"Not yet. We'll compare the fishing line with the line from the other two victims. But we still don't know where any of it was bought."

"We don't know much, do we?" Styx said bitterly, with a last look at the white-shrouded torso.

"Could be worse," said the rookie. "We're lucky the bastard didn't leave the head sitting on a table at a sidewalk café."

"Yeah, very lucky," Styx glumly agreed.

But he didn't say what he was thinking: *If he had, how long would it have taken before anybody noticed?*

CHAPTER 3

Raphael Styx spent the rest of that day at his desk in the Alfons Piet-erslaan police station. For years now, the Ostend Police Department had been planning a move to a more modern facililty near the central train station, but construction had been repeatedly delayed.

A bulletin board on one wall was crowded with documents Styx had collected over the past few months, all concerning the latest se-rial killer. After the second victim—Elisa Wouters, thirty-one, a hair-dresser—had been discovered, the newspapers began referring to the murderer as "the Stuffer," and the police adopted the nickname.

Styx leaned back in his chair as comfortably as his hip would allow and stared at the information tacked to the board. At the moment, the man who'd identified himself as Spilliaert was their only lead. It had been three weeks since the Stuffer's last killing. All they'd concluded about the murderer so far was that he was probably a man—slicing open a human body, filling it with sand, and sewing it shut again required a lot of strength. For the same reason, they assumed that the perpetrator was somewhere between twenty and sixty years old, and his familiarity with Ostend suggested that he was likely a local.

Background reports on the murdered women were in a drawer of Styx's desk, but it was a drawer he preferred not to open. He was after the killer; he didn't need to keep looking at the faces of the dead. Those images only distracted him, and distractions weakened him. Styx didn't have time for that—that way lay failure.

During the course of the afternoon, John Crevits stopped by Styx's office and sagged into his visitor's chair.

"No news?" the commissioner said.

"We're waiting for Spilliaert to get back from work."

"And you don't know *where* he works?"

"No. We've got a man staking out his apartment."

"At least that's something to grab onto. Why so gloomy?"

"I'd rather *not* have something to grab onto and skip the third murder."

"I know," sighed Crevits.

The commissioner had survived two heart surgeries, weighed 260 pounds and counting, and was a habitual sigher. A year ago, he'd developed adult-onset diabetes, which was a constant concern. Styx didn't want to think about the insulin injections his superior needed on a regular basis.

"What's your impression of Delacroix?" Crevits asked, his voice taking on a confidential tone.

"What impression would you like?"

Crevits chuckled. Even that sounded like a sigh. "I know you don't like him, but I think the kid's got potential."

"Let's agree to disagree," said Styx.

"Why?"

"He let a tipster slip right through his fingers, John."

"You know there was nothing he could do about that. And it's not like Spilliaert actually *saw* anything. He just discovered the body."

"I wouldn't have let him get away."

"No? What would you have done, reached through the phone and grabbed him?"

"Something like that."

"You're a tough guy, Styx, but you're different from Delacroix. You came up from the streets."

"Where'd *he* come from? He's just the umpteenth pretty boy Brussels has fobbed off on us."

Crevits held up his hands, annoyed. Styx thrived on conflict. If there wasn't one handy, he'd invent one. Now he had it in for Delacroix.

More and more, Styx felt he was being discriminated against: at work, in his hometown, within his own family. When he screwed up—which seemed to be happening more often lately—no one cut him any slack. His years of experience were baggage. He'd set a high bar for himself, and now he was expected to give 110 percent all the time.

All he wanted was to sit quietly at his desk and eat the chicken curry sandwich he'd picked up at Knapp, his favorite takeaway shop in the Zandvoordestraat. He unwrapped the sandwich and took a bite, hoping to distract himself from the pain in his creaking joints. A drop of curry sauce stained his chin yellow-green, like a festering sore leaking pus.

"Whether you like it or not, we need new blood like him, Styx," Crevits sighed.

"What do you mean?"

"You and I won't last forever. The new generation's getting ready to take over."

"I just turned forty, John."

"I can see that."

"What's that supposed to mean?"

"Let me ask you something: Can you pick up that piece of paper on the floor there with your toes?"

"No."

"Why not?"

"Because I'm not a monkey. A man uses his hands."

"Sure, but then you'd have to bend down to the floor."

"What do you need the paper for, John?"

"The question is what *you* need."

"I don't need anything."

"I hear you need a new hip. Don't be so macho. You said it yourself: you're forty. Doesn't mean you have to have a midlife crisis. You're just starting the next phase of your life. But I'm warning you, you have to take care of yourself. You don't treat your body right, you'll never make it to retirement."

Styx muttered a protest, but Crevits wasn't finished:

"What are you worried about? I've been under the knife twice. You think you're immortal? We're all gonna wind up bionic, the way things are going. You, me, everybody. These days, there's nothing to it. They give you a little shot, you go beddy-bye, and when you wake up you've got a brand-new hip that makes you the center of attention every time you walk through a metal detector. What are you afraid of? You know I can give you three months' sick leave."

"The surgery doesn't scare me," said Styx.

"What, then?"

"It's not the hip. I know they can fix it. My orthopedist, Dr. Vrancken, says the prostheses work better than the original factory equipment. But I can't handle the anesthetic."

"Don't be a baby."

"I don't want them knocking me out, John. I know it sounds crazy, but I've never had a general anesthetic. Never needed one. And once they put you out, well, you know, you hear stories about people who never come out of it, never wake up again."

"Sometimes," Crevits said, "that's for the best. Would you *want* to wake up if you were going to spend the rest of your life crawling around on all fours?"

The commissioner got to his feet, more easily despite his bulk than Raphael Styx could have managed it.

"Look at me," said Crevits. "If I hadn't listened to my doctor, I wouldn't be sitting here talking to you. If I was you, I'd get on the phone to that orthopedist and schedule the operation. They're doctors, Styx. They're there to help. They're not going to leave you sitting in the dark."

Styx didn't want to think about it anymore. He went over to the bulletin board and studied the snapshots of the human statues the Stuffer had created, a catalog of the exhibition. For the hundredth time, the women's empty eyes returned his gaze.

The first victim, Reinhilde Debels, had been found in the sculpture garden behind the Mu.ZEE, Ostend's museum of modern art. She'd been tucked in among the other statues, an ordinary greeting card leaning against her left foot. At first, the museum's visitors had mistaken the corpse for a work of performance art or perhaps something to do with the *Bodies* exhibition, which used polymer preservation to turn actual human remains into works of scientific art. But those bodies hadn't been murdered, let alone murdered and then stuffed with sand.

The carefully handprinted words on the Stuffer's first message had read: #1 IN A SERIES: A BRAND-NEW STATUE FOR YOUR LOVELY GARDEN.

Styx remembered the morning that police forensic pathologist Tobias Ornelis had cut Reinhilde Debels open in the morgue. In his capacity as homicide detective, he'd been present when Ornelis had laid her out on a gurney and sliced through her skin with a surgical scalpel like a butcher laying open a hog.

There'd been no blood, no intestines or other organs spilling out of the body, just sand.

Sand, as if the woman were a shattered hourglass.

Styx had no idea if he was supposed to find the sight disgusting, vulgar, or simply weird. In fact, it had been peaceful. Unreal, yet somehow serene. He stood there for long seconds as the grains of sand slowly leaked out of the dead body and cascaded over the edge of the gurney to the morgue's tiled floor.

It all unfolded in utter silence, like the action in a silent film. And the damn sand just kept on coming. How much fucking sand had the murderer managed to pack inside the body, and how long had it taken him to do it?

That outré moment had given him nightmares for most of the next week. It was a stranger, more gruesome sight than the bloodiest crime scenes he'd investigated in his sixteen years on the Ostend police.

Styx had come to one conclusion: whoever the Stuffer was, he was a man of intense passion. Only a man of passion could be so driven. When he was finally able to tear his eyes away from the dead woman, his shoes were half-buried in sand. It covered the floor of the morgue, dancing beneath the air-conditioning like a miniature sandstorm.

CHAPTER 4

An hour later Styx was still standing in front of the bulletin board when Joachim Delacroix came into his office with an update. He could see that the young Congolese immigrant had just come on shift. That was the new generation for you: you could haul them out of bed in the middle of the night, but they'd keep track of their hours and put in for comp time if you worked them a minute longer than they were paid for. It was sad to see things heading in that direction.

Beneath the fluorescent lighting, the rookie stood there in a dapper charcoal-gray pinstriped suit. On his own time Delacroix dressed in colorful three-piece suits with matching ties and brilliantly polished shoes, never the same outfit twice. Luckily, Styx hadn't witnessed that spectacle all too often, just at the occasional after-hours birthday and retirement parties. Who even *wears* a tie anymore, Styx had wondered more than once.

Today, Delacroix's thick dreadlocks were set off by a pair of bright orange sunglasses. He looked like he'd stolen them from an American film star.

"You get anywhere canvassing the neighborhood?" asked Styx.

"Yeah, but it's not good news. Nobody saw or heard a thing. That early in the morning, you wouldn't expect any different."

"Nobody except Spilliaert, you mean?"

"Except Spilliaert, right."

"He back from work yet? What does he do, anyway?"

Delacroix shook his head. "Our guy's still watching the house, but Spilliaert hasn't shown up."

"Our" guy, Styx thought, as if he and Delacroix were equals.

"What has he got, three jobs? He should be home by now."

"The apartment he called from, in the Hofstraat? He rents it. We contacted the owner, and he confirms that the place is leased to a Mr. L. Spilliaert who pays his rent on the first of every month, like clockwork. A perfect tenant, apparently."

"I guess so," Styx drawled, "seeing as how he's never there. And you've checked with Spilliaert's bank?"

"There's no bank."

"What do you mean there's no bank?"

"He pays in cash, drops an envelope in the landlord's mailbox."

"Shit. So it's off the books?"

Styx eyed the young man, but there was no response.

"Well, welcome to Belgium," he sighed.

"Anything from Toxicology?" asked Delacroix.

Styx looked up sharply. The fucking dandy ought to keep his mind on his own work. The toxicology report was none of his business. But

Styx could see he'd sunk his teeth into the case and wasn't about to let go. The new goddamn generation.

Styx didn't want to give too much away. He preferred flying solo. That limited the risks. Styx couldn't dodge the thought that he'd spent sixteen years building a career in this department, while this newbie'd been around for one year and was trying to pass himself off as Dirty Harry.

"No, not really. Victim died a few hours before we got there. Coroner estimates the time of death around midnight."

Delacroix changed the subject. "According to people who knew her, Madeleine Bohy was well liked."

"Aren't we all?" said Styx, not counting himself.

He went back to his desk. Dr. Vrancken had instructed him to keep moving when he could, to prevent his hip from locking up. Stand a bit, sit a bit, stand a bit, sit a bit. Raphael Styx, the human metronome.

"What do you want me to do next?" asked Delacroix, suddenly ceremonious, standing stiffly in the doorway as if he was afraid to cross the threshold into Chief Inspector Styx's unfamiliar underworld.

"I want you to do your job and let me do mine," said Styx. *That ought to get rid of the punk*, he thought. He didn't bother looking up as the rookie made his exit. But then Delacroix turned and came back.

"A hundred and ten pounds," he said.

"What?"

"A hundred and ten pounds."

"A hundred and ten pounds of what?"

"Sand. In the body."

Styx stared at him, speechless.

"You said you wanted to know, so I checked. A hundred and ten pounds. That's a little more than five full twenty-pound buckets."

"I can do the math," said Styx, and he waved the detective out of his office.

Raphael Styx had trained himself to treat both victims and criminals like the figures in a wax museum, not people. Only in that way was he able to focus on his job. He had to keep it all at a distance, which over the years had turned him into something of a robot. And now Joachim Delacroix was trying to lure him out of his protective hiding place with this little personal detail.

A hundred and ten pounds of sand.

"Bastard," Styx muttered.

He tried to concentrate on the reports, the interviews with the neighbors, the lab results, the facts. But that number kept intruding. A hundred and ten pounds. What drove a man like the Stuffer—assuming it *was* a man—to commit such horrifying crimes? Was he trying to shock the city awake? Was that his message?

Styx got back to his feet, restless now, and tacked a photograph of Madeleine Bohy beside the pictures of the two previous victims. They formed a lugubrious triptych, there on the bulletin board, and Styx eyed them emotionlessly, like a visitor to the City Museum considering a piece of abstract art.

At four PM *he sat in his Cabrio outside Our Lady Academy in the Vin*-dictivelaan, waiting for Victor. These last weeks, picking his son up from school had been torture: the ride home was like a silent funeral procession.

Today was no different. The boy slid into the passenger seat and, without bothering to ask permission, changed the radio station, slitting Schumann's throat and replacing him with a Studio Brussels DJ who introduced Daft Punk's "Around the World."

"How was your exam?" asked Styx, turning down the volume.

Victor shrugged, and turned it back up to full blast.

"What subject was it again? History?"

"Art history." Those two words seemed to cost the boy enormous effort.

Styx watched his son out of the corner of his eye. Thirteen years old, and a royal pain in the ass—just, he admitted, like his old man.

Victor stared out the window.

"And? What was it about?"

"Art history, duh."

"Well, what period?"

"All of them."

"Surrealism? The Belgian painters? Ensor? Magritte? Delvaux?"

"Yeah," said Victor.

"Good thing it wasn't an oral exam," Styx tried.

But his son was too busy hating him to appreciate the joke. The unanticipated death of Grandpa Marc and its aftermath remained a thick curtain that hung between them.

"What's tomorrow's test?"

"A different subject," said Victor coldly.

Styx was desperate to find a way to make things right, but how was he supposed to do that?

This was the first time the boy had ever dealt with death—a subject that formed an integral part of Styx's everyday life. So then why wouldn't Victor talk about it with him? Why couldn't he trust his own father?

It was tearing Styx apart, and all he could do was hit the gas and get his son home as fast as possible—as if he were some juvenile delinquent.

Styx felt like an outsider, more so than ever. Victor's connection with his grandfather had been so strong that the two of them could understand each other without even speaking, while Styx needed a dictionary just to get his son to pass the butter.

"Say, is that stuff I got you doing any good?"

"What stuff?"

"From the drugstore."

"No, it's crap."

"The ads say it—"

"I threw it away."

"What?"

"It didn't work."

"Well, you have to use it for at least three weeks. It's not magic, Vic. You can't expect it to make everything disappear in two days."

"What do *you* care?" Victor demanded.

"I just thought it'd help if you gave it a fair shot."

The thirteen-year-old beside him was changing, not only on the inside, but on the outside. His nose was taking a more prominent place on his face, his skin was getting oilier, and pimples were becoming more of a problem for him than for the other boys his age. His grandfather had suffered from acute acne, too, and it had left permanent scars on both cheeks. To spare his child the same disfigurement, Styx had brought home a special salve the pharmacist had promised him would protect the boy from the worst of it, but that was the problem with kids these days: no patience.

"I wish you'd asked me before you threw it out."

"Why?"

"Because it was really expensive," said Styx.

"I didn't want to bother you, *Dad*," Victor replied, putting sarcastic emphasis on the last word. "I know you've been really busy dealing with the funeral and the lawyers and the will and everything. Are you in it, Grampa's will?"

Styx didn't respond. He pulled into the parking area at the Milho Apartments in the Godtschalckstraat and tried to be the first one out of the car, but his hip wouldn't cooperate.

For the rest of the afternoon, Victor Styx stayed closeted in his bedroom, avoiding the daylight, as if afraid that even a millisecond of illumination would cause the whiteheads that dotted his face to explode.

*At eight PM, well after dinner, John Crevits called Styx at home to re*port that they'd been trying Spilliaert's phone number without success.

Styx's stomach was upset—the oral Voltaren he took three times a day for pain always left him feeling bloated. "What difference does it make?" he said, resigned. "You said it yourself, John, he just found the body. What could he tell us that we don't already know?"

"He's a key part of the investigation. Maybe there were things he saw that were gone by the time we got there."

"Like what?"

"How do I know?"

"Listen, John. This is just more of the same thing we've already been through. Serial killers don't change their spots. They're predictable. They play the same song, over and over. All we know is that Madeleine Bohy was well liked, lived to help others, practically a saint, just like the other two victims. Spilliaert isn't going to tell us any different."

"You sound tired."

"You'd be tired too if you were in my shoes."

"Madeleine Bohy was strangled," said Crevits, out of the blue. "It was hard to tell, because of the beheading, but they found evidence of strangulation on what was left of her neck."

"What's your point?"

"I wasn't sure you knew."

"I didn't notice," said Styx. "I was busy looking at that fishing line."

"You given any more thought to taking some time off?"

"John, we're in the middle of a homicide investigation, in case you've forgotten."

Styx knew the meaning of the silence that followed. The commissioner didn't have to say it aloud: no cop was irreplaceable. So far, there'd been three murders, and Styx had gotten precisely nowhere. Was Crevits suggesting that it was time to turn the reins over to someone else? That was hitting below the belt. But it wouldn't be the first time the commissioner had pulled an inspector who wasn't getting results off a case.

"Maybe you're right," Crevits said at last. "Maybe we should be concentrating on the killer instead of a possible witness."

"The bastard's trying to be the next Banksy."

"The next what?"

"Banksy. He's a street artist, goes around the world painting graffiti."

For some reason, Styx found himself wondering if Victor had studied Banksy in art history. Or maybe the current generation of artists hadn't made it into the textbooks yet.

After hanging up with Crevits, Styx took the dog, Shelley, out for his nightly walk in the dunes. He kept a tight grip on the leash, since he knew the pit bull had a short fuse. A year ago, Shelley had gone after a resident of the neighborhood so violently that the man had had no choice but to defend himself with the ferrule of his umbrella. Since that incident, Shelley had gone through life with only one eye.

"They need to put that rotten beast down," most of the residents of the Milho Apartments would have agreed. "It's dangerous."

But Styx couldn't bring himself to part with the dog. He believed that even the world's lowest creatures deserved a guardian angel. So every evening he and Shelley strolled along the dike, out onto the beach, and then back home past the Kursaal. It was either that or a lethal injection—if dogs could suffer from dementia, then Shelley had it bad, and the "new and improved" Shelley grew meaner and more aggressive by the day.

"Why can't you just let the poor thing go?" Isabelle had asked him more than once. Shelley was yet another bone of contention between them. "He's had it, can't you see that? You keep him alive for yourself, Rafe, not for him."

"That's not true," said Styx.

But the more time passed, the more the animal's temperment came to resemble its owner's.

"The exercise helps my hip," he argued.

And above all else, their half-hour walk—late in the evening, when the streets were quiet and peaceful—gave Styx an opportunity to think.

It also gave him a reason to visit the harbor once a week, to stroll past the cargo ships painted in primary colors and between the long rows of containers, stacked in their hundreds like so many giant Legos. Styx knew that the Ostend harbor was riddled with crime, everything from drug smuggling to weapons dealing and even human trafficking. Last year, a dozen refugees had been discovered trapped in a mildewed container. Half of them hadn't survived their confinement, and the half who had were deported back where they came from—in that case Kosovo.

The only thing that distinguished Ostend's harbor from others around the world was Gino Tersago, a notorious crook who over the years had served Styx as a valued stoolie in exchange for the cop's willingness to overlook certain of Tersago's malfeasances. What goes around comes around.

Tonight, they met by appointment in the rusted dark-blue container in Sector D that served as Tersago's headquarters. Tersago had washed up in Ostend after washing out as the owner of a pizzeria elsewhere in Belgium. These days Tersago dealt mainly in counterfeit designer goods he imported from China and Thailand.

With Shelley on the leash, Styx slipped into the container, where he found the tall, rail-thin gangster with the black brush cut and the scar from a surgically corrected harelip sitting at a rickety metal table, sipping from a can of beer.

"Yo, look what the wind blew in: Chief Inspector Styx."

"Terry," said Styx. He checked behind him to make sure no harbor police were in the area.

"Welcome to my world. To what do I owe this honor?"

Honor, Styx thought. *Nope, honor's got nothing to do with it.*

"Where's your crew?"

"I was just closing up shop," said Tersago. "It's dead tonight. I sent 'em all home. You can see they put in a full day today."

Tersago waved a hand at the empty container, as if it were a chic boutique on the day after Black Friday.

"What's new, Styxie?"

"I was about to ask you."

"Oh?"

"You haven't heard? The Stuffer's notched up another one."

"Yeah, I heard it on the radio," said Tersago. He'd told Styx once that his childhood dream was to be a policeman. "Didn't happen on my beat, though."

On his beat, as if he actually *was* a cop on patrol.

"You didn't see anything?" asked Styx.

"If I had, my friend, you don't think you'd already know about it? What, you don't trust me anymore?"

"Just making sure, Terry, that's all. This case is really starting to piss me off."

"I know where you're comin' from," said Tersago empathetically, as if he and Styx were buddies, "but I've got something else for you, man. Something to take away your pain and put you in a better mood."

Styx was so preoccupied with the investigation into the third murder that he'd completely forgotten today was payday. Tersago pulled a bulging white envelope from an inside pocket.

"Don't spend it all in one place," he grinned.

Styx looked at the outstretched hand and the envelope it held, but made no move to take it.

"Yeah, I almost forgot."

"Almost forgot? What's the matter with you? You don't need it? What, did you win the Lotto? Get a raise?"

"I just forgot," said Styx.

"You really *don't* trust me anymore, do you?"

"It's got nothing to do with trust," said Styx.

"No? What, then? There's three thousand euros here, Styxie. That's a month's pay for doing nothing. *Specifically* for doing nothing."

"I know, but—"

"But what? You understand it usually works the other way around, right? *You* pay *me* for information, if information's what you're after."

Styx stared so intently at the thick white rectangle that Tersago finally looked down at it, too, as if he didn't know how it had gotten into his hand. Shelley barked, putting his own two cents in, and Styx took the envelope. The dog's barking echoed off the walls of the container.

"Good boy," Tersago told them both. "Your friend there smells a treat."

Styx stuffed the envelope in his back pocket. This wasn't the first time he'd been greased to keep his mouth shut about the shady goings-on in the harbor, but it was beginning to eat at him that he did so little to earn the bribes he received. He didn't even have to look the other way. All he did was pass along a container number and location, and let Terry know when the harbor patrol would be making their rounds on the other side of the harbor.

"I think this is the last time," said Styx.

"What?" Tersago looked stunned. In the empty container, his voice rang out like thunder. "I'm not paying you enough?"

"That's not it."

"You want more?"

That *wasn't* it. It was something that had almost completely died away, but that still hung on in a dark corner of the broken-down wreck called Raphael Styx: one last shred of human decency.

"This got something to do with Amanda?"

"No," said Styx.

"What, then?"

"How is she?"

"I have no idea. Last I heard from her, she was in Thailand. I didn't send her in a container, in case you're wondering. I bought her a plane ticket, straight up. I heard she's got some rich fuck there wants to marry her."

"Yeah, well," said Styx. "Nothing to do with me."

Tersago sighed.

"Look, I don't know anything about the fuckin' Stuffer, Styxie. But I'll ask around, okay? If it'll make you feel any better."

"Thanks," said Styx. "I appreciate it."

Tersago got to his feet. "It was just a bunch of counterfeit shit, man." Tersago sounded almost apologetic.

"What?"

"Italian fake-leather handbags, designer jeans, cigarettes, the usual shit."

Styx put up a palm. "That's none of my business, either."

"Calm down," said Tersago, laying a hand on Styx's shoulder.

"I *am* calm."

"You just let me know about the next job. End of the month, I'm getting in a load of cars from the East Bloc. I figure I'll need two, maybe three containers. You'll take care of your contact in customs, right?"

Styx wanted to say, *Don't worry about it.* But he couldn't get the words out. When Tersago locked up the container behind them, the emptiness within looked way too much like Raphael Styx's life. Something had to change, but how long had he been handing himself that line? Too long.

Maybe it was too late for him to change. What was he doing, messing around with a second-rate thug like Gino Tersago? Styx was prostituting himself, and the harbor was his whorehouse.

"I don't know," he said. "You might have to set that up with my replacement."

Tersago's hand dropped to his wrist and held it tightly.

"Hey, Styxie, you're not gonna nark on me, are you?"

Styx didn't answer.

"I pay you, man."

"Yeah, you do."

"Well?"

"Don't worry, Terry, I won't rat you out."

Why would he betray Tersago's trust? Even that seemed too low for him.

Heading for home, he walked along the dike, past the fancy hotels, some new, others old and in disrepair, their glory days behind them. He was about to come down the steps to the street when he turned around and looked back. He'd walked right past it without realizing where he was.

He retraced his steps to the Rubens apartment building in the

Hofstraat. Where was the officer who was supposedly staking the place out? Nowhere to be seen. *Typical,* Styx thought. *The idiot's shift ended, and he went home.* He would rub Joachim Delacroix's nose in it in the morning.

Styx led Shelley into the lobby and checked the list of tenants. The pit bull plopped himself down on the floor.

Styx pressed the bell labeled SPILLIAERT.

CHAPTER 5

"Yes?"

"Mr. Spilliaert?"

"Who is it?"

"My name's Raphael Styx, chief inspector with the Ostend police."

"And?"

"I wonder if you can spare a few minutes?"

"For what?"

"Can I come up? My understanding is that you reported a crime this morning."

"That's right," the voice said.

"A woman was murdered."

There was no response. Styx expected to hear the door click open, but it didn't happen.

"I need to ask you a few follow-up questions, sir. It's urgent."

"I told the police everything I know this morning."

"Yes, we've spent the whole day trying to reach you, but—"

"I've been at work. I just got home."

Still no buzzer. Styx's hip began to protest. Shelley was also getting impatient, and he pulled on his leash. He wanted to go back outside, back to the beach. He'd had enough of this stuffy foyer. Styx looked into the lobby camera's lens and could feel Spilliaert looking back at him.

"I can show you my ID," Styx offered.

"That won't be necessary," said Spilliaert's voice. "I know who you are, Chief Inspector. What exactly do you need to ask me?"

"If you don't mind, I'd rather not discuss it like this," said Styx.

"Why not? I can see you."

"Yes, but I can't see *you*, and that's not the way we do things."

"I can imagine," the voice said, suddenly tinged with irony.

"Excuse me?"

"I can imagine that's not the way you do things."

"How do you mean?"

"You like to have the upper hand."

Styx said nothing, looked straight into the lens. He jerked on Shelley's leash to settle the dog down.

"I'm sorry?" he said, as if he hadn't heard Spilliaert's last comment.

"I said, Chief Inspector Styx, that you're a man who doesn't like to be messed with. But that's exactly what's been going on these last months, isn't it? It must be frustrating for you."

"What are you talking about?"

"These serial murders. The Stuffer."

Styx edged a bit to one side, tried to move out of the camera's field of view. "And what do you know about the case?"

"I read the papers, Inspector. You haven't gotten anywhere, have you? That's why you're here. You're hoping I can help you, but all I can tell you is what I saw when I came out of the sea this morning."

Styx forgot the stiffness in his side. "Do you always take an early swim?"

"You don't need to act like you still don't know who you're talking to, Inspector."

"I'm talking to Mr. Spilliaert, aren't I?"

Styx heard a knowing laugh, distorted by the intercom's speaker.

"If you like."

"Just a second," said Styx. "Is your name Spilliaert or not?"

"What do you think? You know the masters, don't you? You know that Léon Spilliaert, one of Ostend's Surrealists, has been dead for more than sixty years?"

There was the taste of bile in Styx's mouth, and he finally realized what was going on.

"I'll be whoever you want me to be, Inspector."

Styx swallowed. He was about to reach for his cell and call the squad, until he remembered that he never carried a phone when he was out with Shelley. A matter of principle, a rare chance to relish being cut off from the world. Meanwhile, Spilliaert-but-not-Spilliaert could see him, and would be gone long before backup could get there.

"Okay," said Styx. "Let's start over." He pressed the buzzer and said, "Who am I speaking with, please?"

"I told you I just got home from work, Chief Inspector."

It wasn't the words the man said or even the words he *didn't* say. It was the way he said them—and didn't say them. No other man would laugh with such confident abandon. Styx pushed the entry door, but it held fast.

"I'll let you in when I'm good and ready."

"Open up, you fuck!" Styx yelled.

He beat on the door.

"And we were getting along so well," the voice said sadly.

"Let me in!"

And then the voice took on a new tone—harder, more dangerous. "Come on, Styx, you don't expect me to sit here waiting while you send out for a battering ram?"

"Why did you call us?"

"I was getting bored, *Monsieur l'Inspecteur*. I thought you'd all forgotten about me and gone on to other playmates. A true artist has to make himself heard from time to time. He's got to get through to the stupid zombies who waste their lives staring at a computer screen. In this society we've created, he can't afford to lock himself up in an ivory tower."

Styx pounded on the door with his fist. With his other hand, he rang every buzzer on the board. A confusion of voices came through the speaker, each wanting to know who was there. There was no time to explain the situation. He yelled out his name, but there was no answering click. One resident announced: "If you don't go away, I'm calling the police."

"I *am* the police!" screamed Styx. "Open the fucking door!"

And at that moment, he finally heard the click. He flung the door open and, vaguely, behind him, heard the voice of the man who couldn't be anyone else but the Stuffer:

"What's taking you so long, Styx? Come on up. You think I'm going to wait all night?"

There was no time to think. He unclipped Shelley's leash and jumped into an elevator, leaving the pit bull behind.

"Go home, Shelley!" he ordered, pressing the button for the fifth floor. If only he had his phone, he could call John Crevits, call the squad, call that dashing young prick Delacroix, who at this moment was probably standing before a full-length mirror, primping and pimping himself up for a night on the town.

"Come on," he urged the creaky machinery. "Come *on!*"

The numbers above the door blinked on and off slowly. Two . . . three . . . four . . .

"Goddammit!"

He'd just risen above the fourth floor when, through the Plexiglas window in the door, he saw a sudden movement. A shadow flickered past, and he heard rapid footsteps on the stairs. Going down. The bastard was getting away! He'd waited just long enough to make sure that Styx had boarded the elevator, and then *he'd* taken the stairs. From below, he could hear Shelley barking. Styx swore and beat impotently on the elevator door.

"Christ, this is bullshit!"

The door slid open. At the end of the corridor, Spilliaert's apartment door gaped wide.

Downstairs, his fool dog was still howling.

"Shelley!" he bellowed.

Styx raced down the hall into the apartment and searched wildly for a telephone, a cell phone, a tablet or computer that could send an e-mail, anything—but there was nothing. The apartment was completely empty. He stood stock-still before the broad window that gave out onto a balcony with a view of the North Sea. On the horizon, a brilliant orange sun extinguished itself in the water. Four stories down, a figure in what looked like a yellow fisherman's oilskin jacket and sou'wester hat hurried out of the building and away to the west.

The Stuffer.

There were two alternatives. He could find a neighbor who would let him call the station, but by the time the police turned up, the Stuffer would be long gone. Or he could go after the man himself.

Styx didn't hesitate. Within a minute, he burst out of the elevator at ground level and gave chase. The farther he got from the city center, the fewer people were out and about. The beachgoers—at this time of year mostly older couples and families with small children—had packed it in for the day hours earlier. Gone were the surfers and sailboarders. Styx couldn't see the Stuffer, but he knew the man was out there somewhere and quickened his pace. With each passing minute, his shadow lengthened on the dike's pale-yellow tiles.

At last he was forced to stop, gasping for breath, propped up against a stone pillar in the Venetian Galleries. The pain in his hip was excruciating.

"Goddamnit!" he swore.

It would be pointless to try to continue. The killer had several minutes' head start, and there was no guarantee he'd come this way in the first place. Styx's choice of direction had been a wild guess. The Stuffer could have turned off the dike down any of a dozen side streets and by now might have lost himself in Ostend's shopping district.

And yet . . .

And yet Raphael Styx had a feeling he was close by. He staggered forward—and saw a long shadow painted on the marble flooring.

"Hello?"

He approached the figure half-hidden behind a column, but then saw a second shadow, the two of them woven together confusingly. It was the magic hour, between nine and nine thirty. The sun was down, and a golden glow bathed the Venetian Galleries, enchanted them, turned them into the perfect backdrop for a photo shoot.

"Spilliaert?"

Styx barely had time to draw his weapon before the two shadows were upon him, and he saw that it was only a couple of teenagers.

"Sorry," he said, but the boy and girl—young lovers, perhaps, saying their last good-byes before heading off in separate directions for the summer—were already gone, strolling arm in arm toward the sea.

"Shit," Styx muttered.

He holstered his gun and turned back in the direction he'd come.

Styx crossed the dike and took the first wooden staircase down to the beach. He sat on the bottom step and pulled off his shoes, then began the slow walk back through the soft sand.

Léon Spilliaert, he thought.

Of course.

Spilliaert the painter might well have left descendants behind, but Styx was willing to bet that the Stuffer wasn't one of them.

He walked between two rows of rental cabanas, all shut up tight for the night. You could almost shoot a Western here, with beach sand instead of desert sand and the cabanas standing in for saloons.

He saw the gun sticking out between two cabanas just a moment too late.

"Why do I have the feeling you're trying to avoid me, Chief Inspector?" a voice said. "Aren't you supposed to be trying to catch me?"

CHAPTER 6

Styx stared at the gap, the opening, the space between the two wooden huts. He saw the Stuffer's silhouette deep in the shadows, the face concealed beneath the yellow sou'wester hat.

"You're just making it harder on yourself," he began carefully. "First you call in this morning to invite us to the showing of your latest piece, then you disappear for the rest of the day, and then you lead me out here. Why didn't you just come to the station if you wanted to talk?"

"Who says I want to talk?" said the Stuffer.

"Then what are we doing here?"

"We're talking *now*, true."

Styx kept his eye on the gun. The Stuffer had committed all three of the murders with his bare hands. The women had either been strangled or stabbed to death. There'd been no shell casings, no gunshot wounds.

Yet now he was standing eye to eye with a revolver. Even serial killers sometimes change their patterns.

"So you'd like to have a little chat?" the Stuffer continued, his tone casual. "Fine, then. What should we talk about?"

"How about pointing that thing somewhere else?"

"You think I'm an idiot? If you can't come up with more stimulating conversation than that, I'm going to use it."

"Why are you doing this?"

"You know too much, Styx. I'm beginning to understand you. You've got anger-management issues. You're not like the rest of them. You're an outsider, like me. An outlaw, who plays the game by his own rules."

"With a few differences."

"Really? Name one."

"I'm not a murderer."

"You're a stubborn bastard, Styx, I'll give you that. You're as committed to stopping me as I am to carrying on, and that's dangerous. You're starting to get in my way, and it's time to do something about it. Plus, I'm getting bored. I need a little action."

Styx knew he had to keep the madman talking. They were at the far end of the beach, but sooner or later someone would come along. An old man with a metal detector, a dad coming back for a beach ball or kite his kid had left behind.

Through the space between the cabanas, he saw people walking along the dike in the distance. He could shout and attract their attention, but he had a feeling the Stuffer would pull the trigger if he did.

"I don't mean why did you get me out here," he said. "I mean, why the whole thing? The murders. The sand sculptures."

"Sand sculptures?" the Stuffer chuckled. Styx saw the gun barrel bob up and down. "I like that. You mind if I use it?"

"Be my guest," said Styx. "But your exhibition is just about over."

"You think so? I beg to differ. I've got at least twenty more projects in mind. It's going to be a really *big* show."

"What's the point?" Styx demanded.

"What are you, an art critic? What's the point of *your* life, Chief Inspector Styx?"

"I don't know."

"Well, *this* is the point of mine. It reminds me that I'm alive. It makes my life interesting. What have *you* got?"

Styx shrugged. In principle, he could draw his own gun in one swift motion, and then they'd be on equal ground. But there was a problem: his hip. He wasn't a cowboy, it wouldn't let him get away with a quick draw.

"What keeps my life interesting?" he said.

"Right—and stop stalling for time."

His first thought was: *my wife, my son, my family.* But he couldn't bring himself to say it. He wanted it to be the truth, but he knew that it wasn't.

"My job," he said. "That's all I have. My job, and my body."

"I figured. And your body's not looking too good. The body's a machine, Styx, like a car. How many years have you got on your odometer? Forty?"

Shit, how did the fucker know so much about him?

"You need to look at yourself in the mirror from time to time," said the Stuffer, "compare today's you with the you that you used to be. That's what I want to show the world with my, I like the way you put it, my 'sand sculptures.' Each one of them's a mirror. We're all works of art, Styx, every single one of us. We're each unique, but, you know what? We're better looking when we're dead. Only after death does our true beauty really—"

"If I want an art lesson," said Styx, "I'll go to a museum."

He knew he was taking a huge risk, but the words were out of his mouth before he could stop them.

Suddenly, Styx felt very strange. He was paralyzed, but not, for once, because of his hip.

He knew that something very bad was about to happen, and he knew there was nothing he could do to stop it.

He was intensely aware of his surroundings. It was as if he'd grown a pair of antennae, as if his perceptive ability had suddenly tripled. He could hear a cruise ship's foghorn miles out at sea. He could taste the salt in the air. He could feel each individual grain of sand pressing against the soles of his bare feet.

He realized he was still holding his shoes and socks in his hand. He let them fall, as if he was throwing in the towel. He hardly dared to look at the shadow between the cabanas.

"What good is killing me going to do?" he said softly.

"Who says I'm going to kill you? You can just turn around and walk away."

This was exactly what he'd wanted to hear, that the Stuffer wasn't going to shoot him. Of course he wouldn't. Why *should* he? Without Styx to pursue him, the game wouldn't be any fun.

But then he heard the Stuffer cock the hammer of his revolver.

Raphael Styx had heard that sound many times before, but he was almost always the one doing the cocking. Now the tables were turned, and, for the first time in his life, he felt afraid.

His feet were made of lead.

"They say life begins at forty," the Stuffer said lightly.

"You can't—"

"I'm doing you a favor, you stupid fuck."

Styx heard the shot as if in a dream, hollow, echoing. At the same moment came the blast of an air horn, the sort of thing you'd hear at the Arena when the Ostend basketball team sank a three-pointer.

The air horn swallowed the sound of the shot, and no one passing by on the dike paid any attention.

Styx didn't sink immediately to his knees. No, this once his hip supported him. When he looked down, though, he could see the bullet hole in his belly. He tasted blood in his mouth and knew that he was in trouble.

"You can't fucking kill me," he said.

The second shot hit him in the chest, just missing his heart. The bullet punctured a lung and brought him down to one knee. He dropped a hand to the surface of the sand to hold himself up, and now the blood wasn't just in his mouth. It was everywhere, dripping from his body like wax from a burning candle. His eyes focused on a broken mussel shell that lay beside his knee. There were thousands of them on the beach. Millions. This stupid shell wouldn't be the last thing he ever saw, would it?

"I can do whatever I want," the Stuffer told him, stepping out of the shadows. When Styx raised his head, his vision was blurred. He felt very sleepy. His life was leaking from the holes in his stomach and chest. He felt light, like a kite waiting for the wind to pick it up and carry it into the sky.

His vision cleared for a moment, and he saw that the Stuffer was wearing a plastic mask of the painter James Ensor.

"You'll thank me for this," the mask said. "I'm saving you from hell. It's only halftime, Styx, but the game's over and you lose. I promise you, though: I'm going to give you a beautiful send-off. You'll be the star of the show."

Styx toppled over onto his back.

He thought of Isabelle, of his son, Victor, and wondered what would become of them. And Shelley? What had happened to him? Would he be able to find his way home?

His eyelids were so heavy. He couldn't keep them open any longer.

He let them close, and, in the darkness, everything was peaceful and quiet.

There was no tunnel, no white light, no cinematic montage of scenes from his life, no spirit soaring free of his shattered body.

There was nothing. It was all blown away by the Stuffer's third shot, the coup de grâce, which drilled straight through his heart and blew it to pieces.

Raphael Styx sighed out his final breath.

The Stuffer knew he didn't have much time. His air horn had drowned out the sound of the first shot, but the second and third shots had surely not gone unnoticed.

He whipped off his mask and dragged Styx's body into the darkness between two cabanas. He hadn't meant to kill the cop. Well, not yet. Eventually, it would have come to that, but not so soon. He felt like he'd lost his only worthy adversary.

Poor bastard, he thought, gazing down at the motionless, empty face in the sand. *Your life was shitty enough as it was, and then I had to come along.*

With the butt of his revolver, he knocked the lock off one of the cabana's doors. These wooden shacks that looked so quaint on postcards were so cheaply made it was hardly worthwhile locking them in the first place. A child of eight could huff and puff and practically blow the house down.

On the inside, this one was the same as all the rest. A couple of folded beach chairs. An assortment of plastic buckets and shovels and sieves. In the corner, a crab net, a grown-up shovel, and an air mattress. Everything you needed to survive a day on the Ostend beach.

"Sorry, Styx," said the Stuffer, half-aloud, half to himself, "but you'll have to hang out here for a while. I'll fetch my equipment and come back. And when I'm done with you I'll find someplace extra special to put you, so everyone can see just how handsome I've made you."

He dragged the body into the cabana. A lock of Styx's hair caught on a nailhead that had popped up a bit from the floor, and he had to yank hard to pull the policeman free.

"Right smack on the dike, I think, with a lovely view of the sea. Won't that be nice?"

He sighed with excitement and examined the body, which lay there splayed across the wooden floorboards. The cop's black hair was dotted with sand, his trouser legs and feet dark red with blood. That last shot had taken the poor fuck right in the heart.

Just to be safe, he wrestled the body into a corner and lay the air mattress over it.

"Oh, before I forget!"

He fished his iPhone from a trouser pocket.

"Say 'cheese,' " he smiled, and took two photos of the dead policeman, one showing his full body and then a close-up of the lifeless face.

He left the cabana and pulled the door shut as if nothing whatsoever had happened and he'd merely been changing into his swimsuit for a little late-night dip in the sea.

Before anything else, he had to pick out the perfect spot for the display. The final resting place for Raphael Styx, *Untitled #4* (2014).

To make sure he'd recognize the cabana later, he left a little rock propped against the door.

CHAPTER 7

When Raphael Styx opened his eyes, he figured he was dead. He had to be. He'd been shot, three times, twice in the chest, and everything was dark.

At best, he was balanced precariously on the borderline between life and death, at that crucial tipping point where the soul crosses from this world to the next. But shouldn't he be floating up in the sky, looking down at his lifeless body on the beach?

Wait, he wasn't *on* the beach anymore. He could feel a hard floor beneath him and, strangest of all, the usual pain in his hip.

He closed his eyes again and decided it was pointless to try to figure it out. Whatever would be, would be.

But ten seconds later he opened them again. He couldn't just lie there. He was breathing, and that was bizarre. He felt pins and needles in his fingers. His muscles were sore, and he still had the taste of blood in his mouth, although it was dried blood now.

He wasn't about to lie there waiting for death. *Might as well give it a shot*, he thought, and tried to get up, assuming there wasn't the slightest chance he could make it.

And yet he did.

It was still pitch-dark, but he managed to work himself into a half-sitting position and, despite his hip, bend forward far enough to touch his toes.

What the fuck was going on? On hands and knees he felt his way around the enclosed space, searching for something he could use to hoist himself to his feet. In the dark he was like an animal trapped in a cage.

He bumped into something soft and heard it flop lightly to the floor. He explored it with his fingertips and identified it as an air mattress. He moved past it and came to a wooden wall. He pushed at it and discovered that it was a door. He pushed harder and it creaked open.

Outside it was still dark, but this was the darkness of night, not the grave. From the sound of the surf on the shore and the smell of the salt, he knew exactly where he was, still on the Ostend beach.

He was inside a cabana.

Okay.

He struggled to his feet, holding on to the door for support. It was hard work, but he made it. He stood bent slightly at the waist to reduce the strain on his hip. He could see moonlight dancing on the water and the running lights of ships in the distance.

"What the—?"

He searched for an explanation but came up empty. Was this the Great Beyond? If it was, it looked remarkably like the Ordinary Here and Now. But why, if he could feel his hip, couldn't he feel the agony of the Stuffer's three bullets?

"That shitbag," he said aloud.

Apparently he wasn't dead. *Au contraire*, the killer had chosen to let him live. But why?

There's no thrill of the chase if there's nobody chasing you.

It sure as hell wasn't the bulletproof vest he'd left at the police station. Styx refused to wear one after he'd fired in a shoot-out near the market square three years ago. A round had ricocheted and wounded an innocent bystander, a six-year-old girl. The girl had lain in a coma for a month before her family had pulled the plug, and Styx had never once had the guts or the common decency to visit the girl or her family. Both Internal Affairs and the department psychologist had stood ready to help him through it, but he'd shaken off their repeated offers of emotional support. Shit happens, and this was about as shitty as it got, but all he'd done was his job, and the little girl's death was neither his responsibility nor his fault.

What nobody knew was that, since the day of the accident, he'd refused to put on the Kevlar. If he was going to have to pay for what he'd done, then let him pay.

Had the Stuffer fired blanks? Possible. The Stuffer had been hiding in the shadows, and Styx had only caught a glimpse of his revolver.

Sure, it was possible.

But why would the Stuffer run the risk of shooting Chief Inspector Raphael Styx, a cop—and why in the *world* would he carry a gun loaded with blanks?

"The sick fuck," Styx said, and coughed up a laugh.

He realized that he'd pissed his pants, but, fine, anything was better than a meeting with the Grim Reaper. For those last few seconds, he'd really thought that this was the end of the line.

He remembered the broken mussel shell. It seemed ridiculous now to think that he'd knelt there, practically worshiping it, thinking it would be the last thing he'd ever see. It was a shell. There'd be thousands more of them in the years to come.

Yet he'd been ready to give up, to roll over and play dead.

Was that what the Stuffer wanted? To humiliate him? To put him eyeball-to-eyeball with Death and terrify him into giving up the hunt, maybe even turn in his badge and leave the force?

"If you think I'm falling for that shit," he muttered, "you can think again."

He staggered out of the cabana, moving even more slowly and woodenly than usual. Spend a couple hours flat on your forty-year-old ass, though, and who *wouldn't* pay a price?

He pulled an old pocket watch from his breast pocket, wondering if that might have been what saved him, but there wasn't a scratch on it. It had belonged to his father-in-law, an antique from La Belle Époque—and, like so much in Styx's life, it was broken. He'd taken it from Grandpa Marc's house with the intention of selling it at the flea market, but for one reason or another he'd held on to it and begun carrying it around. A sort of rabbit's foot.

But what about the blood? Imagination? No, he'd really seen blood. Or had he? He'd tasted it in his mouth, sweet as honey, thick as molasses. Had he simply bitten his tongue out of fear? But then what about the bloodstains on his clothes? He couldn't see it now in the dark, but when the first bullet had hit him, a dark-red flower had blossomed on his shirt front.

Hadn't it?

You heard about people hallucinating in extreme situations, like when they were staring the Man with the Scythe in the eyes.

He patted his shirt and trousers experimentally. His clothes felt wet and heavy, but then it had been damp in the wooden cabana, and he'd apparently been dragged there through the rain.

Oh, fuck it, he thought.

The important thing was that he wasn't dead.

And that feeling, man, there was nothing like it. He wouldn't recommend it, but thinking you'd breathed your last breath and then realizing it had all just been one giant sick joke . . . priceless.

The adrenaline coursed through his body, and he understood how race-car drivers must feel, putting their lives on the line and living out there on the edge.

He felt reborn. He'd been given a second chance. The Stuffer had been wrong: his second half was still to be played, and, now that he'd seen how quickly it *could* all come to an end, he was going to play it to win.

The shock of his resurrection—and it *was* a shock, that was undeniable—almost nailed him to the ground. A full-grown man with a full-blown midlife crisis, a chief inspector with the Ostend police who'd peed his pants with terror, and here he was, stumbling toward a new horizon on bare feet.

Isabelle, he thought. *Victor.*

He felt for his phone to call them and tell them he was okay. They didn't have to worry about him. He wasn't dead. He was coming home.

But then he remembered that he'd left it at home, remembered what had happened, remembered the pursuit across the sand.

God, Ostend's beautiful when you're not dead, he thought.

He turned his back on the sea and wondered how he would explain it all to Isabelle. The feelings, the sensations of his near-death experience. It was as if he'd survived a horrible car crash or been rescued at the last second from an attempted suicide.

Isabelle would understand. As the chief of nursing of the geriatrics ward at Damiaan Hospital, she saw it every day. How many times had she told him of bringing a patient back from death's door? How many times had she wished she could do the same for their dying marriage?

His hip twinged painfully, and Styx—to his surprise—was glad.

It took Styx an eternity to climb the steps to the dike. He had to stop twice to catch his breath, and, by the time he reached the top, his limbs were aching. He couldn't lift his right leg from the ground but had to drag it along behind him. At least he could still feel it.

From the dike, he looked out across Ostend, the queen of the Belgian seaside resorts, out past the stately buildings and empty streets shrouded in darkness to the Maria Hendrika Park in the distance.

He felt free, free—now that he wasn't dead—from the fear of death. He felt like the monarch of all he surveyed. He stood there, admiring the night and the moon, much as, a few hours earlier, he'd stood at the Stuffer's window and marveled at the beauty of the setting sun.

Halfway down the street, he saw three figures approaching. They wove drunkenly left and right, bumped into one another and bounced off in opposite directions, on their way from Pub A to Pub B—or, by now, from Pub X to Pub Y. They laughed unselfconsciously, exuberantly, at each collision.

As he came down the last few steps, he tried to avoid them, but in the dim glow of the streetlights they drifted closer.

"Jesus, get a load of this guy," one of them giggled.

"What happened to you, man?" said another.

The third one only stared. Styx stared back at him. Under other circumstances, he would have arrested them for public drunkenness, but not tonight.

"What hole did you crawl out of, you ugly fuck?" the first one challenged him.

Styx didn't respond. His tongue felt heavy, his mouth still clogged with dried blood.

"Lay off," said the third man, breaking his silence. "Can't you see the guy's hurt?"

The third man's hand clamped down on his shoulder. "You okay, buddy?" he asked, his mouth so close to Styx's ear that he could feel his breath.

His shoulder jerked upward involuntarily, as if the drunk had touched a raw nerve.

"Calm down," the man said. "I just wanna know if you need us to get you to the hops—the hospital."

"Leave 'im be," the first man slurred. "He jus' had hisself a rough night, like us. Right, buddy?"

Styx looked the three caballeros up and down.

"I'm okay," he said.

"Say, whyn't you join us for a li'l nightcap?" the first one proposed. "One more drink before beddy-byes."

But the other two demurred. They were done for the day.

"You sure we can't drop you someplace?"

"I'm just heading home," said Styx.

They were eyeballing him like he'd been marinating in a bucket of tar. The third one seemed reluctant to abandon him. He staggered right up to Styx and held up a hand and waved it in little circles, as if trying to decide what part of him to pet. His cheek? His lips? His hair?

"Somebody really did a number on you, huh? Lemme guess. The new bouncer in the Cocoon Club, right? He's a real prick."

"Don't worry about it," said Styx.

"We got nothin' against you, man. We're jus' sym . . . pathetic."

Styx turned away and walked off—or shuffled off. His right leg was deadweight, but Dr. Vrancken had promised him that a little exercise would be the ticket. One step at a time.

". . . oughta take a look in a mirror," he heard one of the drunkards say.

He passed the darkened shop windows of the Kapellestraat and saw his silhouette reflected in the glass. Behind him, the tipsy trio turned a corner and, with a howl that could have come from a wolf in the lost forest of Gistel, disappeared into the night.

Styx pulled up before a clothing store. The display window was populated with mannequins dressed in the latest fashions. Coincidentally, his own reflection almost perfectly lined up with one of the dummies, and it seemed for a moment as if *he* was wearing the colorful suit. Bright colors were in this year, and he looked more like Joachim Delacroix than himself.

It was hard to make out his facial features in the dark, but everything seemed normal: his head was the right shape, no obvious bumps or lumps or contusions. Which made sense, since, as best he could recall, the Stuffer hadn't done anything to his face.

But then what was that about a mirror?

Styx shrugged.

But he hadn't meant to shrug. It had happened all by itself.

It had happened without volition. A sort of tic or reflex.

What the hell was going on?

CHAPTER 8

On his way home Styx considered detouring past the Stuffer's apartment in the Hofstraat but decided to check in with the squad first. He felt tired and empty and wasn't in the mood to take unnecessary chances. His best bet was to talk with John Crevits as soon as possible.

But, no, even that would have to wait. First home to his family, who were probably worried sick by now. First to Isabelle and Victor, to reassure them that everything was fine, that he'd met the serial killer and survived. He could see the scene play out: he'd stumble across the threshold, switch on the hall light, drag himself up the stairs . . . and there would be Isabelle, who would take him in her arms and hold him close.

I thought something must have happened to you, he could hear her whisper.

Isabelle in her low-cut black nightgown. Even if he *was* all drenched in blood, she wouldn't mind.

I thought something awful must have happened to you.

"I'm okay," he heard himself rumble.

How many times have I begged you to take your phone with you?

"It wouldn't have made much difference. Anyway, I'm home now."

And then Victor would be there. He would keep his distance, at first, until Styx gathered him into a group hug.

I'm sorry, Dad, Styx heard. *I'm sorry I've been so weird.*

"Shhh, now, it's okay," he would reassure the boy. "It doesn't matter. The important thing is we're all together."

That's how it would go. Maybe not exactly in that order, but—

But *was* that how it would go?

He and Isabelle had grown apart—but she would still worry about him, right? Maybe he'd find patrol cars in the driveway when he turned onto their street. Maybe Crevits and Delacroix would be there, waiting for him, ready to drape a blanket around his shivering shoulders before questioning him about his encounter with the Stuffer. He was a witness now.

Looking like a lost tourist, he came to the Ostend train station, which was on his path toward home. He heard himself growl, like a dog, a clear sign that he needed to rest. The taste in his mouth was so awful he had to rinse it away.

"Like I drank a bucket of shit," he muttered.

He limped into the cavernous station hall and saw that the arrivals and departures board was completely blank. The ticket windows, kiosks, and bistros were all deserted. Here and there, a hobo lay stretched out on a wooden bench, sleeping.

Styx shuffled into the men's room. He thought of Shelley's awful morning breath. This, he thought, was worse. Where *was* Shelley, anyway?

He leaned on one of the white porcelain sinks, his eyes adjusting to the glare of the neon lighting. He squinted, then cracked open the taps to wash his hands. The water was cold. He scrubbed off the dried blood and stuck his head under the tap. He gulped greedily and swallowed. He almost choked and found himself coughing.

Blood splattered the porcelain. He was coughing up blood. Was that bad? Was he bleeding internally? He ducked his head back into the stream of water and cleaned himself as best he could.

When he stood up and got a good look at himself in the mirror, his heart stood still.

"Jesus God!"

What the fuck was *wrong* with him? His healthy complexion had taken on a greenish tint, the color of withered weeds. His pupils were unnaturally large, like a cat's, but the whites of his eyes had gone yellow and were crisscrossed with ominous red veins.

Styx had spent an unusual amount of time examining himself in mirrors these last few months. Ever since he turned forty, there was always something new to worry about. A wrinkle here, a liver spot there. And his eyes seemed to be receding into his skull. But the years, he felt, were adding character to his face. Some men were lucky that way, and he was apparently one of them.

But now, in the middle of the night in the station lavatory, Raphael Styx couldn't believe what he saw.

It didn't make any sense. The dark circles ringing his eyes, the red and purple sores, the bruises, the scar tissue. His lips were black, like some Gothic rock star. He grimaced at the mirror and saw that his teeth were yellow and plastered with patches of dried blood.

This is insane, he thought.

He rinsed his mouth, but couldn't get rid of the gunk. It was baked on, ineradicable.

He backed away from the mirror in horror, and now, beneath the bright artificial lights, got his first clear look at the rest of himself. There was blood all over his shirt, his jacket, his pants.

Okay, so not blanks, he thought.

He tried to unbutton his shirt—no simple task, since he found that he had little control of his fingers. They were unsteady, almost impossible to manage. Like his shoulder.

At last he ripped the shirt open, and his breath caught in his throat. The wounds.

Real bullet wounds. He saw the holes where the three shots had hit him. Stomach, chest, and heart.

I just wanna know if you need us to get you to the hops—the hospital.

Styx touched the gaping wounds with trembling fingers.

I thought something awful must have happened to you.

He half closed his eyes against the monstrousness of what he was about to do and pushed the tip of his index finger into one of the holes. He could feel his finger slide deep inside his body.

I'm sorry, Dad. I thought you were dead.

He pulled his finger free. It made a sickening sucking sound as it emerged from his body. The bullets must still be inside him, he realized. What the fuck was going on? Was he somehow immune to hot lead, like some people were immune to AIDS?

This is nuts. I must be dreaming.

He looked at his wristwatch. It was 2:13 AM. He unclasped it from his wrist so he could wash his arm, but stood there watching the seconds tick by.

Tick, tick, tick . . .

His shoulder spasmed. *Another kind of tic*, he thought.

He laughed hysterically.

He didn't want to believe what he was thinking, but knew there was a way to find out for sure.

He pressed the index and middle fingers of his right hand to his left wrist and held them there.

"Come on," he urged himself. "Come *on!*"

It always took a while to find it. He was never sure exactly where he was supposed to feel it.

He moved his fingers side to side, up and down the inside of his wrist.

Nothing.

Absolutely nothing.

At the police academy they'd made the recruits check their pulses every day—after every twelve-minute Cooper test, after each scuba lesson, during the damn first-aid lectures—but he never did get the hang of it.

"Come *on*, dammit!"

He let go of his wrist and pressed his fingertips to the side of his neck, feeling for the external carotid artery.

Nothing.

There had to be *something*, dammit. Otherwise, he wouldn't be standing here. Where the fuck was his pulse?

He still had a heart, didn't he? After all, he'd taken a bullet to it!

And then he realized what that meant, what it implied, and his wristwatch slipped from his fingers and fell into the sink.

His legs gave out from under him and, for the second time that night, he lost consciousness.

But this time he knew as he dropped that he would wake up again. Not as the old Raphael Styx, an Ostend policeman with a beautiful wife and son, but as a new man, a new *kind* of man.

There was a word for what he had become, but he cracked his head on the washroom floor and his blackened lips fell still and silent.

CHAPTER 9

When Styx awoke, he found himself on the floor of the train station men's room. It wasn't a cabana on the beach, but it wasn't much of an improvement. Shrouded in darkness, his superstition and fear gave way to certainty.

Raphael Styx is dead, he thought. *But he lives again, a revenant.*

A zombie.

He clawed his way to his feet but didn't dare return to the mirror. Nothing had changed, and he didn't need a mirror to be sure.

He shuffled out of the public toilets and heard the first train of the new day rumble into the station. He felt for his father-in-law's pocket watch and looked around for a trash barrel, convinced it had brought him only bad luck. But then he noticed something strange.

The watch was a half-hunter, with a small crystal circle set into its hinged lid to allow its hands to be seen even when the lid was shut. Through the crystal he saw that the second hand was moving.

. He stared at the watch, clicked it open for a better view of the hands. And, yes, the second hand was slowly circling the dial.

"How—?"

The entry hall was still deserted. Even the bums had moved on from their benches. Styx stood in the shadow of an alcove, bewildered by this bizarre new turn his life had taken, when the voices of the day's first travelers echoed through the enormous hall. Footsteps sounded on the marble flooring. And then he saw them.

"This way, Your Majesty, *s'il vous plaît*. Our program for today begins with a visit to the first asphalt roadway connecting Ostend with Wenduine. After we enjoy a buffet luncheon at the Nouveau Theatre Royal, we shall proceed to the new port of Ostend, and then to the casino."

Styx stared at the small procession of partygoers, open-mouthed. There were men in three-piece suits, wearing top hats and carrying canes. The women wore hoop skirts, narrow boots, and wide hats, and carried fans. They all spoke French. In the middle of the cortege was a tall man with an immense squared-off white beard and a sharp nose.

What was *this*? A theater troupe, just arrived from France, here for a performance at the Theater Aan Zee? Styx watched the parade draw nearer, the women giggling, the men talking rapidly and gesticulating broadly. The man with the beard only nodded, and occasionally pointed out a feature of the station hall's construction with the tip of his parasol.

"And if we have time, perhaps we can take in the Promenade and the Parc Léopold . . ."

The atmosphere was genial, the conversations of the men rebounded through the hall and fell on the ear like song. Styx stood in his corner, watching all the girls go by. He was so riveted by the spectacle that, for a moment, he forgot who he was. Or *what* he was, what he had become.

It was odd: the mood, the people, their clothing, the ambiance; it all reminded him of another Ostend, an Ostend that was as dead as he was. The Ostend of La Belle Époque, when Leopold II ruled the land from his Royal Palace. The train station was the same as always, but it was bathed in the glow of an earlier time.

I'm going nuts, Styx thought. *I haven't just gone beyond the pale— I've gone around the bend. This has to be some kind of nightmare.*

He was so preoccupied with his own situation that he barely looked up when the procession moved past him. The men gave him polite nods, but two of the women in the company edged away from him.

"Here, you poor man," another woman said, holding out a coin. She didn't dare risk brushing his hand, though, and dropped her offering at his feet. It tinkled to the ground, and the sound reverberated through the hall like wind chimes in a summer breeze.

"*Ostende doit devenir la capitale de la côte Belgique et la plus belle ville,*" the king said.

"*Mais bien sûr, Monsieur Le Roi,*" a member of the entourage replied. "*Ça c'est certain.*"

They remained gathered around him, and Styx couldn't understand their nonchalance. Weren't they horrified by his appearance? Or were they so caught up in their roles that they saw him as just an ordinary beggar instead of the decrepit syphilitic horror he had become?

"*Mais maintenant on va quand même fêter?*" said the king, a little louder now. "*C'est pour ca que je ne vais jamais au Congo. Pourquoi visiter le Congo si il y a des pauvres imbeciles à Ostende?*"

They moved on, and their laughter disappeared around a corner. Styx bent down and picked up the coin. It was heavier than a euro and seemed made of gold. A profile of Leopold II's head and neck faced to the right. When this group played a part, they played to *win*.

He dropped the coin in his pocket and left his niche. Just before stepping out of the station into the bright sunshine, he turned back to the arrivals and departures board. The letters and numbers weren't clacking electronically, as they always did. Instead, the destinations and times were painted onto wooden slats and hung from pins attached to the board, just like in the olden days.

Styx did some math in his head.

More than two hours from Ostend to Brussels?

That trip wouldn't take two hours unless you traveled by steam engine.

Styx wasn't sure what to do next. He ought to go straight to the police station. Even before heading home, he ought to fill Crevits in on the events of the previous evening. He could report his face-to-face encounter with the Stuffer. He could report that he'd taken three bullets. He could report—

Report what? That he no longer had a pulse? That his flesh was beginning to rot away, that he was starting to stink like the walking dead? What good would that do? And besides, he was no longer sure Crevits could be trusted.

Styx thought back to his previous life, the life he'd already begun to ruin when he still had one to live. John Crevits had twice betrayed him. The first time, Crevits was forced to call in Internal Affairs after a complaint that Styx had used excessive force on a suspect. The second betrayal had been more personal, when Crevits—whether on purpose or accidentally—had let Isabelle know about his affair with Amanda. He'd tried to make it seem like he'd done it for Styx's own good and the good of his family. Crevits, the guardian angel, that was the idea—but Styx knew better. From that day forward, things between the chief inspector and the commissioner had never been the same.

No, maybe he'd better not bring Crevits up to speed. What if, the minute his boss saw the new Styx, he notified his superiors of the situation? Crevits was a company man, always had been, and he'd relish the fame this incredible revelation would bring him.

No, he finally decided, John Crevits—like everything else—belonged to the life he'd left behind.

Styx clapped Grandpa Marc's watch shut and shuffled out into the streets of Ostend. It was a smallish city, which would make it harder for him to hide. From time to time, he saw people looking at him. Two kids on the way to school with their mother stood stock-still in the middle of a crosswalk and pointed at the funny man limping along the pavement.

It didn't take him long to come to a decision. The sun was up, and in his condition, he couldn't go on wandering around in the open. That would attract more attention than he felt he could handle.

But where could he hide?

With the remnants of mental clarity he still had, he considered the current state of affairs:

The Stuffer had shot him.

The Stuffer thought he was dead.

Therefore, although he wasn't sure exactly how it might work, he had an advantage, a trump card he might find a way to play.

But what about Isabelle? And Victor? They need to know I'm not dead.

"You *are* dead," the voice in his head reminded him. "That's the problem."

But I can't hide from the world forever.

"For now, though, it makes sense to keep a low profile."

Why? Because of the fucking Stuffer?

"Exactly. The bastard killed me."

And your point is?

"He must know by now I'm missing, and that's got to piss him off. Serial killers hate being a step behind the learning curve. They want to *be* a mystery, not solve one."

Where are your brains, you moron? Look at yourself! You need help.

"No one can help me. It's too late for that."

You stink, man! And so does your plan to go into hiding.

"What else can I do? It's the only way I can think of for us to trick the Stuffer out of his nest."

Us? Who else is there? You're on your own, Styx, there's no "us." If you're really dead, then there's nobody left on your side, not even that nitwit Delacroix.

Styx listened to the voice of his other self. The human Styx, the rational Styx, the old Styx who shunned his fellow man, who had been nothing more than a doom-and-gloom hypochondriacal misogynist.

Well, this wasn't a rational situation. It was a situation, but there was no rational way to deal with it.

So what's your plan, if you don't mind my asking? Prowl around Ostend like a werewolf until you find him?

"I'm not the Stuffer," he told himself, "and I can't beat him at his own game. No, I'll have to wait him out, wait till he shows himself."

Without further thought, Styx turned into the Adolf Buylstraat, a pedestrian shopping zone lined with expensive, exclusive stores. In Leopold II's time, he would have been surrounded by wealthy ladies in long dresses. Today, though, it was early enough that the shops were only just opening and the street was still relatively empty.

He slipped into Kruidvat, one of the chain drugstores that carried a little bit of everything and was big enough for him to lose himself in its maze of displays. Better that than the ICI Paris XL, a compact boutique where his face would have given the coquettish salesclerks a heart attack. He hurried up and down the aisles as quickly as his condition allowed, grabbing a few cans of deodorant—Garnier Men's, "don't sweat the small stuff!"—a bottle of aftershave, and the largest jar of foundation he could find in the makeup department.

He held his bank card at the ready to speed up his passage through the checkout line. The cashier barely looked at him as she scanned his items. He swiped his card, tapped in his PIN—and felt the nail at the end of his index finger break halfway free.

Back on the street, he was proud of himself for getting in and out without attracting unwanted attention. If the airhead at the register had been awake, she probably would have called the cops on him.

But then he asked himself: Why? He hadn't done anything wrong. Maybe he looked like a disaster, but he was just doing a little innocent shopping. There was nothing the police could do to him. He hadn't even disturbed the peace.

A few doors down, he slunk into an H&M. He realized by now that he could probably get away with his appearance for another day or two. Sure, his clothes were in tatters and his face was a minefield of dried blood and hollow eyes, plastered with drool, but he hadn't gone into all-out zombie mode, not yet.

Not too long ago he'd come in late one night to find Victor in the living room, watching some silly horror movie when he was supposed to be in bed. Lumbering zombies, missing arms and legs. Writhing, spastic, vomiting blood. But that wasn't him.

Not yet.

In a dressing room at the back of the H&M he saw that, except for the three gunshot wounds, there were no other indications of violence on his body. And he hadn't really begun to decay. No, examining himself now in the mirror, he saw a man in a nice linen suit (tan jacket and matching trousers that he'd grabbed from a nearby rack) and an immaculate white dress shirt. He looked like a guy who'd had a rough night—but a *guy*, not a character in a splatter film.

He took a can of Garnier from his Kruidvat bag and sprayed it all over himself, misting his new clothes, his hair, his face. He doused all visible skin—face, hands, wrists—with aftershave, and rinsed out his mouth with the vile brew.

Now for the last part of the makeover. For the first time in his life he unscrewed a jar of foundation. No, actually, wrong: he'd opened one three weeks ago. Not for Isabelle, who had a natural beauty, with creamy skin that didn't need any help from Estée Lauder. Nope, that jar had been for Victor, who'd awakened that morning with a giant zit on his nose and refused to go to school until it had been camouflaged.

He should see what I look like, Styx thought sadly.

He eyed himself in the mirror and began to rub the cream gently into the worst places: the black rings around his eyes, the burst blood vessels on and to the sides of his nose, the blackened lips.

But that barely made a difference, he saw, so he started over, smearing a thick layer of makeup over his whole face. He felt like an artist who, too poor to afford a fresh canvas, bought a cheap old portrait at the flea market and simply painted over it.

He replaced his deathly pallor with what might just pass for a normal complexion.

It took the entire jar of foundation to do it.

Styx wiped his hands clean on his bloody old clothes and hid them in his shopping bag. He took one last look at himself in the mirror.

He would pass.

Maybe Raphael Styx *was* a zombie, but he *looked* like the man of the hour.

He nodded to himself and tried to laugh, but the sound echoed hollow and dead in the little cubicle.

CHAPTER 10

Isabelle Gerard held out until five AM before calling Commissioner John Crevits and hauling *him* out of bed for a change. She sat on the sofa with Shelley beside her. The pit bull had awakened her in the middle of the night, howling like a banshee outside the front door. Victor, bless him, had slept right through the commotion. He had another exam in the morning, so he needed the rest.

"Styx?"

"No, it's Isabelle."

"Isabelle?"

"I'm sorry to call so early, John," she said, not really sorry at all. Crevits had been a friend of the family, once, but Isabelle thought of him now as the man whose big mouth had driven the last nail into the coffin of her marriage.

"What's up? I thought it must be your husband."

"He's not here, John. That's why I'm calling."

She could hear Crevits come fully awake.

"This isn't the first time he's stayed out all night, Isabelle, we both know that."

"This isn't just one of his . . . exploits."

"How do you know? He'll turn up—he always does. Remember that time last year when you went to work and found him about three-quarters crocked in the ER?"

Isabelle remembered it perfectly: the shame of it, the humiliation. That time had been the last straw: Styx dragged into the hospital by some scrawny hooker he'd found in the gutter. Barely coherent, he'd tried to tell Isabelle the bitch was an informant, but she knew better. She'd needed half a Valium to calm herself down.

"I'm telling you, this is different," she insisted. "He took Shelley out for a walk, sometime around nine or ten last night, and he never came home."

"He's probably sleeping it off in—"

"Shelley showed up around one in the morning, John."

"Ah, well, that's good."

"Alone."

"Yeah, that's not so good."

While Crevits considered the situation, Isabelle sat there petting the stupid dog. She couldn't stand the mangy creature. It reminded her more and more of her husband: an obstinate beast, with an emphasis on the "beast," and an animalistic temper.

"Have you tried calling him?"

"He didn't take his phone. It's sitting right here. You know he doesn't want to be bothered when the two of them are out walking."

"And *he* hasn't called *you*?"

"No."

"I don't like the sound of this," Crevits sighed.

"I don't know what to do, John."

"Listen, I know you don't want to hear this, but there's another possibility."

"You're right: I don't want to hear it."

"Have you called her?"

"Called who?"

"You know who. Amanda."

"No, I haven't called her, and I'm not *going* to call her."

"He might be there, Isabelle. I know he broke it off with her, and I don't want to rake up old coals, but maybe . . ."

No, no maybes. She would rather die than call that whore. Amanda had been one of her husband's many conquests, but she'd also been the girlfriend of Gino Tersago, the young thug who ran three nightclubs and more than a dozen cathouses in and around the Ostend harbor. Styx had run across her during a stakeout and had interrogated her.

In, as Isabelle later learned, the backseat of his car.

One thing led to another, and Styx eventually reported that she was working for him, helping to make a case against Tersago and his criminal associates. Amanda was apparently sick of Tersago, but pretty much everyone on the detective squad—pretty much everyone in Ostend except Isabelle—knew she was giving Raphael Styx more than information. There was station-house gossip about them, but there was also talk of hush money being thrown Styx's way. Since Styx and Amanda had gotten involved, Tersago seemed to be getting away with more than ever.

"I don't mind calling her for you," said Crevits.

"You do and I will kill you."

"Why?"

"I've been embarrassed enough, John."

"Okay, I understand. We don't know anything's happened to him.

My advice is don't panic, try to stay calm. I'll make a few calls and put a couple of men on it. Ten to one we'll find him in some—"

She heard the commissioner stop himself, just in time.

"I hope so. I've had it, John. I want to tell him to his face it's over."

"Isabelle—"

"Don't Isabelle me. I can't take it anymore. He's humiliated me for the last time. If he *does* come home, I'll kick him right out the door."

"And Victor?"

"He's old enough to know the truth."

There was a long silence between them.

"You know the man loves you, Iz. He doesn't mean to be such a shit. . . . It's just the way he is. You have no idea what it's like for a cop. The stress you have to deal with, every goddamn day. The misery you're surrounded by. And you know the statistics: every couple goes through a rough patch after fifteen years."

She could tell that Crevits was only saying what he thought was expected of him. Underneath the bullshit, she knew he was rooting for them to finally divorce. She'd long suspected John had a secret thing for her.

"What about the stress a cop's *wife* has to deal with every goddamn day?" she said fiercely. "Don't try to defend him. If anybody needs a little consideration here, it's me. I work forty hours every week surrounded by misery, and then I'm supposed to cook and clean for that son of a bitch, do his ironing and sit up waiting for him to come home and pass out on the couch? No way, I'm done. He can find himself another sucker."

"You don't mean all that, Isabelle."

"Fuck him, John. And fuck you, too."

While they talked, John Crevits had struggled out of bed and powered up his laptop. When he saw another call coming in on his phone—the squad room—he let it roll over to voice mail rather than asking Isabelle to let him put her on hold. There were two e-mails in his inbox—both from the squad—but before he checked them he clicked quickly to the Ostend police's Facebook page. These days it seemed like everybody over the age of eight was on Facebook.

"Look," he said to Isabelle, the phone nestled uneasily between his ear and shoulder and both hands on his keyboard, "if I can find him and get him home before you have to leave for the hospital, will you at least talk with him?"

"Sure, John, I'll talk with him. I'll tell him to pack a suitcase and call a lawyer."

The Facebook page loaded. Near the bottom of the window, someone had posted a photograph to their page; the top inch peeked up over the bottom of the frame so he'd have to scroll down to see it in its entirety.

When he saw the name of the poster—all capital letters, separated by periods—he got a sick feeling in the pit of his stomach.

S.T.U.F.F.E.R.

"Oh, shit."

"*No* shit," said Isabelle. "He's not getting away with it again, no matter what he—"

"Give me a second here."

"I mean it, John!"

"One second."

Ever since the media had given him the nickname, the Stuffer had posted half a dozen times to the police department's Facebook page, each time creating a different account, each account using a slightly different variant of the name. Mostly he'd put up long self-satisfied screeds, boasting of his "accomplishments" and offering his twisted thoughts on the meaning of art in contemporary society—but he'd also contributed photos of his first two victims.

Was Madeleine Bohy's headless, limbless, lifeless torso now also on display, not just for the city, but for the world at large?

Crevits clicked on the scroll bar at the right of the window and dragged it down, revealing the newly posted image.

He gasped.

"John?"

"Oh, Jesus God!"

Raphael Styx, the man he'd known for all these years, whose career he had nurtured, who he'd pulled out of more ditches more times than he could count, the man with whom he'd shared so many memorable moments, was dead.

"Isabelle," he croaked, his voice broken, "it's not what you think."

"What's the matter, John? Tell me."

But he could find no words for her, not even a sigh. He sat there on the side of his bed, his computer resting on his lap, the phone to his ear, staring at the dead face and lifeless body of Chief Inspector Raphael Styx, his old friend.

"Isabelle, I'm sorry. He's—"

After informing Styx's wife that she was now a widow, Crevits sat there for at least another half hour, staring at the screen. As he watched, new postings appeared on the Facebook page, like mushrooms springing up from a forest floor. One in particular summed up all the rest:

"The Stuffer's got another one."

By the time he arrived at the station at nine AM everyone knew about it. The mood was bizarre, surreal. Crevits called them all together in the canteen, and they stared at him as if they too were dead. They sat there, as motionless as the Stuffer's sand sculptures, waiting for him to address them.

Crevits didn't feel up to giving a speech. What could he say? The usual pep talk: "We all have to go on with our work and continue the search for the Stuffer." That wasn't his style. He wanted to be alone.

He turned around without a word and went back to his office.

An hour later he buzzed his secretary Carla and told her to find Joachim Delacroix and send him in.

"Commissioner?" Delacroix said.

"How far have you gotten with the serial case?"

"Me?"

"Yeah, you."

"But I'm—I mean, I'm just a detective."

"You're a cop, aren't you? An inspector?"

"Yes, sir. But it was Styx's case. God, it's terrible, isn't it?"

"Yeah, terrible. There are no words for how bad it is. But life goes on, Inspector, and so does the Stuffer. I want you to take over for Styx. Congratulations on your promotion. Leave the paperwork to me. From now on, it's *your* case."

Delacroix looked like a safe had fallen on his head.

"But I've only been here for—"

"Did I ask you a question, Delacroix? This is my division, and I make the assignments. Styx had a lot of enemies. He's stepped on a shitload of toes over the years, and I don't want somebody doing a half-assed job because—well, because it was Styx, you get me?"

"I—don't I have to wait for authorization from Brussels?"

"I don't see why. I just told you: I'm in charge here. You're the guy who wanted to get *out* of Brussels. So let's get cracking, okay? Whatever happened with our original suspect, that guy we picked up after the first murder, what was his name?"

Delacroix realized he was being tested and answered immediately: "Karel Rotiers. He knew the victim, went out with her a couple of times. And then we linked him to the second victim, they were Facebook friends. But we haven't found *any* connection between Rotiers and Madeleine Bohy."

"Yet. That doesn't mean there isn't one."

"You may be right, sir. But with all due respect, why me?"

"Why you?" He leaned forward and rested his elbows on his desk and examined the young man closely. "Styx didn't like you, Inspector. He told me that more than once. He *never* told me you're a good cop, but he didn't have to. He knew it, and he knew I knew it."

Delacroix stood up, but Crevits waved him back to his seat.

"Tell me about Rotiers's alibi."

"He hasn't got one for the first two murders. At least, not one that checks out. He's a bit of a Don Juan. Handsome, well-known around the nightclubs. According to our sources, he scores more often than not. They say he's made it with half the women under thirty in Ostend and is hard at work on the second half."

"We're trying to find a serial killer, not a sexoholic. Casanova doesn't really fit the profile."

"I know, but he's pretty heavy into the kinky stuff. Orgies, S&M, bondage, like that. He'll try anything once."

Crevits remembered the original interrogation of Karel Rotiers. He and a few of the other cops lurking behind the one-way mirror while Styx came down hard on the guy.

Rotiers turned the questioning into a vaudeville act, using it as an opportunity to brag about his cocksmanship, and, when Styx asked him straight out if he had any interest in necrophilia, he responded, "No way, man, I don't need your sloppy seconds." Styx lost his cool and slammed the playboy up against the wall.

"You've got a hell of a rep around the clubs, asshole," the cop snarled. "I heard you really made yourself some enemies at the Tantra House. I mean, come on, Karl, an X-Acto knife? Always up for something new, huh, you fucking pervert?"

Rotiers started to give it right back, but Styx slapped him into silence.

"Some of the girls call you the Stamper, I hear. What about the Stuffer, you ever get that one? I know you like stuffing it in 'em whenever you get the chance."

"I'll stuff it in your wife," Rotiers shot back, and by the time they were able to pull Styx off him, Loverboy's face was a bloody mess.

Rotiers had spent two days in the hospital and then two more in police custody before they'd let him go for lack of evidence.

Now Crevits waved a dismissive hand at Delacroix and said, "What are you waiting for, a medal? I want to know if that bastard Rotiers has an alibi for Madeleine Bohy's murder."

"You want me to track down where he was last night, too?"

"What am I, your guru? A cop's been murdered, Delacroix. I'm giving you your big chance. Don't fuck it up."

As the rookie was on his way out the door, Crevits called him back a second time. "I want to know *where* Styx was killed. That photo's real, but it could have been taken anywhere. I don't like to think of him lying somewhere, waiting for that sick fuck to come back and, well, you know. Styx had his problems, but he was one of us. We can't let him end up like those three women."

CHAPTER **11**

Styx stepped out of the dressing room, his bag in his hand, his top shirt button casually undone, and left the store. The mall was crowded, and hordes of shoppers streamed past him like zombies, unaware of the world around them, their eyes glazed, paying him not the slightest attention. It was ten AM, and a dozen television screens in the window of the electronics shop next door to the H&M caught his attention. The morning news began with a bulletin:

"Last night in Ostend," the perfectly dressed blond presenter said, "the notorious Chief Inspector Raphael Styx was murdered. Styx served for sixteen years on the city police, and for the last several months he led the team investigating what have come to be known as the 'Stuffer' serial killings. Styx's body has not yet been recovered, but traces of violence were found earlier this morning in a cabana on the Ostend beach.

News of the murder came to light when the Stuffer posted a photograph of Styx's lifeless body to the police department's Facebook page."

Styx stood there, stunned, as the report continued.

"Commissioner John Crevits will hold a press conference later today, representing the chief of police, who is out of the country at the moment, but has already expressed his disappointment that his friend and subordinate's death was reported in the media before Chief Inspector Styx's family could be officially notified, and emphasized that, in the absence of a body, it is premature to use the word *murder* in connection with Styx's death. In fact, the case is being treated at this juncture as a disappearance, although police department insiders who have seen the Facebook photo consider it to constitute undeniable proof that Styx was the victim of a violent attack, and tell us that the department is proceeding on the assumption that Styx was indeed the Stuffer's fourth victim."

Styx stared at the bank of screens. It was one thing for *him* to know that he was dead. But it was a different game entirely now that the whole city had the news.

"Commissioner Crevits assures the public that a full investigation is under way, and that the Ostend police will take all possible steps to uncover the truth. He offers his deepest condolences to Chief Inspector Styx's family in these sad circumstances."

Styx's thoughts turned to Isabelle and Victor. He tried to put himself in their place, but he had absolutely no idea how they would take the news. If the roles were reversed, he knew, and he were to hear that his son had been killed in a car crash, it would tear him apart. Same thing if he opened the door one morning to find a colleague there to deliver the news that Isabelle had been run down on her way to the hospital. He hadn't been much of a husband in recent years, but she was still his wife.

"The Raphael Styx case reopens the debate over the responsibility of social media. It has been confirmed that the Stuffer has posted repeatedly to Facebook, using a variety of accounts. Facebook representatives tell us that steps are being taken to prevent the killer from making any additional postings, but such measures will be difficult to implement. Commissioner Crevits further informs us that the gruesome photograph of what appears to be the body of Chief Inspector Styx will be taken down from the Ostend Police Department's Facebook page within the hour. We'll have more on this developing story as—"

Styx wanted to get a look at the picture, and to check his own Facebook page to see what was posted there. It had taken him a while to make peace with Facebook. He'd opened and scrapped two accounts, but finally acknowledged that it was a necessary evil. He could no longer afford to stay under the radar. People who refused to accept citizenship in the virtual world weren't just closing themselves off from other people's awareness. They were erasing themselves. For all practical purposes, they were dead.

He wondered how many people had already seen the picture of his corpse. If the Stuffer had played his cards right—and Styx knew the serial killer was a hell of a card player—he'd not only posted the photo but tagged it with Styx's name. Each of his online "friends"—his colleagues, his family, his *real* friends (as few and far between as they were)—would see his gruesome photograph in their feed:

Raphael Styx was tagged in Stuffer's photos.

Styx felt the life bleed out of him all over again. Life, *his* life, his life with friends, acquaintances, colleagues, and family, had been brutally torn away from him, without him even getting a vote.

Was there any chance he might be able to find a way to—?

No, there was no point speculating. Better to focus on the

undeniable truth. For now, at least, he was trapped. He couldn't run to Crevits, even if he wanted to. The station would be surrounded by media vultures, waiting to pick the bones of this latest sensational story. If they spotted him, the resulting circus would surely throw the Stuffer investigation off the rails.

He had to think this through.

The world thought he was dead. Who was he to say otherwise?

He wasn't a well-known cop outside the city. Yes, his picture had been in the national papers a few times over the years, but not often and not lately.

That would change as the story of his murder spread, but for now he was probably fairly safe, especially with a face full of makeup.

For now, he was not just a zombie but the Invisible Man.

Inspector Joachim Delacroix was inside the beach cabana where Styx had died, not far from the Venetian Galleries.

Yellow police tape protected not only the crime scene but also the cabanas to either side from prying eyes, and a pair of patrolmen were stationed on the dike to keep the rubberneckers moving along.

"Now the fucker's got his *own* Facebook page?" one of the detectives marveled.

"I don't get it," sighed Delacroix. "How does a sick bastard like this wind up with friends?"

"Probably an open profile," said the detective.

"What does that mean?"

"Means anybody can see what he posts, you don't have to be friends with him."

"And who found the page?"

"Inspector Allaert."

"Stany? Where is he now?"

"Clocked out and went home. He was pretty shaken up. He and Styx were friends, one of the few guys Styx really got along with. Been on the force ten years, and he's managed to keep his nose clean despite Styx's influence."

"You seen the photo?" asked Delacroix. Without realizing it, he'd switched to a more confidential tone.

"Negative," the detective said, "and I'll pass, thanks."

"It's pretty awful."

"I'd rather remember Styx the way he was."

Delacroix thought, *You mean a complete asshole?* But what he said was: "We're not one hundred percent sure he's dead."

Although it was broad daylight outside and the cabana door was open, the interior of the wooden shack was only dimly illuminated. They had found bloodstains on the floor, on the air mattress, and on the walls. DNA testing would take awhile, but Delacroix feared the worst.

They'd lucked into the cabana when the elderly couple on vacation had shown up this morning, found the lock broken off, and called it in as a burglary—although there'd been nothing there worth stealing.

If Delacroix closed his eyes, he could still see Styx's body lying crumpled and lifeless on *this* floor, his head half-resting on the edge of *this* air mattress. He could see the three gaping wounds, the blood, Styx's dead eyes staring off into the Great Nothing.

"Any chance it might have been Photoshopped?" asked Paul Breton, who was there representing the Public Prosecution Service.

"Honestly? I don't think so," said Delacroix. "I don't see this guy faking a picture. Why bother?"

"So you didn't know Styx well, huh?" asked Breton.

"I didn't know him *long*," Delacroix admitted.

"He used to be one of the best."

"Used to be?"

"Long time ago."

Hard to imagine, thought Delacroix.

"Then he started spending a little too much time in bars with the scum he was supposed to be putting *behind* bars."

"I've only been here a year."

"Yeah, one of the best I've ever seen. But he turned into a real shitheel. I can't believe he's gone."

Delacroix had no trouble believing it. Maybe it was precisely *because* he'd barely known Styx that Delacroix found the idea of his death so easy to absorb. He wasn't distracted by personal considerations. He had to admit—to himself, although he wouldn't say this to Crevits or Breton—that he didn't care for the chief inspector any more than the chief inspector had cared for him. The guy had been totally corrupt. Delacroix wasn't happy the man was dead, but he saw Styx as the Stuffer's fourth victim and nothing more.

That thing Crevits had said, about Styx knowing he, Delacroix, was a good cop? Delacroix didn't believe a word of it. It was just one of Crevits's tricks. Even if it *was* true, he really didn't give a shit about Styx's opinion of him. Styx might have been a good cop, once upon a time, but he was a bad man—and Delacroix would rather be a good man and a lousy cop than a good cop and a lousy man.

Breton put his phone away. "First report from the lab," he said. "It looks like it *could* be Styx's blood, but they're not ready to say for sure without running some more tests."

"I wonder how he wound up here," said Delacroix.

"I wonder where he is right now."

"Who, the Stuffer?"

"No, Styx. Imagine he turns up tomorrow on the dike. Statue number four. Jesus, I don't want to think about it."

"We have to find him," said Delacroix.

"What happened with that guy yesterday? Guy who found the third victim? Styx was waiting for word about him—what was his name again, Spilliaert?"

Delacroix shook his head. "We haven't caught up with him yet."

He followed Breton out of the cabana. They were momentarily blinded by the sunshine. Before them, the beach was already crowded with day trippers.

"We finally had the owner let us into the apartment," Delacroix continued, "but there was nothing there. We've got a team watching the place around the clock, but he hasn't shown up."

"What else is happening?" asked Breton, who seemed more interested in the case than the usual civil servant.

"We're questioning the owner, Sam Borremans. We checked him out, and he's clean. No record."

"And?"

"He says Spilliaert's been living there for a year, but he only saw him one time, the day they signed the lease. Their only contact since then is the monthly rent payment."

"Automatic bill pay? Then we can find out more from the bank, can't we?"

"No, Styx already looked into that. Spilliaert paid in cash; stuck a wad of bills in an envelope once a month and pushed it through Borremans's mail slot. Always paid on time, never complained about the plumbing, so Borremans never had any reason to see him again.

"The whole thing sounds fishy to me."

"Indeed," Delacroix nodded.

"Would Borremans recognize him if he *did* see him again?"

"He's not sure. And we've tried to check into Spilliaert's background, but there's nothing. He's not registered with the city. No passport, no identity card, no driver's license, no health insurance. He's a ghost."

"What kind of country is this when any asshole without ID can rent an apartment on the Belgian coast?" Breton asked.

Despite himself, Delacroix thought of the many immigrants he'd met over the year since he'd arrived in Ostend, a shocking number of them smuggled in illegally in shipboard containers. He was one of the fortunate ones: thanks to his parents, he was a Belgian citizen, complete with passport and papers.

"Anyway," he went on, "we put Borremans with a police artist and got a sketch. It's not much, but it's not nothing. We've sent copies around to every police department in the country. And by this afternoon they'll start running be-on-the-lookout announcements on TV and radio."

"Any other leads?"

"We know Styx was tight with Gino Tersago, so we'll pull him in for questioning, but I don't expect he'll have anything useful to tell us. Tersago and Karel Rotiers are all we've really got. We're looking for Rotiers, see if he's got an alibi for the third murder and for last night."

"You think Spilliaert may have some connection to the Stuffer?"

Delacroix suddenly realized that the man from the public prosecutor's office was grilling him. But this was *his* case now. He had to prove himself. He didn't want to give too much away.

"Well?" Breton said with a hint of impatience.

"You figure Spilliaert is the Stuffer, then?"

"I'm wondering what *your* thoughts are."

Delacroix shrugged.

"Goddammit, you're going to have to do a lot more than shrug your shoulders to solve this case, Delacroix."

The man from the PPS stalked away across the sand and clambered up the first stairway to the dike. Delacroix followed behind him.

STYX

He wasn't really dressed for the beach. His Italian loafers, crafted from fine camel-colored leather, filled with sand, and before he reached the stairs he was mopping sweat from his forehead with the white silk pocket square from the breast pocket of his azure suit coat.

Despite the uncomfortable perspiration, Joachim Delacroix felt truly excited for the first time since he'd landed in Ostend a year ago.

His own case.

A chance to prove himself.

This was what he'd been waiting for.

His new life was beginning at last.

CHAPTER **12**

Styx wasn't just suffering a midlife crisis. This was a *life* crisis: he was dead. After the shock he'd received outside the H&M, he'd drifted out into the streets, lost in his own thoughts and eventually in the city, which was as decayed as he was.

He tried to return to the Hofstraat, where the Stuffer maintained his pied-à-terre under the name Spilliaert, but on arrival saw that another detective had the place staked out. Stany Allaert, an honest cop he'd known for almost the entirety of Allaert's career, was fairly well concealed in a doorway across the street from the building, and Styx had sniffed him out in time to back away unseen. He didn't go far, though.

Concealed in a doorway only three doors down from Stany Allaert, Styx kept a close watch on the fifth-floor window across the street.

You in there, Stuffer? Is anybody home?

There was no hint of movement behind the curtains.

Or are you out here on the streets, looking for me?

He would have loved to see the expression on the serial killer's face when he realized Victim #4 had gone for a little stroll.

How do you like me now, you fuck?

He could have waited all day and all night, if he had to. But it was too risky for him to stay where he was. Allaert wasn't the only cop who had the Hofstraat building under surveillance. One by one, Styx spotted a whole team stationed around the neighborhood.

What he *wanted* to do was go home and see his family, but that was impossible. And trying to talk with John Crevits was also out of the question. To Isabelle and Victor and John, he was dead, and he had to go on *being* dead, at least for now.

So he roamed through the city, along the Visserskaai and up the Vindictivelaan, keeping to the shadows as best he could, until at last he found himself in the Hippodroomwijk, where the annual Belle Époque festival was in full swing.

"Of course," Styx muttered, remembering the tableau he'd witnessed that morning in the station hall.

Styx lost himself in the masses of people milling through the streets. He felt comfortably anonymous in the crowd; if he had a heart rate anymore, it would have slowed to normal. He shuffled past stands selling old costume jewelry, watches, toys, postcards from the time of James Ensor, and other trinkets. Many of the vendors were decked out in period costumes.

He pulled up before one of the stands, this one offering a panoply of books and vinyl records. Propped up in the center of the display was a signed copy of Marvin Gaye's *In Our Lifetime*. He remembered that album, released just before Gaye moved into promoter Freddy Cousaert's apartment in the Kemmelbergstraat, right here in Ostend, in 1981. Cousaert had helped the American soul singer kick his cocaine addiction, and urban legend had it that the rhythm on Gaye's comeback single, "Sexual Healing," had been inspired by the sound of the waves on the Ostend beach.

Styx picked up the record, turning it over. The woman running the stand, who was dressed as a fisherman's wife for the occasion, launched into a sales pitch: "That's Marv's last album for Motown. It's worth a lot of money, the autograph's guaranteed authentic."

He examined the singer's elegant photo on the back cover, avoiding the woman's eyes.

"It's thirty-some years ago he washed up here," she went on. "Yeah, he was pretty far gone, but our Freddy helped him get back on his feet. They made a movie about it in the States, shot it right here. Freddy's wife used to cook for him. He was crazy about her chicken and applesauce. He was reborn here."

Reborn, Styx thought.

He paid what she asked for the record and stuck it under his arm.

"You know nobody in Ostend except Freddy and his wife had any idea who he was? He'd walk into the cafés and shoot a game of darts with the locals, and no one knew he was this big American star."

Styx walked on, fiddling with Marc Gerard's pocket watch. There were people everywhere, a hundred lively conversations blurring together all around him, enveloping him in a sea of conversation.

He came to a sudden stop. This was the Flemish part of Belgium, the north, not the Wallonian south, and the Ostenders spoke almost exclusively Dutch.

Then why had those costumed people in the station hall been speaking French? That was strange, now that he thought about it.

He forced himself to shake off the thought. After all, what difference did it make?

He realized he was still holding the pocket watch and slipped it, unopened, back in his pocket.

Where are you scurrying off to, Styx?

He spun around. There was no sign of trouble, just one big happy party.

He continued on his way, bumping into arms and elbows as he pushed through the throngs.

He had to get out of there. His world was turned completely upside down: twenty-four hours ago, he'd been after the Stuffer, but now their roles were reversed.

There's no escape, Styx. I'll find you.

He looked back over his shoulder and for just a moment saw the Stuffer almost hidden in the crowd. A man in a yellow oilskin jacket with hard, deep eyes beneath a sou'wester. Styx could feel those eyes boring into him. How long had the oilskin been following him?

He moved on more quickly, dragging his right leg behind him. When he looked back again, the sou'wester was still there. A hat and rain slicker on a sunny day! Styx felt the sweat and foundation trickling down his face, running like Isabelle's mascara ran when she cried.

He heard a burst of laughter behind him and whirled around.

The man in the jacket and hat had stopped at the last of the market stalls and was chatting animatedly with one of the fisherman's wives.

Styx drew a deep breath and sighed it out slowly.

Styx sat in the living room of his father-in-law's house, the only place in Ostend he could think of to hide.

How many times in the weeks since Marc Gerard's death had Isabelle asked him to clear out her father's place, haul all his unwanted junk to the dump? Her only surviving family was an older sister who'd moved to the south of France years ago. They'd each selected a couple of mementos after the funeral, but neither of them had any interest in their father's furniture or old clothes.

Styx considered the house-cleaning job a punishment, a penance for his many sins, and had found excuses to avoid it. At least now he had a furnished apartment in which to fester.

He tried to get out of the chair, but couldn't do it without the support of his father-in-law's old walking stick. It was a classic piece of woodworking, hand carved from beautiful birch, with a copper grip in the shape of a fish.

"You crippled bastard," Styx said aloud, not sure if he was talking to himself or Marc Gerard, a crotchety devil he'd always hated.

He hobbled back and forth across the living room, testing out the cane. It really did take a lot of the strain off his hip.

There was a sudden noise outside the window and he whirled, half expecting to see the Stuffer lurking there, stalking him. But there was nothing but a tree branch rattling against the window.

Styx asked himself the same question that was probably also on the Stuffer's lips right now:

Where are you? Where the fuck are you hiding?

Half a day earlier, in the middle of the night, the Stuffer had parked his car along the dike, close to the cabana. His equipment was neatly packed into the trailer: sica, scalpel, butcher's knife, fishing line, a miner's lantern, a few other necessities.

There was nothing to be heard but the murmuring of the waves and a loosely tied piece of canvas that fluttered in the breeze. He crept along the line of cabanas, looking for the one where he'd left Raphael Styx. He slowed when he saw that one of the shack doors stood half-open. The silly huts all looked the same, but . . . wasn't that the one he'd selected? He thought he recognized the stone, but beach stones were as alike as beach cabanas, and it was lying now a few inches away, not propped against a closed door as he'd left it.

"Hello?"

He approached cautiously, preparing an explanation for his own presence in case someone had already discovered the body.

"Anyone there?"

No answer.

The Stuffer swung the door wide and held up his lantern.

"Fuck!"

There was nothing in there. No body, no Styx, nothing but bloodstains.

Where the—?

He stood in the middle of the small space, completely dumbfounded.

He'd shot the bastard. Three times! He'd felt for a heartbeat. He'd even taken pictures of the bloody body. Nobody could have faked being dead like that.

He couldn't understand it.

It couldn't be the cops. If they'd found the corpse already, they'd be here waiting for his return. There'd be police tape cordoning off the area. There'd be searchlights. There'd be patrol cars and emergency vehicles on the dike.

Wouldn't there?

It had to be some kind of a trick.

The Stuffer swallowed the sour taste that was suddenly in his mouth. The wind whistled in through the open door, through cracks in the wooden walls.

Goddammit.

Something was very wrong here.

Somebody's fucking with me.

He considered the possibilities.

One: somehow, Styx wasn't dead after all. Wounded, yes, badly wounded, but not dead, and he'd managed to get up and leave the cabana under his own steam.

No. Bullshit, the guy was fucking *dead*, there was no question about that.

Okay, then, two: the cops had found the body and taken it away.

No, if that had happened, he'd be in handcuffs by now, in the back of a patrol car, on his way to jail.

Fine, three: somebody else had stumbled across the body.

But then why hadn't they called in the cops?

Would they have taken the body away on their own, *without* calling it in?

But *why*?

Every pioneer attracts his imitators, he thought. Was this some sort of copycat?

With pride and frustration and forboding swirling around in his brain, the Stuffer left the cabana and strode across the sand toward his car.

He never even considered the fourth possibility.

Who would have?

CHAPTER **13**

At first glance, Gino Tersago thought the police department's interrogation room looked a lot like a container. Only half the size, but otherwise it was just as bare and echoing as the interchangeable offices he had down at the Ostend harbor.

Unfortunately, Tersago wasn't sitting across from one of his clients now, but Commissioner John Crevits.

Tersago was outfitted in his favorite imitation-leather jacket, a red-and-white Michael Schumacher Formula One knockoff he'd set aside for himself off the top of a recent shipment. He wore the collar popped, which he thought made him look tough.

"Look," he said, for the second time in as many minutes, "I'm telling you what I told Styx: I don't know shit about those Stuffer killings. And I haven't talked to Styxie since the last time I saw him."

"And when exactly *was* that, little man?"

"I don't know," Tersago shrugged. "A couple weeks ago, maybe. I haven't seen him much since that shit with Amanda went down. He took it pretty hard when she dumped him."

Crevits lumbered out of his chair and walked around the table, out of sight.

"You sure? You haven't talked to him since then?"

Tersago half turned his head. "I'd remember, wouldn't I?"

"You didn't weld him into one of your fucking containers and ship him out of the country?"

"Why would I do a thing like that?" the petty thug demanded, the picture of offended innocence.

Crevits grabbed the collar of Tersago's jacket and turned it down. His rough hands tenderly smoothed out the fake leather and came to rest on either side of Tersago's neck.

The air went out of Gino Tersago like a balloon.

"I don't know," said Crevits patiently. "Maybe he got sick of working with you—or *for* you—and told you he was turning you in?"

"I don't know what you're—"

Like an old-fashioned schoolteacher smacking down a class clown, Crevits slapped the back of Tersago's head. "Don't fuck with me, son. You and I both know what you did for Styx and what he did for you. If there's one thing I hate, it's disloyalty, especially from a lowlife like you, Gino, and especially after everything Styx did for you."

"Nobody twisted his arm, man."

Crevits picked an invisible speck of lint from Tersago's shoulder. "You want me to twist *yours*, Gino? Don't make me ask you again."

"I swear," Tersago insisted, jerking forward out of Crevits's reach. "I don't know a fucking thing."

"Because if I find out you're lying to me, I'm going to charge you with every piece-of-shit crime you ever committed and about a hundred more I'll make up. Without Styx in your corner, you're dead meat, you know that."

"Exactly!" Tersago cried, spinning his chair around to face the commissioner. "Why would I do anything to get rid of him?"

"Like I said," Crevits reminded him, "he wanted out, and he knew too much."

"Come on, man, you know better than that. The fucker was totally dirty."

And then he saw the rage in Crevits's eyes and leaned back in his chair, bumping so hard into the interrogation table he almost overturned it.

"You think whatever you want about me," Tersago said quickly, "but the fact is I *liked* the bastard. He could be a total prick, but I respected him—more'n I do *you*. He wasn't exactly an honest cop, but you knew that, right? I mean, you busted him yourself."

Crevits had to let that comment pass; everything said in the interrogation room was being recorded. So he returned to his chair and turned the conversation in a new direction. "Maybe he stumbled onto something else?"

"Like what?" Tersago resettled himself in his chair and flipped his collar back up. "Like your wife's a hooker?"

This time, Crevits didn't rise to the bait. The last thing he needed was the distraction of an excessive-force complaint.

"What if he found out you were up to something a little more serious than smuggling?"

"Like *what*?" Tersago said again.

"Like three murders, for example."

"Jesus Christ! You think *I'm* the fucking Stuffer? Shit, I don't have *time* for that, Commissioner. I'm a businessman, we don't like to get our hands dirty."

"Your hands are filthy, son. They're as full of shit as the rest of you."

But Tersago didn't bite, either, and the two of them sat there glaring at each other until Crevits shoved his chair back and threw open the interrogation-room door.

"Get out," he growled. "But leave the jacket here. It's going into evidence: you're under suspicion of receiving stolen property."

The Styxes' apartment was in the Milho complex, former site of the city's military hospital. Joachim Delacroix sat on a plush armchair in the living room facing Isabelle Gerard. Their pit bull lay quietly beside the sofa.

"Shelley's disconsolate," said Styx's wife. "He misses his master."

"You have a nice place here," said Delacroix, unsure how to broach the reason for his visit.

"I like it. I don't think Rafe really paid attention."

She petted the dog, whose chin rested on his forepaws.

"He doesn't—*didn't* much care for new buildings."

Delacroix glanced at his notebook. It still felt weird to be investigating the murder of Raphael Styx. The man's reputation had been almost mythical.

"Why"—Delacroix coughed uncomfortably—"why do you think that was?"

"I don't think he liked *anything* new. He was an old-fashioned, conservative man."

"And you?"

"Well, the longer I knew him, the more obvious it was that we were two completely different types. It was hard for Victor, who takes after me about ninety percent. Lately, he and his father just couldn't see eye to eye."

"Strange."

"Not really. I'm sure you know Rafe always called it as he saw it."

Delacroix glanced around the room, took in the minimalist décor. It was like a museum, but a museum from which all the paintings had been stolen. The mausoleum of a dead marriage.

So far, Delacroix had written down that Isabelle Gerard, born in Wenduine, was the only child of an antiquarian and a lawyer and had enjoyed a happy childhood. She was in her late thirties, impeccably dressed, with short dark hair in a cut that was perhaps a little young for her. Her face was her best feature, effortlessly sensual, with a lovely chin, a small mouth, full lips, flawless pale skin. Like Nicole Kidman in that movie *Birth*, where the kid tries to convince her he's the reincarnation of her dead husband, except with darker hair. She seemed, Delacroix decided, like a woman who'd been a wallflower through her twenties and was only now beginning to come into her own.

"Mrs. Gerard, I know this is painful, but is there anything else you can tell me about your husband's disappearance?"

"Not really. I mean, there was nothing unusual about it until Crevits called."

"Go on."

"He just didn't come home," she said, her eyes dry. "He used to get called a lot in the middle of the night for work, so I was used to him being gone."

"He wasn't working last night, though."

"No. He always took Shelley out for a walk at night. He said it gave him a chance to decompress from his day."

"And that's why he didn't take his phone with him?"

Isabelle smiled. "I suppose. If it were up to him, he would have thrown it in the sea. He hated carrying a phone, but of course he had to for work. He used to say he'd like to live out in the forest, off the grid, no phone, no computer, as far away from the world as he could get."

"After he retired, you mean?"

"No, now. Rafe didn't like people, Inspector Delacroix. I guess you didn't know him very well? He was what you'd call a misanthrope."

Delacroix was fixated on Isabelle Gerard's left eye. A doctor probably would have called it a lazy eye, but he'd say languid, not lazy. It didn't always look where the other one was looking. Delacroix found it sexy.

"Where's his phone now?" he asked.

She stood up. In her simple salmon summer dress and sandals, she looked like a farm girl heading out to pick flowers or collect shells on the beach. She handed him an iPhone and went back to the sofa.

"I've already looked," she said. "No calls."

"Thanks."

Scrolling back through the log, he saw several missed calls, most of them from the detective squad.

"You don't know of any appointments he might have had?"

"No. He didn't really talk about his work at home. *When* he was home."

"And there was nothing at all unusual about last night? Nothing out of the ordinary?"

"Look, Inspector," she said, suddenly more animated, "the *ordinary* at home has been—how can I put this?—not so good lately. Victor was having a rough time with his exams, my husband was busy with the serial murders, and, when he was home, all he really wanted to do was go right back out again with the dog. Are you married?"

The change of subject surprised Delacroix.

"No, not really."

"Not really?"

"I mean, no."

"Well, you spend more than a decade in a marriage, Inspector, and the thrill is basically gone. Rafe and I had some good years, at the beginning, but lately . . . Why do you think it's so empty here? The only thing he was interested in was his work. Rafe's, I don't know, his *soul* just dried up and blew away. There was nothing left. When he was here, he wasn't really *here*, you know? It was just work, work, work. Your boss, Crevits, he called it passion, but that wasn't it. It was *obsession*. That, and pure selfishness."

"No other hobbies?"

She laughed derisively. "Not counting other women, you mean? No, no hobbies. His hobbies were walking the dog and playing hide-and-seek from his family. It had gotten so bad we were thinking about divorce."

" 'We?' Or you?"

"I never actually brought it up, because Victor was having such a hard time and I didn't want to make things worse for him. And I don't think Rafe even knew there was anything wrong; he just went his merry way. But I was at the end of my rope."

Delacroix nodded.

"He changed so much, these last years," she whispered. "I hardly knew him anymore."

"Changed how?"

"A couple of times, he totally lost his temper. You have no idea how aggressive he could be. I mean, there are macho men and macho men, but they don't—"

"Don't—?"

"They don't threaten to hit their wives."

Delacroix looked stricken. "I'm so sorry."

Isabelle said, "He never did actually *hit* me. But sometimes he got so frustrated he had to strike out, and—who knows?—maybe the next time he wouldn't have been able to stop himself. I—I hope not, but I just don't know."

Delacroix stopped writing. He'd known from Day One that he

and Styx were on different wavelengths but he couldn't have guessed at this. The fact that Styx had threatened his wife told him his aversion to the veteran cop had been well-founded.

Isabelle Gerard's milky-white cheeks were flushed now, and her eyes were bright.

"He hasn't made any contact whatsoever since his disappearance?"

She brought her emotions back under control. "No, Inspector, no contact whatsoever. If he *wanted* to drop off the face of the earth, if this is all some kind of plan he set in motion himself, then I'm the *last* person he'd contact."

"I know," said Delacroix. "I'm sorry. I have to consider every possible scenario."

"Well, consider this scenario: my husband isn't coming back, because he hasn't 'disappeared.' He's *dead*. Otherwise, what would you be doing here? I lived with a cop for fifteen years, I know how you people think—and I don't need your pity. Rafe's dead. You think the Stuffer killed him. But I know better: it was his own goddamn obsession that killed him."

She hadn't come right out and said it, but if the woman had told him her husband's death had been at least to some extent a relief, Delacroix would have believed her.

"We don't know that for sure, Mrs. Gerard. We still haven't found a body."

"You don't need his body to be sure. *I'm* sure. And just because our marriage had gone to hell, don't think I don't care. I *do* care. Rafe had his good points, too. It's just . . . that seems so long ago. You know, he actually used to be really romantic."

Styx, romantic? The same guy who'd been called on the carpet again and again for excessive violence during arrests and interrogations, who'd barely survived not one but two Internal Affairs investigations for putting suspects in the hospital?

"He *had* something," said Isabelle softly. "I don't know how to describe it."

Delacroix thought back to the last time he'd seen Styx. Yes, he had to admit, although he couldn't stomach the man personally, Styx definitely *had* something. Maybe it was why they didn't get along.

Because Joachim Delacroix had something, too.

"Would you mind if I took a look around his office?"

One of Shelley's paws was in Isabelle's lap now, and she gently slid out from beneath it. The dog and the man had been two of a kind, Delacroix thought. The detectives often awarded one another affectionate nicknames, and, although they'd never bestowed one on Styx, they could well have called him "the pit bull."

Isabelle slid open a door that separated the living room from a small study. As he joined her, Delacroix asked, "He never said anything about the Stuffer case?"

"Not a word."

"Never talked about work, about any of his colleagues?"

Delacroix had no idea where the question had come from. He felt a need to prove himself, not just to John Crevits, not just to Isabelle Gerard, but somehow to the ghost of Raphael Styx. He needed something to show that his invasion of Styx's home had been worthwhile.

"No, I told you, Inspector. We hardly saw each other. For the last few months, he barely even lived here. He was somewhere else. He just put in an appearance from time to time. Sometimes, in the morning, I'd find a magazine open on the couch or a dirty dish in the sink, a clue that he'd been here, nothing more."

She waved him into Styx's inner sanctum.

"If you want to take anything with you, be my guest," she said. "I can't imagine there's anything here that'll help. If he had anything important, it'd be in his office at the station."

She turned away, as if unwilling to breach the privacy of her husband's space, and went back to the dog, who remained motionless on the sofa.

Delacroix felt uncomfortable in Styx's study. The desk was practically bare. There was a camp bed set up in a corner, and he wondered if Styx would sleep here after an argument with his wife. There was an old wardrobe, and he opened it. There were two black suits on hangers.

Jesus, the guy only had two suits?

He couldn't remember ever seeing Styx in a police uniform. He always wore the same outfit: black jeans, black boots, and a black brushed-velvet sports coat over a black or dark-gray shirt.

Could have used a little more color in his life, Delacroix thought, swinging the wardrobe doors closed.

Since his first promotion, from patrolman to detective, Delacroix hadn't needed to wear the boring Ostend PD uniform either. Like most young men of his social class from the Congo, Delacroix was a *sapeur*, a card-carrying member of La Société des Ambianceurs et des Personnes Élégantes, an informal association of fashionable men who spent half their pay or more on tailor-made colorful suits and expensive leather shoes and, cane in hand, waltzed their way through life like the most elegant of 1940s-era bandleaders.

Poor men in a poor country on a poor continent, the sapeurs lived rich lives beyond their means, lives of joie de vivre. They dined on three-course meals, they partied the nights away as if their lives depended on it, they seized each day in triumphant, joyous hands— and they dressed the part from head to toe, with silver cuff links and ironed pocket squares and a blindingly colorful new suit for every day of the week.

"Thanks for talking with me," he said, a half hour later, as Isabelle Gerard let him out of the apartment. "And for the phone. We'll trace the last calls in and out—discreetly, of course."

"Discretion," said Isabelle of the languid eye. "You know, he forgot my birthday this year."

Delacroix didn't know what to say to that.

"I don't mean forgot it until the next morning. He forgot it altogether, never said a word about it. He just didn't care. I don't think I really existed for him anymore. He was living in another world."

CHAPTER 14

The irritating twitch in Styx's shoulder had gotten worse. He stood across the street from his own apartment. There was a police car parked before the door. He'd waited until full dark to come out and had been there now for more than an hour, hoping for some sign that would allow him—no, *require* him—to hobble through a break in the evening traffic and stick his key in the lock.

But the impulse gradually faded. The longer he stood there, the less he could see himself actually doing it, the less he could even *conceive* of himself walking through that door in his condition. Isabelle would hardly recognize him. He didn't need a mirror to know his skin had gone a color not part of the visible spectrum. You couldn't even call it gray at this point. He was the color of nothingness.

And the corpse-reek his body gave off was getting worse.

It was after eleven when he saw a dark figure stroll out of the Milho Apartments. Styx recognized the jaunty walk: Who else but Joachim Delacroix would stand out so boldly against the night in his pale-green linen suit, a coral scarf draped rakishly around his throat instead of a tie, a collarless Italian shirt unbuttoned halfway down his coal-black chest?

"Jesus," he muttered, "he thinks he's in fucking Miami."

Styx could guess what Delacroix was doing there, the backstabbing bastard. He might be a zombie, but his brain still worked well enough to figure this one out: Delacroix had taken over his case.

Styx watched the young dandy head for his patrol car, beeping it open with a sissified little remote. The prick.

He crossed the street, dragging his right leg like a fallen tree limb. His shoulder jerked spastically, worse than ever. Maybe the twitch was more than a reflex, an autonomic fight against the permanence of death. Maybe it was at least partly mental.

He reached the Opel just as Delacroix started it up, braced himself with a hand on the roof, and leaned down to tap the passenger-side window with an index finger. This time, his nail tore free and dropped to the asphalt.

The window hummed down.

"Can I help you?" Delacroix asked.

Styx was surprised at how casual the rookie sounded. He'd expected him to jump out of his €400 loafers. Then he realized that the garden lights that lined the driveway were too dim to reveal the gruesome truth.

"You don't recognize me, do you?"

"Excuse me?"

"What were you doing in there, Delacroix?"

"Who are you?"

"I'm the man you replaced, Inspector."

"How do you know my name?"

"Comforting the lonely widow, were you?"

"Who *are* you?"

Styx could feel that Delacroix was about to raise the window and back away from the confrontation. He opened the door and slid in beside the rookie, relieved to be off his feet at last. His deep sigh made him sound like a tourist ready for a joyride through nighttime Ostend.

"Can I get a lift?" he asked.

"Get the hell out of my—Jesus, what's that smell?"

"That's me, I'm afraid," said Styx.

"You *stink*, man!"

"Still don't know who I am?"

Delacroix was staring right at him, but the nitwit still had no clue.

"I'll give you a hint," said Styx. "I'm missing."

"Missing?"

"Let me ask you something, Delacroix. How's the Stuffer case coming along? You find anything helpful in that cabana?"

Delacroix stared at him.

"You must have found *something.*"

The young cop opened his mouth, but no words came out.

"I know you didn't find *me.*"

"*Styx?*"

"Bingo! That wasn't so hard, was it?"

"Styx, is it you? Shit!"

"I hope you mean that in a *nice* way."

Styx could hear the rasp in his voice. He wasn't talking so much as mumbling. This was the first time since the incident with the Stuffer—okay, fine, the first time since his *death*—that he'd engaged in an actual conversation.

He reminded himself of John Hurt in *The Elephant Man.*

I . . . am not . . . an animal. I am . . . a human being.

"It—it's not possible," Delacroix stammered.

"Why not?"

"You're dead. Styx is—"

"Dead? Yeah, well, here I am."

"You were murdered. We saw the photos. We saw the blood in the cabana. Who the fuck *are* you?"

"Who the fuck do you *think* I am?"

And at that moment Styx pressed the overhead button that turned on the car's dome light.

"Holy shit!" Delacroix's arms shot up, his hands blocking out the awful sight. The front of one wrist touched the back of the other, forming a crude cross, and Styx wondered if the dandy thought he was a vampire.

Close, he thought. *Guess again!*

The rookie's right hand dropped to his hip, and suddenly he was pointing his service revolver straight at Styx's head.

"What happened to your face? Your eyes? Your mouth? You look like—"

"I look like I got run over by a truck, I know. And then barbecued on a grill. Listen, calm down. I don't know how to explain it. All I can tell you is that I *am* Raphael Styx, and the fucking Stuffer shot me three times, once in the heart. I can show you the wounds if you want to see them, just like in the pictures, but I don't recommend it. I don't know what to do about the stink. My whole body's rotting away. I have no idea how long I'm going to last, but I'm here now, back from the Apparently-Not-Necessarily-Final Darkness."

He leaned in close and put a hand on the barrel of Delacroix's gun and pushed it down.

"I'm back, kid," he said tightly.

"But how—?"

"I don't know how. I just know I *died*. The life leaked out of me there in that cabana, and it was no near-death experience. It was a *death* experience. I was fucking *dead*, and as far as I can tell I still am. Except I'm here. *Undead*."

"Undead," Delacroix repeated dully.

"I know it sounds crazy, but I need you to believe me. You're my only hope."

"Undead? You mean like—?"

He could see Delacroix trying to say the word, but he seemed to worry that saying it would make it real.

"Yeah," Styx nodded, "I mean like."

"I don't believe it," said Delacroix.

"And yet."

"I'm going to puke."

"Save it for later. I need your help."

Styx saw Delacroix's gun hand trembling. The poor schmuck had a decision to make, but Styx didn't have time to wait. He hauled up the old Glock he'd found at his father-in-law's place and pressed the barrel to the young cop's temple.

"I'm going to ask you to take things very slowly now, Delacroix. Try to stay calm. I don't want to hurt you, so please don't make things worse than they already are."

Delacroix laughed hysterically.

"This is bullshit, Styx! It's too weird for words."

"Yeah, well, life's pretty weird at best and, seeing how death's a part of life, I guess it's gonna be weird, too. Come on, put your gun away and start the car. We're gonna take a little ride along the dike. I'll tell you the whole story, best I can."

Delacroix put the gun back in his holster, but did not start the car. He made no move toward the key. Styx watched him sit there behind the wheel in his expensive suit that must have cost him a week's pay. He felt sorry for the young Congolese.

"Look, I know we got off on the wrong foot, you and me. But this is a chance for us to make it right."

"What do you want?" asked Delacroix, struggling to keep his voice steady.

"I want you to start the car. Look, the old Raphael Styx is dead. You can forget about him. The good news is, there's a new Styx in town."

It was hard for Styx to support the weight of the Glock. He wagged the barrel at the steering wheel and waited for Delacroix to start the car.

"You got promoted, huh?" Styx said. "Cool. No hard feelings: my loss is your gain. Except it turns out I'm still on the case, after all."

"What do you mean?"

"I'm gonna get the fuck who did this to me. All it cost him was three lousy bullets, but it cost me everything: my wife, my son, my job, my house, my life. I don't think I just 'came back,' Delacroix. I think I was *sent* back for a reason."

"I never—"

Delacroix didn't finish the sentence. But he didn't have to: Styx had never met a zombie before either.

"And that reason is to take down the Stuffer." When Delacroix backed out into the street, he reached up and snapped off the dome light. "I'm assuming that's what you want, too. Which would be good, because there's no way I can do it without your help."

He lay the Glock on his lap. His arms and legs felt like they were attached to his body with safety pins. It wouldn't have surprised him if his right arm had broken off under the weight of the gun.

They headed south, then east toward the harbor and soon passed the famous *Mercator* ship, which lay gleaming in the light of the full moon. A ghost ship, its decks patrolled by the spirits of many a long-dead pirate.

"Can I ask you where you've been?" said Delacroix after a long silence. "Why didn't you just go home?"

"Jesus, man, you see what I look like!"

"I know, but—"

"No, you *don't* know. You have no idea. I'm a hunk of rotting meat, Delacroix. You think I can inflict this on my wife and son?"

"I got the impression," Delacroix said delicately, "your wife isn't exactly sorry to see you gone."

I'm glad to hear it, Styx wanted to say, but he didn't mean it the way it would have sounded.

"She told me things haven't been the same between you, with you always busy with the job."

Styx looked up. Now *he* was surprised. "She said that?"

"Not in those exact words. Hers were, ah, stronger. She said you don't even know she exists anymore."

"That's a lie."

"She thought you'd react that way," said Delacroix. "She said you have no idea there's anything wrong."

"I love my wife," Styx heard himself say. He clenched his jaw angrily and felt a tooth break off at the root. He swallowed it, and said, "I'd kill for her. I'd die for her."

"She says you threatened her."

"I was an asshole, I admit it. But I never laid a finger on her!"

Delacroix was ready to leave it at that, but Styx wasn't finished. "I'm telling you, my family means everything to me. I don't give a fuck about anything else."

He stared out the window, saw the shimmering water of the harbor. They entered a traffic circle and took the second turnoff, toward the Wellington Racetrack. The roads were deserted.

"You made any progress on the case?" Styx said softly.

"We have a couple of leads. Listen, I have to tell Crevits about this."

"No. What about Karel Rotiers?"

"No connection to Madeleine Bohy. None we can find, anyway. Oh, and he's filing a complaint against the department. He says you attacked him in the interrogation room."

"Shit. The whole world's upside down."

Delacroix kept his eyes on the road.

"I saw him," Styx said. "The Stuffer. I didn't get a good look at him, couldn't see his face, but I saw his shape, his size, his posture."

"Jesus," said Delacroix.

"He was wearing a yellow oilskin slicker and a sou'wester hat. Or maybe the jacket had a hood, I couldn't really tell."

"That doesn't help much. Half of Ostend owns a yellow raincoat and hat."

"Yeah, but they don't wear them when it isn't raining. And they don't walk around in a James Ensor mask."

"James—?"

"Ensor. Painter. Lived here in Ostend, was very well known. You really *are* the new kid in town, aren't you?"

Styx told the story of the previous evening, from the Hofstraat to the encounter outside the cabana on the beach. Delacroix never once took his eyes from the road ahead.

"So you're saying," he finally concluded, "that Spilliaert is definitely the Stuffer."

"No doubt about it. He's been living for a year in that apartment in the Hofstraat. We just don't know who Spilliaert really is."

"So if Karel Rotiers *doesn't* match the sketch we had made from Spilliaert's landlord's description, then we can scratch him?"

"Probably."

"We've got a team staking out that apartment, you know."

"It won't do any good," said Styx. "He won't go back there. He knows we're watching the place."

"But does he know you're not . . . dead?"

It was the first time Delacroix had acknowledged the truth out loud.

"I don't think so. I think he assumes I *am*." Styx wanted to make eye contact with Delacroix. It was a connection, however tenuous, with the land of the living. But the rookie avoided his gaze. "You think that's an advantage for us?"

"It doesn't matter what I think," said Delacroix. "But the Stuffer's dealing with uncertainty for the first time since he started, and that's probably a disadvantage for him. I still think we need to bring Crevits in."

"And I still say no. He'll just figure out a way to use it to his *own* advantage. I don't trust him." Styx sighed in unconscious imitation of the commissioner. "The Stuffer's got to be searching for me," he said. "He'll want to finish what he started. Maybe we can use that to lure him out of his new hiding place. We have to keep my presence secret for now, don't let anyone on the squad know."

"Not even Crevits?"

"Especially not Crevits."

"Okay," said Delacroix with a wry chuckle. "As if they'd believe it anyway."

"So that's one problem resolved," Styx said. "I can't believe Isabelle told you all that shit. She really thinks we've grown apart? I mean, she said that to *you*? You're a total stranger."

"Most people think it's easier to tell their secrets to a stranger than to their nearest and dearest."

"That's bullshit."

He still couldn't believe it. He wanted to ask if Delacroix had talked with Victor, too. But he decided to save that question for later. He was already wound too tight, and his body wasn't happy about it. The twitching continued to get worse, and it was no longer confined to his shoulder. He felt a muscle in his neck acting up, too.

They pulled into the Wellington parking lot.

"I need to get some air," Delacroix said. "You really reek, man."

Styx had almost forgotten about that.

"Go ahead," he said.

But before Delacroix could get out of the car, Styx laid a hand on his arm.

"You haven't answered my question," he said.

"What question?"

"Can I trust you?"

Without answering, Delacroix shook off Styx's twitching hand.

"I have to let this all sink in, man," he said.

As he walked off into the darkness, Styx sat there, his thoughts in a whirl. How could Isabelle have told such intimate personal details to a stranger? And none of it was even *true*, that was the part that was hardest to understand. She must be deep in shock, that was the only explanation that made sense.

With fumbling fingers, he unbuttoned his shirt and looked at the wound on his chest. The blood was completely clotted, but the wound itself was ulcerated. He examined his fingers: three nails were gone, and his fingertips were badly abraded. No, not abrasions but cankerous sores. *Shit, shit, shit.* The disintegration process was well under way, and things were going from bad to worse.

A tiny red glow in the distance told him that Delacroix was out there smoking a cigarette, probably in some fancy holder. He wondered whether or not the rookie believed him—and, if he did, if he was prepared to help him. From Delacroix's perspective, it would probably be better if Styx remained dead.

The point of red arced away and vanished, and Delacroix reappeared, returning to the car. He stood by the open passenger's window, looking in.

"Everything I did was for Isabelle and Victor's own good," Styx said. "I hope you can believe me. I would never put them at risk."

"Well, this is for *your* own good, man."

In the side-view mirror, Styx saw revolving blue roof lights pull into the lot. One—no, two sets of them.

He lifted the Glock from his lap. It was so unnaturally heavy. A strange grin danced across Delacroix's face.

"Put the gun away, man. You're not going to use it."

"What makes you so sure?" Styx asked, though he knew the younger man was right.

"I don't know how much of your bullshit story is true, but I know you're a cop, or used to be. And cops don't shoot other cops. You're not a killer."

"You bastard," said Styx.

He crawled over the gear-shift lever and settled in behind the wheel. Before Delacroix could do anything to stop him, Styx started the engine and raced away from the approaching blue lights.

CHAPTER 15

The world whipped past Raphael Styx at warp speed, and neither his body nor his mind could keep up with the accelerated tempo. His ragged hands gripped the wheel, he could barely depress the accelerator with his clumsy right foot, but he roared out of the Wellington parking lot into the Koningin Astridlaan at full speed. In the rearview mirror he saw the two patrol cars pull up beside the helpless Joachim Delacroix, then take off after him in hot pursuit, blue light bars flashing, sirens howling.

"Bastard," he muttered.

Why had he trusted Delacroix?

He shifted up a gear and raced parallel to the sea, northeast toward the maze of streets that formed the city center, but the cop cars were gaining on him. The yellow streetlights flew past like burning torches. A burst of static came from Delacroix's radio. He reached to snap it off and heard a voice say, "Attention. You are strongly advised to pull over. You are driving a vehicle that belongs to the Ostend police. I repeat: the vehicle you are driving is . . ."

Kiss my ass, Styx thought.

He swung left up a side street that led to the dike.

Still a cop, Delacroix had said. *And cops don't . . .*

But he couldn't concentrate on the rookie's voice in his head. The voice on the radio drowned it out:

"Please identify yourself. I repeat: please identify yourself. The Ostend police are right behind you. If you fail to comply, we'll be forced to use other means to stop you."

Styx wondered what "other means" the dispatcher was talking about. Helicopters, like in the United States? Only once before had he ever been involved in a chase. Not a carjacker, but a guy who'd stuck up an armored bank transport. He'd managed to pull the asshole over right outside the Kursaal and get in a couple of good shots before anyone else caught up with them. When the ambulance finally got there, he'd suggested that the perp must have hit his head on his steering wheel. No idea why the airbag hadn't deployed.

He shut off the radio.

"Fuck you," he told the air.

He checked the rearview mirror. The two cars were still close behind him. He squealed onto the dike, saw apartment buildings and hotels flash by to his right and the sea to his left. In the mirror, he saw the fierce determination on his face. The headlights of the approaching cars reflected larger and larger in his pupils, blinding him.

The sirens were almost on top of him now. A voice yelled "Pull over!" through a megaphone.

Ahead, he saw the metal gate that gave access to one of the dozens of breakwaters which jutted out from the seawall and ran across the beach to the North Sea. He had two choices. He could follow instructions and pull over. But then what? He had no idea how they'd react to his return. What lay ahead: A media circus and imprisonment? The only other option was to try to escape. There was no third way out.

So Styx swung the wheel hard left, bounced across the sidewalk, burst through the gate, and felt the tires thunder onto the uneven wooden surface of the breakwater. His pursuers had slowed down, but they were still behind him. He was getting away from them, but there was one problem: in a few hundred feet, the breakwater came to an end, and all that lay beyond it was the sea.

The headlights in the mirror winked off and on. They were warning him to stop. He *had* to stop, didn't he?

Didn't he?

Something in Raphael Styx kept him flying forward. With less than one hundred feet to the barrier at the end of the breakwater, instead of lifting his battered foot from the accelerator and slamming on the brakes, he pushed harder on the pedal and pinned the speedometer needle to the far right of the dial.

He checked the mirror one last time and saw that the pursuit vehicles had come to a stop. Then, staring out into eternity, he hunched over the wheel and smashed headlong through the barrier at the end of the breakwater.

The car sailed through the air in a sudden eerie silence, straining to hit escape velocity. But gravity had its way, and Joachim Delacroix's cruiser fell crashing into the dark waters of the North Sea.

Raphael Styx sat there, motionless, stunned, as the car filled and sank. A coherent thought formed in his mind: he had to get out before it was too late. He yanked on the door handle and shoved against the panel, but the outside pressure was far stronger than he was. Panicked now, he scrabbled for the button that controlled the windows, but the salt water had already shorted out the car's electrical systems, and the window stayed stubbornly closed.

Again, he flung himself against the door, but he was too weak. He had no strength left in his arms. His blood had curdled, his muscles were stiff and useless, his body was a tumble-down ruin.

The water level rose past his chest, past his neck, over his chin.

Styx kept his mouth tightly shut. During his time at the police academy, he'd gone through a scuba course, and he'd learned then that he was capable of holding his breath for a surprisingly long time. The doctors had told him he had the lungs of a long-distance runner or triathlete, but there were limits to how long even an athlete could survive before drowning.

He was completely underwater now. The world had gone totally still. He felt the pressure on his eardrums increase as the seconds ticked past.

How long had it been? A minute, at least, maybe two.

He knew that, at any moment, he'd have to open his mouth, and the seawater would fill his body like helium swelling a birthday balloon. Like sand filling the bodies of the Stuffer's victims.

But the moment didn't come, and at last the truth dawned on him.

He didn't *need* to breathe!

When he finally parted his rotting lips and unclenched his blackened teeth, he didn't drown.

He was already dead.

He was, in fact, undead.

He had no idea how it worked—it was enough *that* it worked. He sat tight, letting himself calm down and marshaling his remaining strength. Then he swiveled around and saw that the passenger-side window was still open and swam out of the car like a modern-day

Houdini. When he broke the surface of the water, he was far enough from the sunken wreck that the cops at the railing seemed not to notice him.

After Inspector Delacroix's visit, Isabelle Gerard went upstairs to say goodnight to Victor, and then went straight to bed. She was at the edge of sleep when the phone rang.

"Rafe?" she murmured, rolling away from his side of the bed.

That was a reflex—late-night calls were usually for her husband, not her. But then she remembered she was alone in the bed. She fumbled for the receiver and got it on the seventh ring.

"Hello?"

"Mrs. Styx?"

"Yes?"

"This is the Ostend police, ma'am."

She came instantly awake.

"Yes?"

"I'm afraid I have bad news."

She thought of Inspector Joachim Delacroix, who'd been there only an hour before. Was there something he'd forgotten to tell her?

"Does this have something to do with Inspector Delacroix's visit?"

"No, ma'am, I'm calling in regard to the disappearance of your husband, Raphael Styx."

"Who are you?" asked Isabelle. "I'd like to speak with John Crevits, please. Can you put him on?"

"I'm sorry to have to inform you that your husband was killed in the line of duty, ma'am. He's dead."

Isabelle tried to be strong, but, now that the words had at last been spoken aloud, she found herself shaking uncontrollably.

"I know that," she managed to say.

"Oh? Then I expect you also know that he was murdered in a cabana on the beach?"

"I don't want to hear the details," said Isabelle. "I'd like to speak with Commissioner Crevits, please."

"But I *have* to tell you the details, Mrs. Styx," the voice said. "It's my—"

"It's Mrs. Gerard. Isabelle Gerard."

"The problem, Mrs. Gerard—and I hope you'll be able to help me with this—"

And suddenly there came a strange burst of laughter.

"The problem is that his body seems to have disappeared."

"Yes, Inspector Delacroix already told me that."

Something was very wrong. That gruesome laugh seemed to come from some other plane of existence. It was as if she was on the phone with two different people simultaneously.

"Who is this?" she demanded.

"I'm wondering, Mrs. Gerard, if you might know anything more about your husband's disappearance? I thought you might have some information about the police department's plans."

"Wait a minute," said Isabelle. "I thought you were—"

"They've given me a nickname, Mrs. Gerard," the voice said seriously. "I didn't get to pick it myself, but I suppose I have to live with it. Anyway, if you'll play fair with me, then I'm willing to share the exact circumstances of your husband's death with you."

"Please, no," Isabelle begged, realizing at last who was on the other end of the line.

She had never fainted in her life, not even when she'd heard Rafe's death reported on the news. But now all sensation in her legs was suddenly gone, and she felt herself about to keel over.

"Please what?" the voice asked politely.

"I don't want to hear it. How did you get this number?"

"The internet's a beautiful thing, Mrs. Gerard. You're sure you don't want to know what his last words were?"

"No, don't, I can't—"

"I don't mean to be rude, but your name was alas not mentioned. He knew he was looking down the barrel of the gun that was about to send him to hell, and he stood there and pissed his pants. That was all. He didn't say a thing. I'm telling you the truth."

"Stop it," Isabelle choked.

But she couldn't bring herself to hang up the phone. She stood there with the receiver in her hand, shaking. *What am I waiting for*, she thought. Why couldn't she just put the thing back in its cradle?

"I need to know what they're up to!" the voice yelled.

"I don't know anything," she whispered.

"Bullshit! Where is he? Where is that fucking bastard? I have to know! I have to finish my work!"

Isabelle closed her eyes and thought of Victor, sound asleep in his room. And of Joachim Delacroix, the young man in the garish suit who had offered her comfort.

"You tell the cops I won't fall for their trap, you hear me? I'll find out what they're up to. I'll find him. And if it turns out he's in the morgue, I'll go in there and get him. I'll get him, and I'll split him open, head to toe, and cut everything out of him. His goddamn heart, his organs, his muscles, everything, so there's nothing left but one big gaping empty hole, ready for the sand. Do you hear me?"

There was more, but the receiver finally dropped from Isabelle's numb grasp.

It took a full minute before she remembered where she was.

"Victor!" she cried.

She raced down the hall to her son's room and threw open the door. She gathered the sleeping child into her arms, the little boy who from a distance looked so much like his father, the handsome young man the girls were already beginning to notice. He struggled up from sleep, frightened by her sudden appearance.

"What's wrong?" he mumbled, his dark eyes only half-open.

"Nothing," she said, stroking his hair tenderly. "Nothing's wrong, sweetheart. Go back to sleep."

CHAPTER **16**

It took till late that night before they were able to winch the crashed Opel out of the water. Commissioner John Crevits and Inspector Joachim Delacroix stood side by side at the railing as the rescue crew operated the huge crane. When the car finally broke the surface, Delacroix, a poncho draped over his shoulders, leaned forward, staring, as if he expected to see Styx still sitting behind the wheel.

The crane deposited the car, gushing seawater from its open passenger window and door seams, on the breakwater, and uniformed patrolmen threw the doors open and popped the trunk.

The vehicle was empty.

"Well?" Crevits demanded.

"I swear," said Delacroix. "It was him. Styx."

BAVO DHOOGE

"Styx is dead," Crevits said flatly. "We saw the photos. Even if he *isn't* dead, the person you described can't possibly have been him."

"I talked with him," the rookie insisted.

"Let's say you had a little too much to drink, Inspector. If you have any ambition whatsoever, if you want to make anything of yourself on the Ostend police, then I seriously advise you to shut your mouth."

"With all due respect, Commissioner, I saw him and talked with him. He was dead, but he wasn't."

"He was dead but he wasn't? What kind of bullshit is that?"

"I can't explain it," said Delacroix. "I didn't believe it either, at first—"

"Look, Delacroix. I don't care what clothes you wear. I don't care what you do on your nights off. But I'm not going to let you turn the murder of one of the best cops this police force has ever had into a fucking voodoo sideshow."

Crevits nodded at the ruined Opel, which hulked there like a pre-historic beast.

"You say you saw Styx, dead or alive or both or whatever. I say you didn't. Goddammit, you were just at his apartment, offering your condolences to his widow. So don't hand me this line of crap."

"He was eye to eye with the Stuffer!"

"Stop it!"

"He described him to me. A yellow oilskin slicker and a sou'wester. A James Ensor mask."

"I said *stop*. If that was Raphael Styx who drove off in your car, then why isn't he there now?"

"Because—"

But Delacroix had no explanation. Because the dead can't die? No, there was no way Crevits would accept it.

"Raphael Styx may have been a shit," the commissioner said, "but whatever else he was, he was a cop. A cop who'd do anything to solve a murder."

Delacroix saw that his commissioner was about to lose it. He understood that Crevits and Styx went way back. They'd kept each other's secrets, stood by each other through thick and thin. Till death. So why, then, had Styx come to *him*, and not to Crevits? Why didn't he trust Crevits?

"Whoever stole your car," Crevits snapped, "it wasn't Styx. You ask me, it was some random carjacker, and right now he's at the bottom of the sea."

But Delacroix wasn't asking John Crevits anything.

"It's night, it's dark, you were tired," Crevits went on patiently. "Some crackhead jumped in your car and took off with it. You only saw him for a second, and you thought he looked like somebody you used to know. That's completely understand—"

"I'm telling you I *talked* with him," Delacroix said tightly. "We sat next to each other in the car. I saw him."

He wanted to tell Crevits the whole story, starting in front of Styx's apartment, but Crevits grabbed him by both lapels and pulled him close.

"Listen to me, you stupid bastard. I'm not going to let you fuck with the one molecule of respect Styx still has in this city. Did you not hear what I said? It was a carjacker. He knocked you out and stole your car. There's no shame in that. But it would be a *big* mistake for you to try to blame it on somebody else, especially a dead man. We don't speak ill of the dead around here, and I'm not going to ask you if you got it. I'm *telling* you you got it, you got it?"

"But—"

"One more word and you're on your way back to Brussels," Crevits spat. "I'm giving you a chance to move up, Delacroix. Don't *fuck* it up by turning the whole department into a laughingstock. Styx did enough of that while he was alive. Can you imagine what the media would do with *this* story, if it got out?"

The flood of seawater from the Opel had ebbed to a trickle. Two patrolmen were poking around the soggy interior, looking for—what?

"What about the information he gave me?"

"What information?"

"The yellow rain slicker and hat. The Ensor mask."

"That's all bullshit," said Crevits. "First of all, your 'witness' has disappeared. And second, half—"

"I know, half of Ostend has a yellow slicker and hat. I just thought that—"

"Thought what?" Crevits barked.

Delacroix held his tongue. "Nothing, never mind."

"Now you're starting to make some sense, son. Your imagination ran away with you for a while there. Go home. Sleep it off, and come back with a clear head in the morning. We'll laugh about this tomorrow."

But Delacroix knew there was nothing to laugh about.

"We can't afford to drop the ball on this investigation," said Crevits, resting a fatherly hand on his shoulder. "It's much too important. The department's reputation is at stake—Styx's is already shot. Let's not turn this whole thing into a farce."

Delacroix watched Crevits walk away, past the leaking carcass of the dead patrol car.

Later, still leaning on the railing, Delacroix watched a couple of guys in orange coveralls load the Opel onto a tow truck. They drove off, and the beach settled back into stillness.

Yes, fine, Delacroix had had a drink or two the night before. But he had a drink or two every day: a glass of wine with lunch, a shot of *jenever* during the afternoon, a martini before dinner, and a cognac after. But he was a sapeur, and he could handle it. He hadn't been drunk. He knew what he'd seen, and he knew what he'd heard, straight from the mouth of Raphael Styx:

A yellow oilskin slicker and a sou'wester hat. Or maybe the jacket had a hood, I couldn't really tell.

Long ago, Delacroix knew, you used to see them by the hundreds, all of a type, those hardy fishermen, up at the crack of dawn and out in their yellow uniforms to brave the vagaries of the North Sea.

Half an hour later, he remained at his post. Nothing moved out there save the rolling breakers, but in his imagination the ripples took and gave back the shape of Raphael Styx's face.

He could hear Styx whisper to him from beneath the waves:

Go, Delacroix. Do it. Be a cop. Don't let me down.

A few weeks ago he'd been sent to the forensics lab's pathology department to pick up a copy of the autopsy report on Reinhilde Debels, the Stuffer's first victim, for Crevits.

And he remembered catching the briefest glimpse, through the open door to the chief pathologist's office, of a bright yellow rainjacket hanging on a coat stand.

He stayed at the railing for another ten minutes, watching the place where the Opel had gone into the water, thinking about Raphael Styx and their preternatural encounter.

In the morning, there would be nothing for him to sleep off. But there would be work for him to do. Just like the old fisherfolk, he would be up and out the door early.

Without Crevits's blessing, he was on his own now.

Just like Styx.

CHAPTER 17

The gentle current carried Styx along the coast, and, by the time he squelched out of the sea, he was half a mile south of the point where he'd crashed into it. He wasn't sure if he should rejoice at the discovery that he was apparently immortal or despair at his eternal condemnation to the kingdom of the damned.

Weirdly, he had never felt so completely alive as when he'd sat there talking with Joachim Delacroix. He had almost felt his heart thrumming in his chest—though he knew a bullet had stilled it.

Was it the fact that they'd been talking about Isabelle which had revived his spirits, or the fact that he now saw a possible break in the Stuffer investigation? He tried to convince himself that it had been Isabelle, but he knew better.

For the second night in a row, he hobbled through the deserted streets of Ostend. He didn't even notice his drenched clothing plastered to his body. His lot in life—or rather, death—had become this endless wandering through the city.

He was headed for his father-in-law's house, which seemed destined to serve as his lair. When a distant church clock tolled the hour, he remembered the broken old pocket watch he'd been carrying. It was completely ruined now, surely—but, when he took it from his sopping-wet pocket, it seemed miraculously undamaged. He clicked it open, and a rush of heat went through him, like a furnace turning itself on as the outside temperature fell.

Just past the Belgian Coast Tram's Ravelingen stop, almost halfway back to the place where he'd roared off in Delacroix's patrol car, he saw a figure on the other side of the tracks, an older gentleman with longish gray locks, like Einstein on a good hair day. A tourist who had lost his way? A fisherman out ahead of the pack, waiting for a tram to take him to his boat?

Styx was transfixed. He'd felt this same strange sensation at the train station. He couldn't quite put it into words, but it was at the same time both bizarre and completely comfortable, both real and surreal. A man, all alone, bathed in moonlight beside the tracks.

He wanted to call across to him, to test whether or not the man was just a figment of his imagination. He held himself back, though. He'd already had contact with one living being tonight—Joachim Delacroix—and that hadn't exactly worked out well.

But his feet walked him closer. No need to look left and right for an oncoming tram at that hour of the night. As he approached the stranger, he put his age at about seventy and was surprised to see him standing behind some sort of high-backed chair.

No, he realized as he narrowed the distance between them, it wasn't a chair: it was an easel, and without any conscious intention Styx found himself saying, "Good evening. A good night for painting?"

Not looking up, the man went on sketching pencil lines on his canvas. He took a step back to study the results, and to make room for Styx to get a better view.

"I don't know yet," said the man. "You *never* know, at night. The world at night is a dream: everything looks one way at one moment, and the next moment it's all different. I paint what I see, not what's *there*, and what I see is always changing. Is that a contradiction? A paradox? I don't know. Is that why they call me a Surrealist? I don't really agree with the label."

On the canvas, Styx saw a naked woman against the detailed background of . . . a train station. She stood beside the tracks, lush and lifelike, lit by the moon, staring emotionlessly ahead, a visitor in a world where she didn't belong.

"It's beautiful," said Styx.

"I hope not," the painter replied matter-of-factly. "Beauty is boring. I want it to make you *think*. I'm trying to create an entirely new world. A world between worlds. Do you understand?"

"I think so," Styx said. "I think I know exactly what you mean. A different reality."

"You could call it that. A reality that isn't real. A contradiction."

"Do you do this often?"

"What?"

"Paint in the middle of the night."

"Why not? The Impressionists set up their easels in the middle of a cornfield, so why shouldn't I set my—"

"But you're no Impressionist, are you, Mr. . . . Delvaux?"

The painter leaned in closer to examine his creation's breasts.

"You know me?"

"Your work is well known."

"That would surprise me. But why not? And, as I began to say, why shouldn't a Surrealist—if that's how they're going to insist on pigeonholing me—set *his* easel up where my imaginary model and I can choose to lose ourselves?"

"May I ask you something? Where *are* you when you paint a scene like this? Are you still in this world, or do you go to that other world? Or are you—like your subject—somewhere in between?"

"That's a difficult question," the painter replied.

He turned toward Styx at last. He was smiling peacefully, a reaction Styx wouldn't have expected. The artist switched his pencil to his left hand and put out his paint-smeared right. Styx took it.

"Paul Delvaux."

"Raphael Styx."

Styx was perplexed by the man's calm. Why wasn't he gathering his easel and canvas and paints and brushes together and putting as much distance as he could between himself and a sight far more surreal than a naked woman in a train station: a waterlogged zombie.

But the dead cop was more confused by his surroundings, which he saw now were out of joint. There were no cars on the street, but he had the feeling—no, he was absolutely convinced—that, if there were any cars to be seen, they'd be vintage models from the turn of the twentieth century. Delvaux's easel and supplies were professional and expensive, but they were *old*, not aged but old-fashioned, the type of equipment that had last been in use decades ago or even longer. And then there was the painter himself, the personification of a dream, who, like Styx, had somehow reappeared from the land of the dead.

He glanced at his pocket watch and saw the second hand turning. It couldn't be a coincidence . . .

"You're interested in my work?" said Delvaux.

"It has a few connections to something I'm working on myself."

"May I ask you to explain?"

"She looks familiar to me."

"The nude?"

Styx examined her. "She's striking," he said. "Especially since—"

"Since?"

"She radiates pure beauty. But in the case I'm working on, that beauty has been perverted into horror."

"I'm sorry to hear that."

The Stuffer's first victim, Reinhilde Debels, a prostitute working in the Ostend harbor, had been found naked in the Mu.ZEE sculpture garden in the exact same posture as the woman on Delvaux's canvas. Until now, all that linked the three victims was that they were women. But now . . .

"I don't think our paths crossed tonight by coincidence," said Styx.

"How do you mean?"

"Do you believe in signs, Mr. Delvaux? Visions, omens?"

"My good man, that's *all* I believe in."

"I think this is more than a sign. I think it's a trail, a clue, a signpost to the truth."

"I'm a painter," said Delvaux. "But you are surely a poet?"

"No," Styx told him. "Not at all. I'm a cop, a policeman."

He knew full well he was speaking in the present tense.

As he studied the naked woman in the painting, her pale face seemed to dissolve into the elegant features of Reinhilde Debels.

"A signpost to what truth?" asked Delvaux, bringing him back out of the painting to whatever world this was.

"I'm not sure yet," said Styx. "All I know is it's a clue, but I don't know where it will lead me."

"That is the essence of art, and of Surrealism in particular," said the painter. "Our mission is to stimulate questions, not to answer them."

"First Delvaux, then Ensor, then Magritte," Styx gasped, as he saw at last the link between the Stuffer's first three victims. James Ensor had painted a woman on a flight of seaside stairs, surrounded by masks, the sea a field of blue behind her. And then there was René Magritte's headless, armless, legless nude torso of a woman planted on a sterile beach.

"Why me?" asked the painter.

"I'm sorry?"

"You, too, lump me in with the Surrealists?"

"Not me," said Styx. "Someone else."

"He's made a mistake."

"A costly mistake for the women in your paintings—"

"They're not real women," Delvaux explained patiently.

Not anymore, Styx thought.

The artist returned his attention to his canvas. He was ready to get back to work.

Raphael Styx was, too.

Delvaux stepped closer to his easel. He looked as though he was preparing to dive into his imaginary world. There was so much left to draw, to paint, to create.

"If you don't mind," said the artist, "I'd like to finish this by dawn. Once the sun comes up, I lose interest. It's the moon that moves me. The sunlight makes everything so obvious."

"We disagree there," said Styx, who was hungry for the day to begin.

Delvaux winked at him, and Styx crossed the tracks and set off for the city center, the road to a solution stretching out before him.

A really big *show*, the Stuffer's boast rang in his ears.

The Ostend Surrealists.

He was beginning to understand.

As he trudged on toward his father-in-law's house, he was all alone. Only later did it strike him that he had always worked alone— first as a man, and now as a zombie.

As a zombie, though, would he be on his own by choice, as he'd been in his previous life, or did he even *have* a choice anymore? Were there more of his kind—and, if there were, where were they? An existential loneliness washed over him: even as a zombie, he seemed destined to travel solo. Was that part of his penance? A natural consequence of the way he'd lived his life as a human being?

Or was there another possibility? Could he be some type of dark messiah, *chosen* to walk this dusty road alone? Perhaps his lot was to wander through the darkness as Jesus had wandered through the desert.

No one, not even a zombie, should have to go through life—or death—alone. But once again Raphael Styx seemed to be an exception to the rule.

When he got to the house, he pulled out Marc Gerard's half-hunter and snapped it shut.

He didn't need to look around to know that, by doing so, he had returned himself to his own place in time.

CHAPTER 18

With its bright fluorescent lighting and blank walls, the forensic lab's pathology department was just as cold and sterile at nine AM as it was at midnight. As behooves a true sapeur, Joachim Delacroix had decked himself out to shame the sun in a three-piece suit, striped tie, and silk pocket square in shades of brown, green, and blue.

He was accompanied by a patrolman, Martens or Maertens, who outranked him in age only and was as colorless as—well, a nonsapeur.

"Window shopping?" asked Dr. Tobias Ornelis, chief pathologist, a man with a spartan frame that suggested a refugee from behind the Iron Curtain.

"Not exactly," said Delacroix. "I recently replaced Chief Inspector Styx on the Stuffer case, and I never got to see Madeleine Bohy's body, so I—"

"Sad story, Styx," said Ornelis.

"I don't know whether I'm glad you haven't got him on a slab here or sad we still haven't found him."

"What do you expect to learn from Bohy's corpse? Everything's in the autopsy report. Blood results, descriptions of the wounds, internal bleeding, the sand, everything up to and including the needle and fishing line he used to sew her back together."

"No idea," Delacroix admitted. "I don't know what to look for, and it's probably a waste of time, but—"

"But what?"

"Well, maybe Styx missed something."

"I don't suppose taking another look could hurt," said Ornelis.

"I think we owe it to the chief inspector."

"Still no sign of him?"

"Not a trace," Delacroix lied.

He'd taken a night to sleep on it—as John Crevits had directed—but hadn't actually gotten a wink of sleep. He was too wound up to close his eyes, too eager to get a look at Tobias Ornelis. Delacroix wasn't there because of anything Styx might have missed but because of something the zombie cop claimed to have *seen*: the Stuffer dressed in rain gear and a James Ensor mask.

Ornelis was also obsessed with James Ensor and his masks. He had reproductions all over the place. But then again, this was Ostend, the birthplace of the master painter, so perhaps it wasn't all that unusual for Ornelis to be a fan. Still, two things made the pathologist special. One, he apparently knew the last victim, had a secret crush on her, according to several people Delacroix had questioned. Even dead and lying in his morgue, she seemed to have an unnatural hold on him. Two, people were starting to gossip about Tobias Ornelis and his bizarre relationship with the dead girl.

Ornelis led him into the morgue, its far wall lined with a bank of refrigerated lockers. He unlocked one of the compartments, slid out a long metal drawer, and unzipped the white plastic body bag that lay on it. Madeleine Bohy's head and limbs were all there, not quite touching the torso but ranged around it in their proper positions. Delacroix stood there looking Death in the eye, and for the first time he had absolutely no doubt who it was he'd encountered the previous evening.

Raphael Styx.

He knew it the moment he saw the pigmentation of the dead woman's skin, smelled the grave-reek that rose from her body, felt the changes that being in a room with her wrought in the very atmosphere. They were kinfolk, Bohy and Styx, two of a kind. With one difference: unlike the woman on the slab, Styx was still walking around.

"Crevits gave you a copy of the autopsy report, I assume?"

"Yes," said Delacroix, staring at the severed head.

"She was strangled, unlike the first two victims, both of whom were stabbed to death. Hey, can you tell me what we're supposed to do with the sand? We've got it bagged in a storage closet, but it can't sit there forever."

"Why not?" asked Delacroix. "It's just sand."

"What are we supposed to do with it? Make sand castles?"

"It'll make its way back to the beach eventually," said Delacroix.

Ornelis cocked his head toward Martens or Maertens, who was waiting for them out in the corridor as instructed, on the other side of the viewing window. "How's the new partner working out?"

Delacroix shrugged. "I don't really know him yet."

"He's not as . . . colorful as you."

Delacroix understood that his approach to life must seem completely foreign to Ornelis, a man who spent eight hours a day puttering around among the dead.

"You can zip her back up," Delacroix said, after a perfunctory examination.

"You sure?"

The rookie nodded, and tried to act as if he'd found what he'd been looking for. As Ornelis carefully reclosed the body bag, the young cop wandered apparently aimlessly around the impersonal examination room.

There was a battered metal desk in a corner of the room, and on it was an equally impersonal MacBook Pro. The lid was up, and a screen saver showed a colorful photo of the Ostend shrimpers' annual parade: dozens of men in yellow oilskins and sou'westers on horseback, dragging enormous nets behind them along the beach.

Delacroix had seen the picture on Ornelis's desk a few times. He'd never paid any attention to it before—to each his own obsession—but it certainly caught his eye now. Only once had he noticed Ornelis at a crime scene—and then only from a distance.

"The shrimpers' parade," he said casually. "When is that again?"

He examined his memory more closely, zoomed in mentally on Ornelis's figure in the distance—and, yes, there he stood, protected from the rain by his yellow oilskin jacket and hat. There'd been no reason to notice it at the time—yellow raingear was practically an Ostender's uniform—but now he combined the memory of that crime scene with the more recent memory of Raphael Styx's voice:

I saw him, the Stuffer . . . a yellow oilskin slicker and a sou'wester hat . . . a James Ensor mask.

Behind him, the pathologist said, "I'm not sure what the date is this year. Tell you the truth, I haven't watched it in years."

"You still use that photo as your screen saver, though. When was it taken?"

"Oh, Lord, I don't remember. It's not me, though."

Delacroix turned around. Ornelis had slid the drawer back into its refrigerated compartment and was tapping the lock code into the door.

"The picture, I mean. I didn't take it, and I'm not in it."

"I see," said Delacroix. "Where'd you get it, then?"

"Some website. Probably the city's."

Delacroix turned back to the laptop, studying the yellow rain jackets like the little patch of yellow wall in Vermeer's *View of Delft* that had so affected Marcel Proust. The so-called Stendhal syndrome, the experience of being overwhelmed by beauty.

Delacroix wondered if there was a version of the word for horror. Here in the morgue, he was prepared to believe there was.

"When was the last time you took part in the parade?" he asked. Ornelis seemed not to hear him, and he began to repeat the question: "When was the last time you—?"

"The last time I was in the parade?"

So he *had* heard him. There was something weird about Ornelis, Delacroix thought. He'd heard enough gossip over the past year to know that he wasn't the only one who thought so.

"You haven't met Dr. Death yet, eh, Delacroix?" one of his colleagues had joked, while a bunch of them were catching a beer after their shift, his second week in Ostend. "Never fear: you will. We all do. He's a nutcase. But, I mean, what would it do to *you*, sitting there, day in, day out, nobody around but the dead? Who *else* has he got to talk to?"

Delacroix thought he must have misunderstood. "You mean—?"

"Oh, yes," said another gleefully.

"He *talks* to them?" He assumed the story was an exaggeration, some sort of hazing new members of the city's police force were put through. But the whole group chimed in with its agreement.

"I heard him myself," a third man said. "I was about to open the door, and I heard him in there talking to someone. I figured he had somebody in there with him, but, when I went in, he was all alone."

"Creepy," Delacroix had said.

And then there was the aura the man gave off.

Or, better, the *lack* of one.

Like every pathologist, Tobias Ornelis was more or less required to wear a white lab coat during working hours, but he usually ignored that custom, roaming around in old jeans and a raggedy sweater. He wasn't merely as somber as the Man with the Scythe. He had no personality at all—at least none he allowed anyone around him to see.

"Can I ask you something?" said Delacroix, still focused on the laptop. Ornelis didn't respond. Maybe he was only used to talking when no one else was around. No one *alive*, at any rate. "You still have your jacket and sou'wester?"

"What?"

"That fisherman's gear."

"I'm not a fisherman."

"No, but you used to be in the parade."

Delacroix smiled affably, but the other man was carved out of ice, as cold and stiff as the corpses he worked with.

"Why do you ask?"

"Just curious."

"I don't know. If I still do, I haven't worn them in a while."

A silence fell upon them and lasted long enough to begin to become uncomfortable. Finally, Ornelis added, "I don't go out much."

"It's been pretty busy around here lately, eh?"

"Unfortunately."

"But you have to go out sometimes? I mean, you don't sleep here, do you? And there's been so much rain lately. People tell me they've never seen anything like it. Supposed to be the worst spring since they started keeping records." He let a moment go by, then continued: "You could *use* one of those yellow rain jackets. I hope you didn't throw yours away."

They stood there eyeing each other. Tobias Ornelis, with his hands clasped behind his back, and Joachim Delacroix, placidly watching the doctor, a man who fit the description Styx had provided. Tall, thin, hollow eyes.

"Anything else, Inspector?" Ornelis asked.

"I don't know," Delacroix said. "I'm thinking."

"It's just, I was about to take a break when you came in. I eat my breakfast late, and I like to keep to my schedule."

A slave to routine, Delacroix had heard it said. *A strange, strange man. He lives alone, never married, never had a girlfriend or even been out on a date, far as we know. Had a crush on the last victim. Carries the smell of death around with him. No wonder he's single. Can you imagine going out to dinner with the guy? How could you possibly eat?*

"I don't want to keep you," said Delacroix.

But he couldn't pull himself away. He'd seen Madeleine Bohy's body, and he knew there were other bodies in the other sliding metal compartments. There were cabinets and drawers filled with scalpels, knives, and surgical saws. In the hands of a serial killer, these would be dangerous weapons. Here, though, they were simply tools of the pathologist's trade.

"I don't like to leave strangers in here on their own," said Ornelis.

Apparently Delacroix counted as a stranger.

"It's all right, I'll walk out with you."

"It's just, people usually aren't comfortable in here without me."

Delacroix let the statement hang in the air.

"Why wouldn't I be comfortable?"

"Well, because they—because they're all dead, obviously."

"Doesn't bother me," said Delacroix. "I deal with death every day of the week."

"Then we're two of a kind," Ornelis said, smiling weakly.

"How do you mean?"

"We know the dead can't hurt us. Most people are afraid of them, but we really ought to pity them. If you ask me, we need to do a better job of getting them ready for their journey. You take a living woman, for example. She spends an hour, maybe two, in front of her mirror in the morning, making herself up, smearing gel in her hair, covering up her wrinkles. Once she's dead, though, that all comes to a stop. Except for me. I'm the one who takes over the job. It's like maintaining an old car. It'll never drive again, the motor's shot, maybe even gone altogether like the heart out of a body, but I can still polish her chassis and keep her looking good."

"Although she's dead," said Delacroix.

"At least she ends in beauty."

"I thought morticians were responsible for all that sort of thing."

"Perhaps. But I take my work more seriously than they do. Especially when I know the victim."

So at least some of the rumors were true, then.

"I'll admit," said Delacroix, "when I go, I want to go in style."

"I can see that."

Delacroix could tell that it was time for him to leave. As he strode across the room he spotted a small table half-hidden behind a narrow door he'd barely noticed. On it was an array of what seemed to be medical specimens and personal effects.

He swung open the door for a better overview of the table. There were a dozen airtight plastic Baggies, some containing bits of skin, tissue samples, strands of hair, nail clippings, while others held a lipstick, a compact, a ring of keys, and similar items.

"What's all this?" he asked.

"Evidence," Ornelis responded brusquely. "From the decedent, Madeleine Bohy."

The sapeur delicately lifted one of the Baggies with his thumb and forefinger. It held a length of what looked like wire. On closer inspection, he saw that it was a thick plastic filament. "And this? The fishing line used to hold the body together, right?"

"Yes, I took it all out. I I don't think her family would want to see her buried like that."

Delacroix nodded. He laid the Baggie back in its place and asked, "Who says she's going to be buried? Maybe they'll have her cremated."

"What difference does it make? Either way, it's better without the—"

"Better?" Delacroix spat out the word. "A corpse is a corpse."

"Not to me."

"No, clearly not. I assume you had official permission to cut the line out of her? To make your . . . improvements?"

"Improvements?"

"You have a better word for it? You sewed her back together, I noticed, with surgical thread. That's an improvement on the Stuffer's work, isn't it?"

Delacroix's imagination unspooled a film of Tobias Ornelis here in his workshop, leisurely restitching the sculpture he'd had to hurry through out on the beach. He could see the pathologist patiently sewing, talking pleasantly to the dead girl while he worked.

"I don't think I like your tone," said Ornelis.

"I don't think I much like *you*," said Delacroix.

"As I said, Inspector, I spend most of my time with the dead. I'm not very good with the living. I apologize for my manners."

The doctor had clearly had enough of this particular representative of the living and wanted to be left alone so he could eat his late breakfast. Or early lunch. Delacroix was about to offer the pathologist his hand when he saw it.

The scar. An ugly cut, perpendicular to the wrist on the side of the hand. Delacroix had known a young woman who'd succeeded in slitting her own wrists. In fact, it was because of her that he'd become a sapeur.

His whole life, Delacroix had been a Sunday's child, "bonny and blithe, and good and gay." Everyone around him in Ostend assumed he'd grown up in Brazzaville and emigrated to Belgium as a young adult, and he thought that origin story added to his allure so he did nothing to disabuse them of the notion. But the truth was that he'd been born to a Belgian mother and a Congolese father, and had been raised in one of Brussels' better neighborhoods. He'd coasted through middle school and high school, and was planning to study law and become an attorney.

He was in his first year, wrestling with contracts and judicial remedies when his half-sister Celine, seven years his senior and a classic Jill of all trades, master of none, finally lucked into an internship in Prague. Though this was pre-Facebook, they'd stayed in close contact by e-mail and phone until the day her calls stopped coming.

At first, he assumed Celine had fallen for some hulking Eastern European, but then he got a call from the host family that provided her with room and board. She'd been terribly homesick, they explained in English they barely spoke and he understood with only marginally less difficulty. Ultimately, the depression had driven her to slit her wrists in a public bathroom at school. No one found her until hours had passed and it was far too late to save her.

Joachim thought the call had to be some kind of sick joke. But no one was laughing, and, when the confirmation came, he took a leave of absence from school and a train from Brussels to Frankfurt to Nuremberg to Prague to investigate the matter on his own.

He questioned her friends, her colleagues, and her host family, determined to uncover whatever it was that had driven her to suicide. There had to have been more to it than loneliness. If that was all it was, then why hadn't she simply gotten on a plane and returned home?

He learned that Celine had steeped herself not only in the beauty of the Golden City but also in the darker side of its history, a history stained by occult practices and tragic melancholy. Had she gone mad? He didn't know. He'd finally given up and returned to Brussels, unable to solve the mystery of her death.

He knew from their father and their Congolese friends of the rise of La Sape back in Brazzaville, and to honor his sister's memory he attended her funeral dressed for the first time as a sapeur. With his sister dead now, he wanted somehow to keep her spirit alive, so he dressed up every day, as if he dressed for two. It was months later that the host family in Prague came across a stack of letters she'd written but never sent on the top shelf of the closet in what had been her room. Several of the letters were addressed to him. They were heart-breaking cries for help, permeated with shame and grief and misery as she became convinced that a daughter of racially mixed parentage would always be an outcast.

It was after reading those letters that Joachim Delacroix dropped out of law school and applied to the police academy.

The scar on Tobias Ornelis's wrist was a faint reminder of his lost half-sister Celine.

They shook hands, and, before letting go, Delacroix turned the doctor's arm a bit for a better look.

"Occupational hazard," Ornelis said, noticing Delacroix's attention. "The problem's not the knives and scalpels. It's the thread."

"I wouldn't have thought surgical thread was all that dangerous."

"It isn't," Ornelis laughed uneasily. "I meant the fishing line the victim was sewed up with. It's all thread to me, but that stuff's so stiff it flies all over the place when you try to stitch with it."

"You mean when you took it out of her?"

"Right, of course."

"You said it flies around when you stitch with it."

"I mean it wasn't the thread I used to sew her up the second time that cut me, but—"

"The second time?" asked Delacroix.

"Yes."

"You sewed her up twice?"

"No, the killer sewed her the first time with the fishing line, and then I—"

"So how did you cut yourself?"

Ornelis held the door for him, but Delacroix wasn't about to leave now.

"On the—what difference does it make? I don't really remember. Let's just say it was the fishing line, and it happened when I was removing it from her body."

"Sure," said Delacroix.

He pressed the button for the elevator, and Tobias Ornelis stood and waited with him. He wanted to question the doctor further about the scar on his wrist, which couldn't possibly have been caused by ordinary surgical thread. Certainly not in the case of a man who used the stuff every day at work.

"I'll let you know if I remember, Inspector."

The door slid open at the lobby level and Delacroix stepped in, but the pathologist stayed where he was. As the door began to close, the cop put out a hand and stopped it.

"I thought you were going out for breakfast?"

"No, I bring something from home. And I prefer to eat alone, so, if you'll excuse me . . ."

"Of course," said Delacroix. "I appreciate your time. See you soon."

"Not *too* soon, I hope."

It took Delacroix a moment to get the joke.

"Yeah, right. I'm not in any hurry."

Ornelis returned to his lab and closed the door behind him.

Delacroix stepped back off the elevator and put his ear to the lab door, listening to see if the rumors were true, if the doctor would begin talking to his corpses. But the only sound that came through the door was soft piano music. *Debussy*, Delacroix thought.

"See you *soon*, Ornelis," Delacroix whispered. He pressed the button to recall the elevator, and, while he waited for it, took out his phone to call John Crevits.

CHAPTER **19**

It was pouring yet again in Ostend, and—especially at this time of year—that was bad for business along the coast. Styx was listening to the rain batter his father-in-law's windowpanes when the doorbell rang. He had just finished smearing himself with a tube of Nivea gel moisturizer, not so much to protect his skin as to mask the stench. His H&M suit was already ripe with his new brand of body odor, and he'd had to change into an old one he'd found in one of Marc Gerard's closets. With its wide lapels and sharply pointed collar, it had possibly been in style back in the seventies, and it was at least two sizes too small for him, but it was better than being naked. Though not by much.

He got slowly and painfully to his feet, grabbed his walking stick and dragged himself over to the window. He drew the heavy curtains aside to see who was at the door, but all that was visible through the rain was a dark cap and coat. Whoever it was stood with his back to the house, watching the street.

"Shit," said Styx.

Who knew he was hiding here? The house hadn't yet been put up for sale. Was it some city functionary checking the place out? That didn't seem likely at this time of night.

Could it be the Stuffer, here to finish what he'd begun? No, there wasn't a chance in a thousand he could have linked this address to Raphael Styx. Was there? Anyway, though the color of the unexpected visitor's cap and coat were difficult to determine in the dark, they certainly weren't a yellow sou'wester and oilskin. But Styx clutched his walking stick a bit more firmly, just in case.

Styx thought of his plunge into the chilly waters of the North Sea and decided it couldn't hurt to see who it was. At this point, he had nothing left to lose.

When he eased the door open, a familiar voice said, "Styx. Finally."

Beneath the cap stood Joachim Delacroix, wrapped in an old-fashioned dark-gray three-quarter-length English overcoat. The two men eyed each other for a full half minute, as if neither could believe what he saw.

"I thought I'd never find you."

"Delacroix? How *did* you find me?"

"I'm a cop, Styx. We have ways. Your wife told me you'd been clearing this place out the last few days before you died. Or were supposed to be, anyway. I didn't get the address out of her, but I've got a realtor friend, and I asked him if he knew of any interesting properties that were likely to come on the market soon."

"Solid detective work," said Styx grudgingly. "I couldn't have done better myself."

"You going to let me in or make me stand out here until I drown?"

"Why should I let you in?"

"Because it was a whole lot of trouble finding you."

"Why should I care? And how do I know you won't just turn me in again?" He peered out past Delacroix's shoulder, but there was no one lurking in the street.

"You think I'd pull that twice?"

"Why not?"

"Because the fact you're still standing here proves you weren't lying. You're the real deal, aren't you? I mean, you're exactly what you said you are."

"You can't say the word, can you?" said Styx.

He took a step back to make room for Delacroix to come in. The young cop whipped off his overcoat, which he'd been wearing draped around his shoulders like an aristocrat, and scoped out the foyer, wrinkling his nose at the musty smell.

"Come on," said Styx, and led him into the interior of the house.

Marc Gerard's living room was divided into two distinct areas, a front parlor used only for Sunday company and a second, less formal sitting room. Styx had closed the metal shutters, and the only illumination came from a single table lamp beside the threadbare old armchair in which Styx's father-in-law had passed his lonely evenings watching war documentaries on the National Geographic channel.

"I can't say the situation's gotten any better," Styx said. "You can see that for yourself."

"I can see it and smell it," said Delacroix.

"I'm falling apart."

"Why don't you open a window?"

"What's the use?"

"What happened, Styx? I mean, one minute we were standing there talking, and the next minute you're off like a bat out of hell."

"What happened? You ratted me out is what happened."

"I did what I thought was right," said Delacroix. "I'm still working for Crevits, you know." He waited for an invitation to sit, but Styx dropped into the armchair without a word. "What would *you* have done?"

"I would have heard you out, cop to cop."

"Well, for what it's worth, I'm convinced now, and I'm sorry. And you're right about not telling Crevits. The fewer people who know about this, the better."

"That's nice," Styx said, "but it doesn't do me any good. And it doesn't help bring down the Stuffer, either."

Delacroix bent to switch on another lamp, but the bulb was burned out. It was just an empty glass shell. "I can't get over it," he said. "But I guess I have to, eh?"

"I can tell you," said Styx, "it's no picnic."

"What I don't understand is, where's the rest of them? I mean, you're undead, I get it, but you can't be the only one. In the movies, there's always dozens of them, hundreds, thousands, crawling out of their graves and staggering around looking for people to kill. Is that *you* now? You don't look like you're getting ready to take a bite out of me."

"No," said Styx. "I'm not. And I have no idea if there are more like me out there. I haven't seen any, but I don't know."

"How did it happen, then? You didn't get bit?"

The rain on the roof was the only sound in the room.

"I don't know. I don't think so." Styx thought back to the moment when he'd awoken from the dead in the cabana. He was so preoccupied with the three gunshot wounds and his rotting body that he'd never stopped to think about a possible bite. Delacroix was right: that's the way the legends said it happened. If the stories were true, then he probably *wasn't* the only zombie out there. "I didn't see anybody. But I was out of it for a while."

"Then how?"

"I'm telling you, I don't know. It is what it is. I didn't come crawling out of some graveyard. I don't clomp around with my arms all stretched out, moaning gibberish. And I'm not sitting here hungry for a nice, juicy manchop. Not yet. All I can think is that the shit they show in the movies and on TV is bullshit. What's real is me. Christ, I'm *real*, Delacroix. I'm a fucking zombie."

"I have so many questions."

"You think I don't?" He saw Delacroix studying him, so he shied away from the light. In the dark, his cracking skin, his rotting teeth, his split lips and suppurating wounds were no longer visible.

He knew they were there, though. He could feel them. He could feel himself decomposing.

"You're living like a rat here," said Delacroix. He jumped to his feet and began to straighten up the room. The cardboard box that had held last night's pizza, the empty beer cans and chip bags and Kleenex boxes, the dirty towels—he shoved all of it into a trash bag he found beneath the kitchen sink.

"What do you want me to do?" Styx groused. "Take a bath? I tried. The scrubbing makes my skin peel off; it's disgusting. I tried to take a shower, and I wound up ankle-deep in my own pus."

"I get the point," said Delacroix. "But you can't just give up."

Give up? Styx wanted to *stand* up, but he couldn't summon the strength. He tapped the tip of his walking stick on the floor.

"What do you think you're doing?" he demanded. "This isn't the fucking *Odd Couple*."

"I just want to make things a little nicer for you," said Delacroix. He disappeared back into the kitchen and reemerged pulling on a pair of latex gloves. He picked up Styx's discarded clothes, from socks to necktie, and stuffed them in the plastic trash bag.

"This all goes to the dump," he said. "Tomorrow, I'll bring you a couple of my old suits. I bought two that are too big for me. They're from overseas, so I can't return them. They ought to fit you."

"Why are you doing all this?" asked Styx, his chin resting on the copper fish that formed the walking stick's handle.

"I told you, they don't fit me. And they're not your cheap H&M suits either. Not that it makes any difference, but—"

"You know that's not what I mean. I mean, *all this*. Why did you even come here?"

Delacroix paused, hands on his hips.

"I don't know," he sighed. "Honest, I don't know."

"A couple of days ago," said Styx, "I hated you."

"*That* I know."

"Because you—well, I don't even know why."

"Just as well."

"I mean, because I—"

"I know what you mean. You don't have to say it."

"So *why*, then?"

"Look, Inspector, you turn on one more lamp, I'll probably run right out of here and never look back. But I keep hearing this voice in my head saying, *He doesn't have anybody else.*"

"That's *my* voice," said Styx softly. "You're all I've got."

"Yeah, and, as far as the Stuffer case goes, *you're* all *I've* got. You're right: there's still a case to solve. A serial killer who thinks he's some kind of Rodin is on the loose in Ostend. And he won't stop killing until we stop him."

Styx had no response. There was a murderer to find, and the death of the investigation's lead detective was just a footnote.

"You making any progress?" Styx asked.

"Well, that's the other reason I'm here. I mean, I'm happy to help you, but there is something I need to show you."

Like an eager little boy, he hunkered down by Styx's side. In the dim light of the room, he could see the horror that was Styx's face, see the sunken eyes glisten as he took the photograph from his pocket and handed it over.

"You know who this is?" he asked. It was a studio portrait of a man posing against a bright white background and gazing uncomfortably into the camera's lens. "I found it on a website."

"Of course I know him. It's Ornelis."

"Tobias Ornelis, chief pathologist at our forensics lab."

"Right. Did he tell you something about the Stuffer?"

"He—"

"He found something?"

"No," said Delacroix. "But—"

"But what, dammit!"

"I think Ornelis is more than just a pathologist."

"Such as?"

"A serial killer."

Styx gaped at the portrait. Ornelis? They'd met countless times, but hadn't exchanged more than ten sentences over the years of their acquaintance.

"Are you serious?"

"Yes," said Delacroix.

"That's crazy," he said, handing back the picture, ignoring the greasy stain his fingers had left on the glossy paper.

"He's got a yellow oilskin rain jacket."

"Who doesn't? It's not him, Delacroix."

"He's obsessed with James Ensor. He knew the last victim."

"So what? Ensor was a great artist. And Ostend is a small city, why wouldn't he know her?"

"He acted really strange when I talked with him."

"Ornelis *always* acts strange. He *is* strange. The day Tobias Ornelis *doesn't* act strange, *that'll* be strange. No, I don't believe it. You're barking up the wrong tree."

"Styx," sighed Delacroix impatiently. "He was talking in riddles, nothing he said hung together. And he had a cut on his hand. I think he got it from that fishing line when he was sewing Madeleine Bohy's body back together after he stuffed her full of sand."

"I'm not gonna listen to any more of this," said Styx. "It's total BS. I've known Ornelis for years. Why would the man suddenly go psycho?"

"Why not? He talks to the dead."

"He hasn't said a word to me," Styx said drily.

"You know what I mean. You've heard the stories."

"We've all got our little idiosyncracies. He *talks* to the dead, I *am* dead."

"Ha ha," said Delacroix.

He put the photo back in his inside jacket pocket, and now at last he dared to look Styx in the eye.

"I'm telling you, he almost gave himself away today. He's the closest thing we've got to a viable suspect. And he fits your description."

"You shouldn't take what I said too seriously."

"Why? Because you're a zombie?"

"Because it was dark when I saw the Stuffer. And he was wearing a mask."

"The description matches, Styx."

"Fine, so what's your plan? You going to arrest him? Interrogate him until he confesses?"

"We already have," said Delacroix. "Arrested him, anyway. They're questioning him now."

CHAPTER **20**

Earlier that day, Joachim Delacroix had returned to the pathology department. A few other officers—including Martens or Maertens—accompanied him into the subterranean recesses of the police building to arrest Tobias Ornelis on suspicion of murder. He knew they didn't have a lot to go on, but they had to do *something* with the Stuffer still on the loose, and the first thing he wanted to do was interrogate Ornelis. They came out of the elevator soundlessly and approached the door to the morgue.

Delacroix put a finger to his lips.

He wanted the other cops to hear it, the lugubrious whisper of Ornelis's ongoing conversation with the corpses in his charge.

"On three," Delacroix mouthed. "One, two, . . ."

They could have waited for Ornelis to lock up his abattoir and head for home, but why delay the inevitable? Either way, arresting a man who worked so closely with the Ostend detective squad would be big, and Delacroix didn't want to risk Ornelis somehow hearing about what was coming.

"Three!"

Delacroix rapped sharply on the door and pushed it open without waiting for a response. The team swarmed inside.

They found Ornelis bent over the body of Madeleine Bohy. He was fully dressed, thank God, and put up no resistance.

"Inspector Delacroix?"

"Doctor Ornelis, you're under arrest on suspicion of murder. You have the right to remain silent. Anything you say may be used against you in a court of law. You have the right to an attorney. If you cannot afford to hire an attorney, one will be . . ."

It was Martens or Maertens who shoved the pathologist up against a cabinet to handcuff him. Ornelis struggled to free himself. He pushed off an evidence table and raced out of the lab.

Delacroix went after him and caught up to him halfway down the corridor.

"Don't make it worse than it already is, Doctor. You don't want to make a scene."

But he fought again to get loose, and Delacroix had to wrestle him to the tiled floor. With his cheek pressed into the linoleum, the doctor groaned, "Let me go! Don't make me leave her!"

"You're coming with us, Doc."

"You can't leave her here alone! She needs me! I'm the only one who can help her!"

"You're the one who needs help, you sick bastard." Delacroix hauled him to his feet, threw him up against the wall, pulled his arms behind him, and slapped on the cuffs.

"She doesn't have anyone else. I can't abandon her."

— — —

Delacroix described the arrest to Raphael Styx, described the ghastly look he'd seen in the pathologist's eyes as the elevator door slid closed.

"I'm telling you," said Styx, "it's not Ornelis. Has he said anything?"

"No, nothing."

"Maybe you ought to bring in one of his dead bodies, if he only talks to them."

"Good idea," said Delacroix. "You busy tomorrow?"

"Funny. Look, Ornelis is not the Stuffer. He's not going to say anything helpful, because he doesn't have anything helpful to say. The man's a loser. Yes, I get it, he sees dead people—and talks to them— but that doesn't mean anything. The Stuffer's not a loser. He knows what he's doing, he's smart. He's got good taste, artistic sensibilities, he's distinguished."

"How do you know all this?" asked Delacroix.

"I've been after him for more than half a year, remember?"

"Yeah, but what makes you so sure Ornelis doesn't fit that profile?"

Styx tried to pull himself out of the armchair without barking in pain. He leaned on his walking stick and hobbled over to the low table Marc Gerard had used as a makeshift bar. The bottles of gin and vodka and whiskey were old, but age had been kind to them.

"You want a drink?" Without waiting for an answer, he poured whiskey into two water-spotted glasses and added ice to each. "This is about all I can still taste."

Delacroix threw back his portion in two long gulps.

"You'd be better off pulling in that Casanova Karel Rotiers," Styx said.

"Forget it. True, Rotiers knew the first two victims, but he had absolutely no connection to the third one. And he's got an airtight alibi: he was out of the country when Madeleine Bohy was killed, in Ibiza, adding a couple more señoritas to his stable."

"Shit."

"That's why I'm pinning my hopes on Ornelis. The doctor's the only legitimate suspect I've got, and Crevits is really starting to turn up the heat. I can't just sit around and do nothing."

"It's not Ornelis. It can't be."

"How can you be so sure?" asked Delacroix.

"I don't know exactly how to put this," Styx began. He rattled the ice cubes in his glass, and they tinkled like the bell announcing the start of a new round. "But now that you've gotten a good look at my, ah, condition, maybe you'll be able to swallow it." He took a breath. "Ever since I said farewell to the land of the living, it's not just that I'm still walking around. Somehow or other, I also seem to be able to visit, well, another Ostend."

"Another Ostend? What other Ostend?"

"The Ostend of La Belle Époque."

"You lost me," said Delacroix. He stepped to the bar and poured himself another drink.

Styx, still nursing his first one, explained: the train station, Leopold II and his entourage, the lonely Surrealist painter in the night who'd introduced himself as Paul Delvaux. Styx couldn't quite believe it himself, but his father-in-law's pocket watch seemed to be a key—or, better, a doorway—to the past.

"You don't mean you met the real Paul Delvaux?"

"Why not?"

"Because he's, well, *dead*?"

They let that sink in, and at the same moment they both burst out laughing.

"You sure it wasn't some sort of hallucination?" said Delacroix.

"It seemed awfully real to me."

"Maybe the whole dying thing's got you confused?"

"Could be," said Styx. "Maybe. Maybe my mental ability's fading out, like an Alzheimer's patient."

"So you're fighting against time, trying to solve the case before the little gray cells give up the ghost?"

"I'm no Hercule Poirot."

"I hope not. A zombie Poirot, back from the dead to crack the case—now *that* would be crazy."

"All I can tell you," said Styx, "is that Delvaux got me thinking differently about the murders."

Styx limped over to the only bookcase in the room. It was an old grandmotherly affair, with five shelves behind a pair of glass doors. There were books on the four lower shelves, and the top shelf displayed a collection of knickknacks, souvenirs from family holidays, and a couple of framed photos of the old Ostend, one of them showing a group of fishermen on the beach. Styx bent over and slid a thick art book from the middle shelf. It was heavy, and his back seized up on him for a long, painful moment.

"I want to show you something," he gasped. "When I met Delvaux, he was painting a nude woman, and that's when I saw it."

"Saw what?"

"The connection. The missing link."

Styx opened the book, a study of the Belgian Surrealists. He'd been paging through it in the hours before Delacroix's arrival, and the dog-eared corners made it easy for him to find the pages he wanted.

"Look at this one."

He tapped a reproduction of a Delvaux painting with a sepulchral fingertip.

Nude in a Train Station.

Delacroix saw it immediately: the pose of the woman in the

painting matched the posture of Reinhilde Debels's body in the Mu. ZEE's sculpture garden almost exactly.

"He painted a lot of naked women," Styx said, "in all sorts of strange settings."

"Like the Stuffer leaves his victims in strange places, you mean?"

"Right. He's copying the Surrealists, and not just Delvaux."

"Jesus." Delacroix was leafing through the thick volume. A picture on one of the other dog-eared pages brought him to a standstill. The torso of a naked woman—arms, legs, and head all missing—standing on a deserted beach. It was a Magritte, titled *When the Hour Strikes*.

"Jesus Christ," said Delacroix. "This one's almost exactly like what we found."

"So you don't think I'm hallucinating?"

"No," Delacroix said firmly. "This is absolutely a legitimate lead."

"And you understand that Tobias Ornelis had nothing to do with it?"

"I'm not ready to go that far. Like I said: Ornelis is a big Ensor fan. I want to show him these paintings and see how he reacts."

"He won't have any idea what you're driving at," said Styx, closing the book and setting it down on an end table. "Where's his motive? How does it do Ornelis any good to kill a few people and fuck around with their bodies? He's got all the bodies he wants down in his morgue. No, it just doesn't add up."

They sat side by side on the old sofa, thinking and drinking.

"You want another one?" asked Styx after a while. He seemed happy to have Delacroix's company.

"Thanks, no, I've got to get ready for tomorrow's questioning. And I need to do some research, follow up on your leads. Well done, Chief Inspector."

Styx led him to the front door.

"Does this mean we're working together?"

"Let's see what happens tomorrow," Delacroix said. "Then we can decide."

"I'll be right here," said Styx. "I think there's an old computer around somewhere. I can do some research, too. Maybe some of those old Surrealists still have family here in Ostend."

"You think that might be important?"

"Who knows? It's worth a shot. I'm not going anywhere. I have to do *something*. I'll see what I can dig up on collectors, art historians, gallery owners, museum curators. If I come up with anything that seems promising, I'll let you know." He paused. "When I see you, I mean. In this condition, I guess I'll have to wait for you to come to me."

"Sounds like we *are* working together, then," said Delacroix. He didn't want to shake Styx's hand—who knew what pieces might break off if he did—but he touched it gently and fought the urge to whip out his pocket square and wipe off the putrescence. "I'd get some sleep if I were you," he advised. "You look dead tired."

"Dead as your sense of humor," said Styx. "Anyway, I don't seem to need much sleep anymore. I guess I'll sleep when I'm *really* dead."

He hoisted his walking stick, pretending to drive Delacroix out of the house. It was still raining, and the rookie had almost disappeared into the night when Styx called him back.

"I almost forgot," he said, reaching into the pocket of his father-in-law's outdated suit. "I wanted to give you this."

CHAPTER **21**

"What is it, an original Delvaux?" Delacroix joked.

With difficulty, Styx worked a thick yellow envelope out of his pocket.

"It's a letter," he said. "For her."

"For who?"

"Isabelle." He handed it to Delacroix. "If I mail it, they'll know I'm still around. But there are some things I need to tell her. Things I never had the balls or the time to say."

"Inspector, I don't know if I'm the right person to—"

"Of course you are. Who else is there? Not Crevits. And you've already talked with her. Just go back, tell her you've got a few more questions."

"Well, I could bring her your phone. We've listed all your incoming and outgoing calls, so we don't really need it anymore."

Styx hadn't realized that the police had taken his phone in the first place. "You don't have it on you now, do you?"

"No, it's back at the squad."

"I'd actually like to have the phone myself." He hesitated. "There are some texts and voice mails I want to keep."

"From your girlfriends?"

Styx looked abashed. "No. From—"

"From Isabelle," said Delacroix.

Styx nodded, his ruined face melancholic. "Nothing special. I think she called me one time, asked me to pick up a few things at the store."

Delacroix nodded.

"I never did get there. Something came up. As always. But it would mean a lot to me to hear her voice. Will you bring me the phone?"

"Sure. And I'll figure out another reason to drop by the house. You want me to just give her this?"

"No! Hide it someplace where she'll eventually find it. You're a cop. Imagine it's a piece of incriminating evidence you want to plant at a suspect's house."

Delacroix ran a finger across his upper lip. "I've never done that," he said slowly.

Styx looked disgusted. "You're young, you'll learn."

Styx had written and rewritten the letter half a dozen times on the old stationery he'd found in one of Marc Gerard's desk drawers. He was used to writing police reports and witness statements: straight-ahead prose, objective conclusions, without so much as a hint of emotion. And now here he was, a zombie, and for the first time in decades he had to compose a love letter.

"When she goes out to the kitchen to make coffee, stick it under the logs in the fireplace," he said. "She knows that's where my will is. Or, no, better yet, there's a book she gave me on the night table next to the bed. A guidebook for New York. Put it in there."

"I don't know if I'm cut out to play Cyrano de Bergerac."

"Who asked you? *I'm* the Cyrano in this story, rookie. You're just the messenger boy."

"I'll try my best," Delacroix promised.

"Bullshit. There is no try, only do and do not."

Delacroix still looked skeptical.

"Come on, man," Styx pleaded. "I need you to do this for me. It doesn't matter when she finds it, I just want it there for her to find. It might be years from now, but when she *does* find it and read it, she'll understand what she's meant to me. I've been treating her like shit for way too long. My job, my ambition, my fucking appetites—I put all that crap ahead of her and our son." He shook his head sadly. "What an ass I've been. What a total fucking ass."

"Can I ask you something?" said Delacroix.

"Sure, what?"

"All the stories, they said you had pretty strong connections to the Ostend underworld. The mob, the pimps, the dealers, Amanda, Gino Tersago."

"Yeah? What do you want to know?"

"I don't need it all, but you know what they've been saying about you. It's not just that the mobsters were stooling for you. Word is they were paying you off. Hush money, bribes."

"You're saying I was corrupt?"

"I'm telling you what *they* say."

"*That* Styx is dead. He's the guy who treated *you* like a piece of shit, too, but he's gone now. I've been given a second chance, and I won't make the same mistakes this time."

"So you're a *good* zombie?"

"Jesus," he sighed. "I couldn't figure out how to live a good life. But I'm gonna do whatever I can to live a better death."

Delacroix nodded, but he didn't look convinced. Styx leaned his cane against the doorjamb and grabbed the sapeur's shoulders with his moldering hands.

"Promise me you'll take the letter. If I'm sure she'll eventually realize how sorry I am, then maybe I can finally get a little rest."

"I never knew you were such a romantic," said Delacroix.

"I never was," Styx admitted. "I couldn't even figure out what to write. I mean, I've always been an action guy, not a word guy. So I borrowed some stuff from Lord Byron."

"How appropriate."

"Why's that?"

"He was what they call a Romantic."

"Yeah, my favorite period. You know, I was gonna pack it in at one point, change careers, start all over. Actually, it was Isabelle's idea. She hated me getting hauled out of bed every other night to go look at dead bodies. She wanted me to 'reinvent' myself. We talked about it a lot. I was gonna go back to school and everything, study literature, maybe wind up teaching or something. Can you imagine?"

"What happened?"

"I don't know." He shrugged. "What always happens? Life got in the way."

They were both quiet for a moment, the wind whipping around them.

"I'll hide the letter in the house," Delacroix said.

"Thanks. Don't read it, okay?"

"I won't read it. It's none of my business. I just hope you didn't tell her the truth. That wouldn't make things any easier for her."

"I'm not asking her out for coffee, Delacroix. I'm never going to see her again. What we had is gone for good. That's why I wrote the letter."

"Unfinished business?"

"Something like that. I just want to try to make things—it's probably way too late to make them right, but maybe I can make them a little less wrong. I want to, I don't know, whisper in her ear, try to leave her with something better than bad memories, let her know I finally realized she was all I ever really needed out of life, all I ever really wanted. I just wish I'd figured that out before it was too late."

"You're a poet yourself, Styx."

"Yeah, maybe *that'll* be my new career: Raphael Styx, Zombie Poet."

Delacroix tucked the note away in the inside pocket of the English overcoat he had draped over his shoulders like a boxer's robe. Ready for a fight.

With the lights of the house behind him, Styx's silhouette looked perfectly normal. No one passing by on the street would have realized what he really was.

"I'll keep you posted," said Delacroix.

"You know where to find me. And bring my phone, next time. Then we can stay in closer contact."

"Will do. Good luck."

"You're the one who's gonna need it," said Styx, and he watched the young inspector dash across the street through the pelting rain to his car.

He carried Styx's letter in his pocket, next to his heart.

I used to have a heart, Styx thought.

CHAPTER **22**

The atelier was an art school during the daylight hours and hosted an assortment of classes for adult learners from seven to ten PM. It was now a little after midnight, so the place was empty except for Heloise Pignot and the dark man who let her into the building.

Heloise was twenty years old and a student, though not here. She was studying nursing at the university in Kortrijk and had spotted the MODEL WANTED poster on a bulletin board there. As a teenager, she'd competed in several beauty pageants, so she had experience posing, and she'd called the number listed on the flyer. To her surprise, she'd been offered the job over the phone, without a face-to-face interview, without even e-mailing the artist any of the publicity shots that had been taken of her during her short-lived pageant career. That seemed a little strange, but for €50 an hour she could live with strange.

The only request she'd made during their conversation was simple: "I've never posed nude before, so I don't want anyone else around."

"Of course," the painter had told her, "that's perfectly understandable. The important thing is for you to feel comfortable."

They'd agreed to meet at the front entrance of the academy in the Dr. Verhaeghestraat at eleven, because the artist worked mainly during the night. Heloise was right on time, and when the painter didn't show, she wondered if someone had been playing a joke on her. Or maybe she'd ruined it saying she didn't want anyone else around, and he'd found another model. But, I mean, there were limits, weren't there?

She knew a couple of girls at school who stripped in front of a webcam to pick up a bit of extra spending money, and even one who worked weekends in what she called a "gentleman's club"—although, according to her, the men who patronized the place were anything but gentlemen.

But then the man from the flyer showed up and apologized for being late and—now *he* was a gentleman!—opened the door for her.

The smells of oil paint and turpentine were almost overpowering, and there were sketchbooks and canvases and easels and palettes everywhere. A dozen drawing tables were ringed around a small platform that held an armchair and, on a side table, a bowl of fruit that was beginning to go bad.

Heloise took off her coat, and the painter slid a CD into an old player against the far wall.

"I hope you like Debussy," he said. "I find he helps me concentrate."

"I don't mind," said Heloise. "Anything's better than nothing."

"Make yourself at home," said the artist.

Heloise stepped onto the platform and took a seat in the armchair. She kept her clothes on for now.

"You don't really look like a painter," she observed.

"No?"

"In a suit, I mean."

"Many artists wear suits while they work. Borremans, Tuymans. It's nothing new. The great James Ensor—may I assume you know Ensor's work?—he never left his house dressed any other way. He—"

He stopped abruptly.

"Oh, who am I trying to kid? Listen, my dear, I'm not really a painter."

Heloise looked up sharply. For just a moment, she was terrified she'd fallen into some sick rapist's trap. These days, you had to be so careful. What had she been thinking, agreeing to meet a stranger, alone, at midnight?

"I'm just an amateur," he confessed. "If all I ever do is *talk* about art, without rolling up my sleeves and trying to *make* some, then something's seriously wrong with me."

Debussy filled the atelier, and Heloise Pignot felt herself transported to another world.

"I don't want to hurry you," he assured her. "Take your time. Allow yourself to get in the proper mood. Meanwhile, I have a few things to prepare."

She sat there in the armchair, beginning to feel comfortable, her feet tucked beneath her, watching as he slowly, in time to the music, as if enacting some ancient ritual, removed the lid from a large container he set atop one of the drawing tables. He dipped his hand into the pot and scooped out a clump of some gray substance.

"What's that?" said Heloise dreamily.

"Clay," he replied. "I like to work with my hands."

"I thought you said you were a painter?"

"I am, but I've decided to branch out, try something different. Tonight, I haven't made up my mind between painting and sculpting.

It may sound crazy, but I like getting my hands dirty. I'm like a child: the more dirt under my fingernails, the better."

He laughed. She saw the emotion in his eyes and was herself moved by it. This was a man who knew how to give himself over to passion. She was intrigued. "Have you done sculpted figures before?"

"Yes," came his response. "A few times."

"How did they turn out?"

"Let's just say I'm still searching for my own style. My voice. Like every artist."

"I can't wait to see what it looks like," said Heloise.

To be honest, she couldn't wait to get out of her clothes. She saw the sparkle in the artist's eyes. She could tell from the way he considered the mass of clay on the table that he was ready to begin.

"You don't want to put on a smock?"

"No, we'll just see what happens. Sometimes I go into a sort of trance, and I don't even notice till it's all over that my clothes are covered in . . . clay."

"Well, I'm not going to make you wait any longer."

"Yes, let's get started," he said.

She unbuttoned her blouse and removed it slowly, stepped out of her skirt, folded them both neatly and laid them beside her on the platform. She untied her sneakers, unhooked her bra, pulled off her panties. It happened almost automatically, felt completely natural. She didn't think she could have done it in front of any other man.

"Okay," she said enthusiastically. "Now what?"

"Now we need to find the perfect pose," he said.

He turned away from the block of clay and took a pencil from a leather case, held it point up before him, and used it as a sort of measuring stick, moving it from side to side to estimate the proper proportions.

"What should I do?" asked Heloise.

"I don't know. Just move. We'll see."

"I really don't have much experience."

"That's the beauty of it. Just be yourself. That's what I need."

Heloise tried an array of poses. Heloise Pignot resting her cheek on the back of her hand and gazing out into space. Heloise Pignot sprawled across the chair, one hand cupping the back of her head. Heloise Pignot in lotus position.

"Nice," he said. "Yes, lovely. We're almost there."

"I'll have to sit still for a long time, right?"

"As long as possible," the man said. "It's going to take us quite a while."

"But I can have a break if I need one? If I get a cramp or something?"

"Oh, you won't," he said. "We'll make sure of that."

"How about this?" She was lying on her side, one hand resting on her thigh, the other stretched above her head, as if she was swimming.

"Beautiful. That's perfect!"

"I don't know how long I can hold it, but—"

"It's exactly what I want," he said. "Just relax and lie there, and I'll get started."

Heloise breathed deeply, like her doctor had her do when he was checking her lungs. She closed her eyes and let Debussy's piano music carry her off.

When she opened her eyes again, he was standing right beside her. She almost jumped to see him so close. He was still holding the pencil.

"Can you put your other arm next to your body, too? That'll look more natural. Like you washed up on some deserted island."

Heloise did what he asked. "Like this?"

"Yes, terrific," he said.

She watched him return to the drawing table, his head half-hidden behind the easel. The clay was ready for him. He took a few more items from his leather case: a box cutter, a pocket knife, a scalpel, and a sort of dagger with a long curved blade.

"What is all that?"

"Tools, for shaping the clay."

He selected the scalpel, bent over the table, and began carving. With short, quick movements, he shaved the sides of the brick, smoothing them, bringing form out of formlessness. He seemed to be creating a cube.

"You're good with that knife."

"This is just the rough work," he said, not looking up. "The details come later."

He dropped to his knees, so his chin rested on the edge of the table, and began shaping the cube into a suggestion of something more human. And now he began pricking holes in the clay with the point of the scalpel. He poked, prodded, punched the blade into the yielding earthy flesh. From her vantage on the platform, Heloise watched bits of clay fly in all directions as he worked.

"You really know what you're doing, don't you?"

He didn't answer her. Soon there was more clay on the floor than on the table. Heloise saw that he was unsatisfied. Frustrated.

"Should we take a break?"

"Stay where you are," he snapped.

He stepped away and looked back and forth between his sculpture and the girl. For the first time, Heloise felt he saw her more as an object than a person, and she didn't like the feeling. Sculpting didn't seem to be working for him. Maybe he should go back to painting, although she had no idea if he was any better in that medium than this one.

"What's the problem?" she asked. "Is it me?"

"Don't be silly," he said.

He came out from behind the drawing table, the scalpel held

loosely in his hand. He let it tremble between his fingers. He was thinking. Heloise knew she should be quiet, not upset him, but the words were out of her mouth before she could stop them: "I can try another pose, if you'd rather."

"No," the man said, still deep in thought.

Then he came to a decision. He nodded, strode up to Heloise Pignot, and slit her throat with one fluid swipe of the blade. Hot blood spurted from her neck, painted her naked body, soaked the platform. She twitched convulsively, and, as she lay there dying, not understanding what had happened and how quickly the world could change, the Stuffer said, "It's better if you lie completely still. Just a few minutes more. We're almost finished."

When she was dead, lying there with open eyes staring blindly at the misted windows, he wiped the scalpel clean on his trouser leg.

He said, "I like you better when you're quiet."

He pulled on a pair of latex gloves and moved her into a slightly different position. He had no intention of sculpting her in clay. She herself was now ready to be molded into art. Her death was a necessary step along that path. He adjusted her arms and legs a bit more, until she was exactly the way he wanted her. Then he backed away and eyed her contemplatively.

Now what?

He could cut her open with the sica. He could excise her organs and dump them in the sink. He could fill her empty shell with the silica sand the ceramics classes used on their kiln shelves and sew her back together.

It was almost one AM, and he was the only living soul in the atelier. He would have plenty of time.

Or perhaps he should show everyone how angry their mistake had made him.

The article in the newspaper, announcing that a suspect had been detained in connection with the serial killings, had made him sick to his stomach. The fools!

Tobias Ornelis? Who the hell was that? Some ridiculous morgue attendant? How could they insult him like this?

"I'll show them," he said aloud. "I've got to make a statement, move my work in a whole new direction."

That was why he had decided to present his newest piece indoors. He'd broken in through the back door a little after eleven, after the last of the students and instructors had gone, and unlocked the front door from the inside, so that at midnight he could pretend to let himself and the unwitting Heloise Pignot in.

Now that the time had come, he realized that making a break from his original style meant making a break from sand as well.

What else, then? What would be his new medium?

Ah, of course.

Clay.

That would show the world his creative spark flamed more brightly now than ever before.

He approached the girl's body, the curved dagger in his hand. He would unburden her of her useless old soul and deliver unto her a new one, a soul he would design purely and only for her.

No imitation, this time, but a completely original work.

She would be his finest creation, a demonstration of his undeniable artistic authenticity.

"I am reborn," he said.

CHAPTER **23**

It was the flies that woke Raphael Styx late the next morning, hundreds of them, thousands of them, skittering all over him, in his eyes, in his mouth, burrowing into his ears and nostrils.

He bolted upright, screaming.

The metal shutters were closed, so the room was pitch dark. He fumbled for the table lamp and felt insects crawling up and down the lengths of his fingers.

When the light winked on, he saw that they weren't flies after all.

They were maggots, not thousands but dozens of them, little white grubs wriggling in and out of a ragged tear in his left arm. He was rotting, and his hand was barely recognizable. The tips of his fingers tingled and he jumped in disgust when he saw that there were only four of them. His index finger was gone. The realization shocked him less than he would have expected. This was just a part of the process of decay. Something he'd have to learn to, well, "live" with.

He'd known this next step was coming, and in fact it had taken longer than he would have guessed. Slowly, he stuck his head beneath the blanket. There, where it was still dark, his four surviving fingers searched for their wayward brother. They found blood and slime and more maggots, but the finger was gone.

"Goddammit!"

He finally threw off the covers and sat on the edge of the sofa. His index finger was on the floor, half-hidden beneath the end table. It looked like one of Shelley's turds. He bent down, cursing his hip, and picked it up. It had shriveled to half its usual size.

He tried to stick it back where it belonged, but the stump was black and crusty and the finger wouldn't stay put. He stuck it in the pocket of his father-in-law's pajama pants and was brushing off the top layer of bugs when the shutters rattled noisily.

There was someone outside who wanted in.

"Delacroix," Styx tried to call, because who else in Ostend knew where he was? But his voice caught in his throat, blocked by clotted blood and his blistered gums.

He hobbled to the front door and opened it.

"Ta-da!" said Delacroix. He held up a blindingly colorful suit on a hanger. "Good morning, Chief Inspector. This'll be a lot more comfortable than those rags you were wearing yesterday."

He bustled inside like a Meals on Wheels deliveryman.

"Sure," said Styx, limping along behind him. "Give me five minutes to change. We can go parade up and down the dike like a couple of pimps. Why do you wear this shit?"

"I'm not a pimp," said Delacroix. "I'm a sapeur."

"I've heard you say that before, but I have no fucking idea what it means."

"I'm a member of La Sape. The Society for Ambiance and Personal Elegance."

Styx looked him up and down. "You just made that up," he decided.

"Why would I? It's a real thing, started in Brazzaville, where my father came from, and it spread from there to Brussels. Look it up, if you don't believe me."

Delacroix crossed to the couch and bent over to lay out the suit, then jumped back when he saw the pillow infested with grubs. "What the fuck?"

"Never mind," said Styx.

"Jesus, it's getting worse."

"You think death is the end of the road?" said Styx. "It's just the start of a whole new level of misery. Set it down over there."

But, afraid of what he might find inhabiting the table Styx was pointing to, Delacroix held on to the hanger and launched into a commentary:

"Today's special is the uniform of the true sapeur. A gray-green houndstooth blazer by Boss, paired with beige flannel trousers with a light-brown stripe by Lagerfeld and a wine-red vest by Hilfiger. Some people talk about a sound mind in a sound body, but we prefer a sound body in a sound suit. The shoes are by J.M. Weston, and they retail for about two thousand euros, so I want them back and please try not to mess them up."

Styx examined the outfit. He hadn't understood half of what Delacroix had said, and couldn't see himself wearing any of it, truly not.

"Well?" said Delacroix.

"You don't actually expect me to put that shit on?"

"Why not?" The rookie snapped his fingers. "Oh, of course, sorry. I forgot the pièces de résistance: silver cuff links by Armani and a gold tie clip by Gaultier."

Styx allowed himself to be nagged into trying the clothes on, and, while he changed, Delacroix found a whisk broom and dust pan under the kitchen sink and cleared the maggots from the couch. "Much better," he said proudly, when the transformation was complete. "You may be dead, but at least you're dressed well."

They got down to cases. Styx explained that he'd stayed awake most of the night. He'd gotten his father-in-law's old computer up and running, and had done some research into Surrealism in old Ostend. By doing a search on the names Spilliaert, Ensor, Magritte, and Delvaux, he'd come across some interesting information—special exhibits at the Mu.ZEE on local Surrealist filmmaker Henri Storck and the sponsor of the first Surrealist expositions in Ostend, but nothing that seemed particularly relevant to the current investigation.

"The city's pretty much forgotten the grand old masters, except for those crazy Ensor masks," he said.

"You think the Stuffer might be upset about that?"

"It could be a motive. Maybe he's making some kind of statement. A protest."

"Couldn't he just carry a picket sign?" said Delacroix. "Less deadly."

"Maybe we're overthinking things," said Styx, gently stroking the index finger he'd transferred from his pajamas to his jacket pocket for luck. "Maybe Surrealism's not the point, or just *one* point."

"You're the one who met Paul Delvaux."

Styx thought about it.

"I'm betting it *does* have something to do with art," said Delacroix.

"What makes you so sure?"

"We found a fourth victim this morning."

"Christ."

"Yeah. Found her in an art school. He cut her throat. But here's the weird part. There was plenty of sand there on the premises—they use it in their kilns—but he didn't touch it. He tried to stuff her with potter's clay instead. Total fail."

"You sure it was the Stuffer and not a copycat?"

"Almost everything else matched. Concierge found the body early this morning and called it in. You can imagine what would have happened if the first class of the day had walked into that studio with her still there. Twelve-year-olds."

Styx shuddered. "Okay, but why clay?"

"That's what I want to know. Maybe he's branching out, but maybe he's starting to make mistakes."

"Everybody makes mistakes," said Styx, thinking immediately of his life with Isabelle. Man, the mistakes he'd made in his marriage. You couldn't count them on the fingers of both hands—not even if you included the one in his pocket.

"Something else," said Delacroix. "I guess we can let Tobias Ornelis go. He was in a cell at the time of the murder. The perfect alibi."

"I've been saying it all along: Ornelis is strange, but he's not a killer. He'll be glad to get back to his bodies. He'll have a lot to tell them." Styx frowned. "Wait a second. You said *almost* everything matched."

"Right. There was one other difference. He didn't leave a greeting card this time. Instead, he painted a message directly onto the girl's body."

" 'Number four in a series'?"

"Right," Delacroix said. "Then, after that, 'Art for art's sake.' "

"Jesus."

"And this time he signed it."

Styx looked up hopefully. "He *signed* it?"

"Not with a real name. With the name the newspapers gave him. The Stuffer."

Styx stared down at his €2000 shoes. He wiped up a splash of zombie slime that had already dripped onto the light-brown leather.

"So where are we?" he asked.

"Pretty much nowhere. The girl's name was Heloise Pignot. She was twenty, in nursing school. No apparent connection to the other victims—at least, nothing we've found so far."

Styx tried to imagine what it must have been like to look the serial killer straight in the eyes. He was almost jealous of Heloise Pignot. Had the Stuffer worn the Ensor mask? Styx would give his life to unmask that scumbag. What was he thinking: he *had* given his life. His helplessness ate away at him, more ravenous than the post-death decay he was already undergoing.

"I've made a few notes," said Styx, handing over a sheet of blood-smeared paper. "Things you might be able to track down. I think the last item on the list might be the most promising."

"Paul Delvaux? Didn't he die like twenty years ago? You're not telling me he's another—"

"No, this is a different Paul Delvaux, still living. He's fifty-five, has an apartment right here in Ostend, took early retirement a couple years ago. He worked in banking and got out with a golden parachute right before the downturn. Severance package, big bonus, and he sank a lot of it into art. He wound up getting named chairman of this fancy association, the SOB."

"You've met him?"

"No, no. The Surrealists of Ostend, Belgium. I think the name was their idea of a surrealistic joke."

"Where did you get all this?" asked Delacroix.

"The association has a website, and Delvaux has a Facebook page. Open profile, so anyone can check him out. Mr. Delvaux seems eager to reawaken local interest in Surrealism. He's trying to raise funds for a museum, permanent exhibitions, you name it. He's applying for government subsidies, and he's hitting up his high-class friends to put the SOB in their wills. He says his mission is to keep Surrealism alive."

"By killing half the women in Ostend?"

"I'm not sure I'd go that far. But I think he's worth a closer look. What's especially intriguing is that Paul Delvaux's not his original name. His wife, her name's Justine Delvaux, but he was born Paul Nollet. He took her name when they got married, to make the connection to Surrealism."

"That was convenient," said Delacroix. "You think it's possible Mr. Nollet's declared war to defend Belgian Surrealism?"

"I don't know," said Styx thoughtfully. "I just know he's become a pretty controversial figure. You should read his speeches and manifestos and Facebook posts. He passes himself off as a sort of guerilla fighter. I mean, he puts up selfies with a knife clenched between his teeth."

"Come on."

"No, really, take a look. It's pretty creepy."

"It doesn't make him the Stuffer, though. Might just be a coincidence."

"Sure, and he's not the only Paul Delvaux you can find online. But this one is the most promising. He claims to be a direct descendant of the painter. Everybody knows it's his wife's name, not his, but he sticks to his story."

"Maybe he wants it so much he's begun to believe it."

"Possible," Styx said. "The Surrealists said that dreams become reality and reality is a dream."

"I'll check it out," said Delacroix. "I'll be busy with the Pignot murder today, canvassing the neighborhood, the autopsy report, you know the drill. I might be able to make time to see Delvaux this afternoon. You don't happen to know his address?"

Delacroix stood up and took a good look at Styx. In his sapeur outfit, his hands clasped on the head of his walking stick, he looked like a ghoulish Oscar Wilde.

"I do. It's a penthouse apartment overlooking the city. I wrote it down for you."

"Shit, you *have* been busy. How did you find it?"

"Never underestimate the power of the internet."

Styx returned his protégé's intense gaze.

"So now it's *your* turn to meet Paul Delvaux," he said.

CHAPTER 24

"Almost forgot," Delacroix said, "I brought you a phone." He couldn't resist straightening the knot in Styx's tie. "It's a new one—your old one's evidence, so they're holding on to it. If something comes up, call me. If you find anything else online, call me. If you need a fresh suit—"

"I get it," said Styx. "I'll call you."

Delacroix turned once again to go, but Styx wasn't ready to be left alone. "Hang on, there *is* something else."

"You want a spare shirt?"

Styx ignored him. "Did you drop off my note?"

"You only gave it to me yesterday."

"I know. It's just, if you decide you don't want to do it, you can tell me, okay?"

Delacroix glanced down at his shoe. "I figured I'd get it over with, so I *did* drop by, early this morning. I told her I'd forgotten to give her my contact number. It was around eight, just before we got the call-out on the new murder. I didn't stay long."

"But you hid the note somewhere in the house?"

After all Delacroix had heard about Raphael Styx it would have been easy to think that he'd gotten exactly what was coming to him. But the more time he spent with him now, the more human he appeared. Death seemed to have changed Styx for the better.

"Yes," he said, "I did."

The dead man's eyes sparked with something suggesting life.

"I wonder when she'll find it."

"When the time's right," said Delacroix, but he was thinking *Don't count on it.*

"How did she look? How's she dealing with it?"

"How do you think?" said Delacroix, returning the serve. He didn't want to say any more. In fact, Isabelle had been on her way out the door when he'd gotten there. She'd decided not to take compassionate leave and was on her way to work.

She'd looked ravishing in her white uniform, her short black hair pulled back in a Roman style that emphasized her long slender neck and gave her a profile that would inspire any painter.

"I guess it'll take awhile to get over it," said Styx.

"I guess," Delacroix nodded.

Dammit, the lie was for Styx's own good.

Earlier that morning, Isabelle Gerard was running about ten minutes behind schedule. She was at the front door, waiting for Victor, who had his English final today.

The previous evening she'd told him that, under the circumstances, they could arrange for him to take the rest of his exams late. The school would surely understand. But he'd refused.

Was he trying to be strong? Or proving how estranged he'd grown from his father? Isabelle tried to talk him around, but the boy stuck to his guns. He seemed to have no reaction at all to the news of Styx's death. Either he was in shock, or he'd consciously decided to put off his mourning until he was done with his finals.

In any case, when the doorbell rang, he was still in his room, studying for today's test.

Isabelle opened the door and found Joachim Delacroix in full regalia on the stoop.

"Good morning, ma'am. I'm sorry to bother you again so early, but I was in the neighborhood."

"It's not a problem," she said. "I'm on my way out."

She looked up the staircase, and Delacroix mirrored the movement of her head.

"How's he taking it?" he asked.

"The school said he could have the week off and do his exams in September, but he said no. I think he needs something to focus on so he doesn't fall apart."

"I forgot to leave you my phone number," said Delacroix.

Isabelle hoped she didn't look completely punch-drunk from the sleeping pills she'd taken the night before. She'd never felt the slightest attraction to dandified men with their ascots and pocket squares and bells and whistles. But behind Delacroix's colorful façade she saw a young man with a passion for living, a man who wanted the world to know that he was seizing not just the day in general but every single second of it in particular.

How different from Rafe, her dead husband, who had lived only for his work, who'd buried any suggestion of emotion. And who'd thought nothing of wearing the same black shirt and jeans three days in a row. *Ick.*

"You didn't have to make a special trip," she said. "You've got our home phone number, don't you?"

"I had to be in the area, anyway. Like I said."

"You *did* say, didn't you?" She felt a little light-headed, maybe from the pills.

"I hope you got some sleep."

"Some," said Isabelle.

They found themselves in a conversational twilight zone and, for a long moment, let the silence speak for them.

Then Isabelle seemed to shake herself awake. She turned back to the staircase and found Victor on the second step.

"There you are," she smiled. "This is Inspector Delacroix."

"Joachim Delacroix," the sapeur introduced himself.

The boy nodded politely but left it at that. He'd apparently smeared his face with some sort of lotion which had left his skin shining. He squeezed past the policeman and climbed into the car.

Delacroix fished in his pocket. "I should give you this," he said.

She watched him pull out an old-fashioned yellow envelope with a scalloped flap. His fingers were long and slender and almost jet black. There was a silver ring on his index finger and another on his pinkie.

He shifted the envelope clumsily to his other hand and dug back in his pocket, at last producing a card.

"My number," he said.

"In case I need you," said Isabelle.

"Just in case."

She watched him return the envelope to his pocket. Whatever it was, it was none of her business.

"Thanks," she said. "You might be hearing from me."

"If there's anything I can do. Anything at all."

"You're very kind."

"It's no trouble," he said.

There was more he wanted to say, but he held it back.

The car horn sounded. Victor, for once telling *her* to get a move on.

"This'll sound weird," Isabelle said, stepping outside and locking the door behind her. "But do you think you might like to have dinner with us sometime? Nothing special, just spaghetti or something. I'm not really much of a cook."

"That's very nice of you," said Delacroix slowly, "but I'm not sure it's such a good idea."

"I understand."

"It might not be—"

"I know. I just thought . . . maybe you could talk to us about Rafe. His last days. I don't know if that would get Victor to open up, but I thought—"

As if by fate or prior arrangement, his phone rang.

"The squad," he smiled, but didn't answer it.

"Well, it was just an idea," Isabelle said. "You know what? I'll call you, now I have your number. I know how you guys eat: sandwiches, pizza, fries. Remember, I lived with a cop for years."

"I appreciate the offer," said Delacroix.

"I'm always at the service of the Ostend police," she said gaily, and got into the car.

When the door slammed shut, Victor asked, "Who's that?"

"A detective," she said. "Didn't you hear me? I introduced you."

"I wasn't awake."

Isabelle took her son's hand and held it to her breast. "I'm sorry, sweetie."

"It's not a big deal, Ma."

But she was apologizing for more than he knew.

Rafe was gone, but he was *usually* gone. The only real difference was that now she knew he wouldn't suddenly reappear drunk in the middle of the night.

CHAPTER **25**

Paul Delvaux—the art lover and retired banker, not the painter—was your clichéd early retiree. He'd let his gray hair grow out of its businessman's crew cut, traded in his button-down shirt and tie for an open collar and a gold chain around his neck and his three-piece suit and dress shoes for casual linen slacks and sandals.

When he admitted Joachim Delacroix to his penthouse apartment in the Leopold III-laan his only concession to the formality of the occasion was a wrinkled blazer.

Delacroix wasn't interested in the man's wardrobe. He was interested in alibis.

"And how might I be able to help you, Inspector?" asked Delvaux politely.

"As you may know, sir, we're investigating a series of murders that may be connected to Surrealist art."

"Really? That's a particular interest of mine."

"Yes, sir," said Delacroix, "that's our understanding. I wonder if you'd be willing to answer a few questions."

"Certainly, if I can."

"Well, it seems that the perpetrator, the serial killer, has been inspired by certain iconic images painted by the Surrealists."

"Seriously? I haven't seen anything about that in the papers."

"No, sir, we've been withholding it. But it's one possible lead we're exploring."

Delvaux took a contemplative sip of champagne and laid a manicured hand on a metal sculpture, the only artwork on his spacious terrace. It was a rectangular steel plate with the silhouette of a man cut out of its center, like something out of a Magritte painting.

"And how do you think I might be able to help?"

"I'm pretty much a layman when it comes to Surrealism," said Delacroix.

"There are many art books you could consult."

"Of course. But it's been suggested to me that you've devoted your life to the study of the Surrealist movement in Ostend. You even took your wife's last name to emphasize your interest, isn't that right?"

Delvaux frowned. "That's just a triviality," he said. "But it's true that I'm considered *the* expert on the subject—both locally and, I'd like to think, farther afield. I'm not an artist myself, and I've had no academic training, but during my career in bank management I began buying original artworks and reproductions for our offices around the country."

"Why?"

"Why? Look around you, Inspector. Look down there. Walk straight up the Kapellestraat and in ten minutes you'll come to James Ensor's mother's old shop. You can almost see it from here. Ensor was one of Ostend's most important artists, and that shop now serves as a museum to his memory and his art, but do you think the average Ostender has ever been there? Do you think he even knows it exists?"

"You're not satisfied with the current level of interest in Surrealism?"

"To say the least. It's an outrage, Inspector, I'm sure you agree. How many masters has this city contributed to the world of fine art? Ensor, Spilliaert, the list goes on. *We* were the wellspring of Belgian Surrealism, not Brussels. And I'll tell you why: it's because Ostend is on the coast, on the sea, and the sea itself is surreal, as impossible to capture as a dream. It's an infinite mystery that Man can never unravel."

"And you want to fight that?" asked Delacroix carefully.

"Fight it? Fight what? There's nothing to fight."

"Then what *do* you want?"

"I want to stand up for the rights of the masters, since they can no longer stand up for themselves. They're all dead, you know. Dead and forgotten. Even Henri Storck, whose first documentaries were shot right here and who lived almost to the dawn of the new millennium. Do you think the city preserved those wonderful films of the twenties and thirties? No, they're all lost. It's completely scandalous!"

"With all respect, sir, was there really anything the city could have done about that?"

But the dam had broken, and the flood was on the rise. Paul Delvaux's champagne was gone, and he was working himself into a fury. He patted down his thin gray hair, but the wind on the terrace had other ideas. He crossed from the steel sculpture to lean his back against the railing.

"We'll never know, Inspector, will we, since they didn't even bother to try. But I tell you this: Ostend is sound asleep, it's been sleeping for a hundred years. Look at all the beautiful buildings left empty and decaying, all the monuments in need of loving repair, the once-famous hotels now crumbling into ruin. I swear, if it were up to me, I . . . I—"

Delacroix waited, but the end of the sentence blew away in the wind. Delvaux turned his back on the inspector and looked out across the city.

"You're here to ask about Surrealism, yes? This isn't an interrogation?"

"No, sir, not at all. Please go on."

"Every age has its norms, Inspector, its customs and mores and laws. And every city has its attractions. But Ostend—what does Ostend have to offer but a few decadent discos and a nude beach? Who do *we* attract, beyond a smattering of young immigrant riffraff?"

Delacroix waited for the banker to assure him that he didn't mean to sound like a racist, but no such explanation came.

"If it were up to me, I'd at least try to restore the city—the Queen of the Seaside Resorts—to its former glory. Yes, the city government took over the Thermae Palace, but the renovations they promised haven't even begun. We have to remember that we were once the most important city in Belgium, and of Leopold II's empire."

"Yeah, well, look what *he* accomplished."

Leopold II had founded the laughably misnamed Congo Free State and conscripted its population as his own personal mercenary army.

Delvaux spun back to face him, enraged.

Delacroix had to force himself not to add coal to the fire. This elite snob was hot enough already.

"I don't know what that's supposed to mean," Delvaux snapped. "But I'm telling you this city used to *matter* in the world. The sea, the beach, James Ensor's masks."

"And now you think those masks should be ripped away, so the world can—"

"I'm not sure what you're implying."

"I'm asking *you* what *you're* implying, sir."

"I think we need to look back to the days of the old bourgeoisie, when there was still a ruling class and we had some standing in the world. Would that be so bad? I don't think so. But I thought you wanted to talk about Surrealism."

"Well, as long as we've moved away from that subject," said Delacroix without a moment's hesitation, "where were you last night between ten PM and two AM?"

Paul Delvaux was too stunned to reply.

Could be a pose, Delacroix thought. Actually, he'd surprised himself a bit with the boldness of the question. This was the first time he'd ever met Delvaux, and they were in the man's own home. Asking for an alibi was practically an accusation, and a step beyond the bounds of propriety. But he knew that Raphael Styx was racing to beat some supernatural deadline, and there was no time to waste on polite beating around the bush.

"I refuse to answer," said Delvaux, "and I believe this conversation is at an end. If there's anything more you need to know about Surrealism, I recommend the public library. If you have questions about where I was last night, I'll give you the number of my attorney."

"I'm just asking, sir, same as I could ask you where you were a week ago or—"

"And I'm telling you that it's time for you to go."

"Fine. I'm not accusing you of anything, Mr. Delvaux, but this is a homicide investigation, and I'm going to need you to account for your whereabouts at the time of each of the murders."

Delvaux sputtered, "This is—"

He seemed unable to find the word he was searching for, and Delacroix provided it: "Surreal?"

"Precisely!"

"I understand. But I'm afraid I'm going to have to insist that you report to the station for further questioning."

Delacroix couldn't really see the retired banker slashing the organs from a dead body in his expensively casual haute couture blazer and €100 manicure, but that was just the point: anything was possible in the world of Surrealism.

And what he *could* see, as he allowed the man to usher him briskly through the living room toward the elevator, was a pair of dark-green Crocs shoved almost out of sight beneath the leather sofa. They didn't seem to fit Delvaux's idea of style. Delacroix only saw them for a second, but it looked like the soles were caked with dried sand.

"You'll get your answers." Delvaux bit each word off individually. "All in good time. But now you need to be on your way, or I'll—"

"You'll what, sir? Lose your temper?"

"Quite."

The elevator was halfway to the street when Delacroix realized there was something else of importance he'd seen, perhaps even more interesting than the Crocs.

The locations where the Stuffer's victims had been discovered were all visible from Delvaux's terrace.

The Mu.ZEE, where Reinhilde Debels had been posed in the sculpture garden like the original Delvaux's nude by the railroad tracks, lay to the southwest. The Kapellestraat, where Elisa Wouters was surrounded by early morning shoppers like Ensor's old woman ringed by masks, was directly below. The breakwater, where Madeleine Bohy had been planted on the beach like Magritte's limbless, headless torso, was to the north. And the art academy, where poor Heloise Pignot had, for reasons they had yet to discover, broken several of the Stuffer's patterns, could just be seen in the distance, to the south. Even the cabana where Raphael Styx's bullet-riddled corpse had reanimated was within sight.

You could stroll around that terrace, Delacroix thought, *and have the whole city under your watchful eye.*

Like a sniper.

CHAPTER 26

Raphael Styx did something he should never have dared to do: under cover of darkness, he left his hiding place and returned to the land of the living, cloaked in the camouflage of Joachim Delacroix's ridiculous clothing.

Styx had never felt much need for human companionship. He'd always been satisfied with an inner circle of two: Isabelle and Victor.

Leaning heavily on his stick, he made his way haltingly in the direction of the dunes behind the Milho complex. From the dunes he could observe the back of his own apartment, where his wife and son still lived.

He'd tried to wait for news from Joachim Delacroix but had finally reached the limit of his patience. He needed his family. Just the sight of them would be as restorative as a blood transfusion. And he had to know how they were dealing with his absence. Had Isabelle already found his note?

He thought back to the early days of their courtship, before they married, before Victor was born. How long had that romantic idyll lasted? Two years? Three? Afterward, all their passion drained gradually away.

From his vantage point in the dunes, he saw her pass before the apartment's back window.

"Isabelle," he whispered.

Her face was made up, and she wore a black summer dress with an open collar. Was she in mourning? Was this how she would dress for his funeral? Had those arrangements been made?

"Isabelle."

When was the last time he'd pronounced her name? He sat half-hidden behind a mound of grassy sand, a voyeur stalking his own family.

Victor wasn't in the living room. Where was he? Hiding from the world in the privacy of his bedroom? Or had he gone to a friend's house for the evening? Styx had lost track of what day it was. In death, every day was Sunday. Or Monday, or Tuesday—what difference did it make?

He saw her again. She held something in her hands. A dish? A tray? Christ, he could almost reach out and touch her, she was so close. And so very familiar.

His house. His family. Everything he'd worked for. Tears welled in his eyes, and he wondered how that was even possible in his state.

It was torture to see her. His heart no longer beat, yet he seemed to feel it pounding in his chest.

He lay on his belly to ease the ache in his hip and reached out his four-fingered hand toward her. If he closed one eye—the goatish eye he could barely see out of, anyway—her body fit neatly between his thumb and middle finger, and he could pretend to hold her.

But then a second figure entered the living room.

A man.

Did she have a *date*? So soon? He wasn't even cold and buried, and she had another man in the house? He could barely believe it. The unexpected visitor had his back to the window, but Styx knew at once who it was.

"Delacroix?"

The flashy pink suit, the light-blue cuffs and collar, the nonchalant strut of the sapeur . . .

Perhaps there was something he'd forgotten to ask? Or, no, wait: Perhaps Isabelle had invited him over to show him the mysterious note she'd found? Sure, that was it. He could appreciate her need for a confidant, since the message he'd written was cryptic at best:

My darling, some day you'll realize that death does not exist. I won't just live on figuratively in your memories. Sometimes love can reach across the raging river. I'll be waiting for the moment when I will see you again, in all your . . .

And so on. He couldn't remember it all verbatim. He'd told Delacroix that he'd borrowed some of the language from Lord Byron, but he'd only said that in case the dandy read the letter and wound up thinking Styx had gone soft in his old age. In fact, he'd written every word himself. Maybe he *had* gone soft. The hard-boiled Raphael Styx, reborn as a romantic poet.

Apparently Isabelle had invited the sapeur to dinner. Styx crept around the dune and inched closer to the window. He couldn't see any sign of his note.

"You fucking hypocrite," he muttered.

They were sitting at the dining table. At *his* table. And they were eating—no, not just eating. They were *dining*. Isabelle had outdone herself. This wasn't police business. Isabelle was doing most of the talking, and Delacroix listened attentively, nodding at whatever it was she was saying.

Something inside his body stirred. He still had feelings. He was not entirely dead.

He waited until Isabelle carried their empty appetizer plates into the kitchen, then dialed Delacroix's cell.

"Come on, you fuck, pick up!"

From his hiding place, he saw Delacroix take his phone from his pocket and check the screen, saw him turn toward the kitchen and call something out to Isabelle.

"Answer the phone, you cocksucker!"

Delacroix stood up and walked over to the plateglass window. He punched a button.

"Yes?"

"It's me, Styx."

"I know who it is. What's up?"

Styx swallowed uncomfortably. "Where are you?"

"What difference does it make?"

Just answer the question, Styx thought.

"At the office?"

"No," said Delacroix, "it's late."

"I thought you were coming by."

"I was going to, but something came up. Maybe I can still make it. Probably not till midnight."

"I might be asleep by then."

"Bullshit." He saw Delacroix cup his free hand around the phone and heard him lower his voice. "You don't sleep, Styx, remember? Listen, I'm hanging up. I'm with people."

People, Styx thought. He watched the sapeur stand there at the window.

"I just wanted to know if you got to see Paul Delvaux," he said quickly.

"Yeah, I was there this afternoon. He's a remarkable man. You could be right. We'll have to keep an eye on him."

"What happened?"

"He's got some pretty strong ideas," Delacroix said. "He thinks we all ought to go back in time to when the rich got richer and the poor got poorer."

"Get rid of the social-welfare state, that sort of thing?"

"Well, he didn't say it in so many words, but he came off as pretty radical."

"What else?"

"Nothing," said Delacroix. "I'll see you later. Or else tomorrow."

Isabelle came back from the kitchen, and Delacroix turned to face her. She was carrying a covered serving platter and wearing a pair of matching oven mitts, the last gift Raphael Styx had ever given her— and that was years ago. It was typical of the old Styx: those mitts were like handcuffs, intended to chain her to the stove, though he'd wound up being the one who used them the most, since she rarely cooked.

"I have to go," said Delacroix.

"No other news?"

"No."

"What about my note?"

There was a pause.

"I'm working on it," Delacroix said flatly.

Right, I can see that. "It's just," he said, and watched Delacroix return to his place at the table as Isabelle took the lid from the platter. It was obvious he wanted to get off the phone so he could help her. "It's just—"

"Just what?"

"I really miss her," Styx admitted. "I never thought I'd say something like that, but I do, I miss her. Weird, isn't it? When I was still alive, I wouldn't give her the time of day, and now that I'm dead, she's all I can think about."

"I know," said Delacroix, and Styx saw him as his own mirror image, the living man taking the place of the dead one, at his table, in his house, with his wife, with his son. "Try to think of something else. The case. The Stuffer."

"I'm not having a lot of luck," said Styx. *Unlike some people*, he stopped himself from adding.

Truth be told, part of him was glad to see Isabelle freed of him at last. In life, he'd been a ball and chain, dragging her down. Now that he was gone, she would have a chance to float back to the surface.

And she deserved it. Why should she go on being miserable when she had a right to so much more?

"I'll see you," Delacroix said.

"Okay," Styx sighed. "Bon appétit."

They broke the connection simultaneously, and Styx wondered if he'd heard those last two words.

It was time to go.

As he struggled to his feet, a light winked on upstairs, in Victor's room.

The curtains were shoved aside, and there stood his son in the window, looking out. Had the boy spotted him, out in the dunes, hunched over his cane like a crippled leper? It would be so easy to raise a hand and wave to him, give him a sign that his dad was still looking out for him.

Still?

When had he *ever* put his son's interests before his own?

Not for years.

I'm sorry, Victor, he thought. *I'm so sorry.*

He stood there, motionless as a scarecrow.

He didn't see me. He doesn't see me.

Victor turned away and disappeared from the window, and another character made his entrance: Shelley, who propped his forepaws on the windowsill and howled. The dog's reflection in the pane turned him into Cerberus, the three-headed hellhound.

No sound reached Styx through the thick glass, but he could see his old friend barking wildly. Was it possible that Shelley had smelled him?

Isabelle rose from the table and went upstairs. He saw her at Victor's window, trying to calm Shelley down. When that didn't work, she pulled him downstairs by his collar and closed him up in the kitchen.

Styx had had enough.

He'd already died once over the last few days, and now he died yet again.

This second death was even more painful than the first.

CHAPTER **27**

Styx couldn't stand the thought of going back to his father-in-law's deserted house, so he decided to walk a while. He half expected to be transported back to La Belle Époque, but the city remained as it was. The locals were asleep in their beds. Tomorrow was a workday. The tourists were tucked in at their hotels and B&Bs.

He wandered through the entertainment district, where a bit of life still ebbed and flowed. He came to a halt before the entrance to a club whose bright-red neon sign identified it as The Groove. The front door was open, and a soulful voice wafted out on the breeze over a hypnotic backbeat.

"I want you the right way, baby . . ."

It was the voice of Marvin Gaye, the doomed soul singer who'd washed up in Ostend a few short years before he was shot to death by his own father. Whoever was deejaying tonight had excellent taste, Styx thought, and he shambled through the door, along a narrow entry hall with velour walls and into the main room, which—luckily for him—was almost completely dark. A disco ball hanging from the ceiling spun slowly, and the four pinpoint spotlights that hit it turned the dance floor into a swirling galaxy of stars.

The place was packed. Styx pushed through the crowd to the bar.

"Whiskey," he said, raising his voice above the music and the din of a hundred shouted conversations. "Rocks."

The bartender, a ponytailed giant with a snake tattooed on his right arm, looked at him strangely.

"Please," said Styx. "I'm dying here."

He'd given up feeling embarrassed about the way he looked. When he got his drink, he tossed it off in a single swallow. The place was mobbed, and he wanted to turn around and leave, but the crowd somehow absorbed him, swallowed him whole, enfolded him in a whirling mass of strangers, drunkards, and crazies, the freaks of the night.

Surrounded, Styx felt his palsied, creaky body begin—almost against his will—to sway in time to the Marvin Gaye song. As he dipped and twirled, the others backed off and gave him room, until he was dancing solo in the middle of the floor, ringed by a throng of intoxicated spectators who clapped in time to the music and cheered him on.

A girl who'd been standing alone against the wall wormed her way through the crowd and joined him. She was young and blond, but her hair was stringy, her teeth were yellowed by nicotine, and she stank of sweat. Her short skirt was stained and she wore tattered espadrilles on her feet.

"You come here often?" she asked, eyes half-closed, fully under the spell of the music.

"No," said Styx, bobbing his head.

"Why not?"

"I'm a zombie."

He waited for her scream, but what he heard was a peal of delighted laughter. "Who isn't, man?"

Before he knew what was happening, her arms were around him and they were slow dancing. He couldn't understand it. Didn't she see how ghastly he was? Wasn't she repelled by his unholy stench? Or could she actually be attracted to his degenerate flesh, as Eros was drawn insatiably to Thanatos?

"Shhh," she soothed him, her hand on the back of his neck.

"You have no idea who I am," Styx whispered in her ear.

"It doesn't matter."

"It *does* matter."

Her hands dropped to his backside and pulled him closer. She ground her crotch against him. Styx felt his bones about to shatter, but at the same time he felt the old hunger stir within him. His body had been stiff with death for days, but now, that one last limp organ—his penis, his dick, his cock, his tool—was stiffening with life. He wondered how that was even possible.

"If you're a zombie," the girl laughed, grabbing him, "how come *this* thing's not dead?"

"Maybe it's like hair and nails," Styx moaned. "They keep growing after you die, don't they?"

"No, they don't. They just *look* like they're growing, because the rest of the body starts shrinking after death."

One hand holding him tightly, the other crushing his mouth to hers. Her tongue flickered across his crusted lips. Styx tasted the sweetness of lust through the toxicity of his own fetid breath.

It's gonna fall right off, he thought, *like my finger.*

But before he could do anything about it, the girl released him and pushed him off her.

"What the fuck is *this*?"

She stuck out her tongue and plucked a rotted tooth from the tip of it, held it up to catch the sparkle from the disco ball and stared at it in horror. Styx thought she might faint or scream, but she simply dropped the tooth to the dance floor and slapped him, as if she were punishing him for having having told her the truth. He actually *was* a zombie, the bastard. She turned away and disappeared into the crowd.

Probably a good thing she split, thought Styx. For just a moment there he had felt the glimmer of deep desire, and not for sex. No, this was a more primal, more unquenchable hunger.

Tongue to tongue, teeth to skin. However unappetizing her appearance, he had *wanted* her. What would have happened if she hadn't fled? Would he have sunk his teeth into the soft flesh of her neck? No, that was vampires, they were after the blood. Her brains, then? But, Jesus, she was such a skank! And yet, to him, she had looked . . . delicious, that was the only word for it.

Was it possible that death was not an ending but a beginning, a gateway to new experiences Styx would much rather avoid?

He checked Marc Gerard's pocket watch, found it still running, then shut his eyes and went into a trance, barely feeling his uncontrollable tics and twitches melt seamlessly into dance moves. Eyes still closed tightly, a frown spread across his battered face, an expression of both physical and spiritual pain that stretched into a grimace as he reached skyward like a sleeper awakening from a century's slumber. He rose on his toes and grabbed for the ceiling, jerking spasmodically within an imaginary prison of regret, self-pity, pain.

"Hey," a deep male voice whispered in his ear. "What's goin' on, brother?"

He opened his eyes and saw that he was almost alone in the club. A knot of stragglers lingered at the bar, but he and the stranger were the only two people left on the dance floor.

"When did she stop lovin' you?" the deep voice asked.

In the dark Styx saw that the bearded man was none other than Marvin Gaye himself. He was wearing the Adidas tracksuit and Jamaican knit cap Styx knew he'd worn every morning to jog through the Ostend dunes as he fought his way free from his drug addiction. He was probably on his way to the dunes now for his morning run.

Except.

Except that was more than thirty years ago, and the soul legend had been dead since the mid-eighties.

Had Styx been transported to yet *another* Ostend, segued through time by some inexplicable enchantment the way a DJ segued between songs?

For the first time Styx wondered if it might have been more than mere chance that had pushed him in pursuit of the Stuffer on the beach that night, just as some felt that Marvin Gaye had manipulated his father, a minister of the House of God, into firing the shots that had killed him. In police parlance, they called it "suicide by cop" when an individual with a death wish provokes a law-enforcement officer into killing him. In the troubled singer's life, it could perhaps have been suicide by parent. In Styx's case, could it have been suicide by serial killer, a way to free himself from the ruin he'd made of his own life?

"Let me give you a bit of free advice, my friend," the angelic voice went on. "It's never too late to change."

Styx wanted answers. His tortured relationship with Isabelle, the Stuffer investigation. He *needed* some free advice, but he didn't know what to ask, or how.

"It's time to make things right. To stand up, my man."

With these last words, the Prince of Soul faded away, and Styx felt a firm hand on his shoulder. He never knew if it was the bartender or a bouncer. All he knew was that he was dragged off the dance floor and shoved through the narrow entryway and out into the street.

"And don't come back!" an angry voice yelled after him.

Styx wasn't sure what happened next, but when he regained his senses, he lay in the gutter, curled up in the fetal position, in agony, humiliated, gathering his strength.

It was time to stand up.

It was time to make things right.

It was time to rise from the dead, once and for all.

He found his stick in the street beside him and scrabbled painfully to his feet. There was something very wrong with his body. He felt like he'd been sawn in half and the pieces glued together out of alignment.

My hip, he thought. Throughout his decay, the pain in his hip had stayed with him, like a tether to the old world, but now it felt different. It had finally happened. He'd made it this far, but now there was no doubt.

I broke my fucking hip.

He staggered off toward his father-in-law's house like a marionette whose strings had been cut.

But his face was set in grim determination.

He was down, but he wasn't out.

He could handle the pain.

He could handle whatever shit they threw at him.

And he had work to do.

CHAPTER **28**

Joachim Delacroix always had the same dream. He was in an endless corridor lined with doors that all opened into bathrooms. In each room someone had committed suicide. Some of the victims had overdosed on pills, some had jumped out of the narrow bathroom window, some had slit their wrists in the tub.

In the corridor dreams his mission was to find his half-sister Celine. He proceeded down the line, opening unlocked doors and battering down the locked ones, sometimes surprising the living in the act of self-destruction but more often arriving on the scene mere moments too late.

The corridor always seemed infinite, but he always came eventually to one final door. It was always locked, and he always heard Celine's muffled voice pleading for help on the other side. And as he was about to kick it in or put his shoulder to it or shoot out the lock, he would jerk awake.

It was no different tonight—except that, as he sat upright in his bed, shaking with frustration at yet another failure, his doorbell rang.

He plodded down the finite hall of his apartment in midnight-blue silk Peter Hahn pajamas and a wine-red velvet Hugh Hefner smoking jacket to the videophone beside his front door.

"Yes?"

"It's me," a voice said.

The monitor showed a figure with its back to the surveillance camera.

"Me who?"

"Who the fuck do you think?"

The face remained invisible. All he could make out was a black ski mask and a pair of dark eyes.

"Styx?" he said.

"No, it's the fucking Stuffer." The voice was disgusted. "Let me in."

Delacroix hesitated. For a second he thought about the last two words Styx had muttered last night over the phone. *Bon appétit.* Could it be the zombie knew he'd had dinner with his widow? *Nah,* thought Delacroix. Anyway, he wouldn't mention it to Styx. The ex-cop had other things on his mind.

Delacroix had grown acclimated to the sepulchral sight of Raphael Styx's discolored face, but now that the monster was hidden behind a tenebrous mask, he seemed somehow more pestilential and horrific.

"Goddammit, would you let me in?" Styx growled. He leaned closer to the camera and his bloodshot eyes filled the screen.

Delacroix pressed the buzzer.

A minute later Styx dragged himself through the door. "I know," he said, "I look like shit. I thought about buying one of those masks from the gift shop at the Ensor house, but they won't be open for hours. You checked, right, to see who *has* bought them the last couple months?"

"Of course I checked. I'm not an—"

"Well?"

"They sell dozens of them every day. Way too many to track."

"Pity."

Delacroix shook his head. "You look like a bank robber."

"If I could get into the hospital, I could get one of those burn masks they put on patients who've survived—"

"I'm not talking about the ski mask," said Delacroix. "The ski mask isn't bad. I'm talking about your clothes."

Styx looked down at the torn jeans and black shirt he'd substituted for Delacroix's grotesque sapeur rig. "Oh, these."

"Those," said Delacroix. "What happened to—?"

"Relax, your shit's at the house. I'll get it all dry-cleaned tomorrow."

"Why'd you change?"

"These are *my* kind of clothes, Delacroix. I'm sick of hiding out in yours."

It must be broiling hot under that mask, Delacroix thought, then realized Styx must be long past the point where such things mattered.

"What are you going to do? Why are you here?"

"I'm ready to show myself," said Styx.

"To who?"

"To you. To him. To the world."

"You mean the Stuffer?"

"I'm not going to go on hiding from that fuck."

Delacroix saw him balancing his weight on his left leg, struggling to stay erect. "What happened to your hip?"

"I threw it out. Don't worry about it."

Something was different about the man. Styx seemed calmer, more at peace with his condition. It was like he'd taken a Valium—or a couple of belts of good scotch.

"What's that on your shirt?"

"That's another story."

"Tell me."

"You don't want to know," said Styx, thinking back to what had happened an hour ago.

"Is that dried blood? Is that the shirt you were wearing when he shot you?"

"No," Styx sighed. "This is a different one."

"For God's sake, man, what happened?"

An hour ago, at the port, after a quick stop at Marc Gerard's house to change, Styx had hobbled into the container where Gino Tersago maintained his "office," his stomach rumbling with a hunger unlike anything he'd ever felt before in his life, a hunger for—he fought back a wave of nausea at the very thought of it—for human flesh. At the bar, he'd been able to fight against it, but the more time passed, the more insistent the sick craving became. It was a cliché, he knew, an overdone trope straight out of every zombie movie he'd ever seen, but there it was. He needed to feed, needed it far more desperately than he'd needed liquor, drugs, and women in his previous life. To slake this new and horrible demon inside him, he'd decided to pay a little call on Terry Tersago, a bastard if ever there was one, a lowlife who only just barely qualified as "human."

And who knows? Perhaps, if Tersago was lucky, he'd wind up receiving the same second chance at a fresh start Styx himself had been granted. Tersago, ready to close up shop for the night, was deep in conversation with two stolid men who could have been twins. He was gesticulating broadly and didn't notice Styx come in.

"Terry," one of them said sharply, but Tersago seemed not to hear him. "Terry! You got company."

The gangster didn't bother to turn around. He raised a warning hand and said, "Tell him I'm busy."

"What with?" Styx growled. "Stolen cars from the East Bloc?"

Now the man spun around. The container was almost as dark as the night, and Tersago could see only a tall, dark figure silhouetted in the doorway.

"Who the fuck—?"

"Terry," said Styx calmly, "it's me."

He limped closer. No ski mask, no shame. Before Tersago could make another sound, the twins hurried past Styx and fled into the night, like untied balloons released by a child.

Tersago gabbled wordlessly, and Styx grabbed the man's cheeks between the four nailless fingers of his rotting right hand and massaged them.

"Say it, Terry. Say my name."

But Gino Tersago was struck dumb. He quaked with terror, stared into the blighted eyes, the ruined face that steamed with miasmal vapors.

"Styx?" he croaked at last. "But you're . . . dead?"

"Don't believe everything you hear," said Styx.

Styx wanted to have a nice cozy chat about the good old days—the deals, the bribes, the corruption, the meetings in unused containers at harborside—but there were two problems.

One: there was no way his hip would let him get cozy.

And two: the hunger was getting worse.

Styx felt like a predator operating on pure instinct.

He was so achingly hungry.

"Well, what the fuck happened?"

"It's none of your business, Terry."

As if Gino Tersago dealt with stinking, moldering gargoyles every night of his life, he seemed satisfied with Styx's nonanswer.

"Okay by me," he said. "I got my own problems."

"Excuse me?"

"I don't know where you been these last days, but I sure coulda used you around here."

Styx stood riveted to the ground, not by his hip for once but by simple astonishment. "I'm sorry my personal situation interfered with your plans," he said.

"What interfered? You think you can't be replaced, Styxie? Trust me, *nobody* is irreplaceable. But your fuckin' guys almost nabbed me. Some cop got wind of what was goin' down, and if I was as stupid as he thought I was, I would have walked right smack into a trap, and this minute I'd be schmoozing with that fuck Crevits instead of you."

"So what happened?"

"I must have some kind of sixth sense. I just felt like somethin' wasn't kosher, so I blew off the deal in the nick a time. That didn't make me too popular with my business associates, though." He tugged at his upper lip with his bottom teeth. "And that's *your* fault, Styxie, for not bein' here when I needed you."

"Aw, shucks," Styx said. Somewhere inside him it was nice to think that *someone* still needed him.

"I mean, what do you think I was doin', playin' charades with Tweedledum and Tweedledumber just now? Those guys don't speak Flemish, Dutch, English, French, nothing. You don't talk Commie, do you? Maybe you can explain 'em the fuckup was your fault, not mine."

"I told you I was changing my ways, Terry."

"You think I'm not onto you?" the gangster continued. "You got everybody thinkin' the fuckin' Stuffer took you down, but you just been hidin' out from him, you coward. Is that why I haven't seen you? You know that schmuck Crevits gave me the third degree for like two hours? He thought *I* was the fuckin' Stuffer!"

"You still don't understand," Styx interrupted him, "do you?"

"I oughta beat the crap outa you just for that, Styx. You got any idea what it's like to spend two hours cooped up with a sweat bucket like that Crevits?"

"You don't understand," Styx repeated slowly, shaking his head.

"Don't understand *what*?"

"This," said Styx. "Me. It's real, Terry, not a game."

"What's real? You? You're not real, man, you're a fuckin' joke."

"I don't hear anyone laughing."

Tersago turned away from him, looking for his associates, but they were long gone. He returned his attention to Styx. "Are you tellin' me you're really *dead*? You expect me to believe that shit?"

Styx took a step closer and leaned in as far as his hip allowed. "You want proof, Terry?" he whispered into Tersago's ear. He was so close he could smell the man's blood, sweet and coppery. The hunger he'd felt earlier was growing louder.

Tersago pulled back. "Jesus! You go to hell, buddy. I'm—"

"I just came from there," said Styx, and without warning he lunged forward and bit off the gangster's ear.

Tersago screamed. But Styx grabbed him with both arms and bit into the side of his head, gouging down to the bone. He tasted flesh and blood and heard Tersago shrieking in a voice that was no longer human, "Jesus fucking Christ! Get the fuck *off* me!"

But there was no one around to help him.

Styx wrestled with the gangster and fell on top of him, gnawing greedily at his cheeks and nose and chin until his ravenous hunger was finally stilled.

Gino Tersago twitched spastically on the floor, not quite dead. Blood poured from a hundred face wounds.

Styx got to his knees, panting.

The metal floor of the container was drenched with blood.

"What do you say, Terry?" he gasped. "You believe me now?"

He wondered how much time would pass before a new Gino Tersago staggered to his feet and lurched off into the night. That was how it happened in the movies, but Styx had no idea what the rules were out here in the real world. Maybe, once Tersago bled out, he'd be gone for good.

He didn't have time to stick around and find out.

It wasn't until later, on his way to Delacroix's apartment, that he realized his midnight meal had not only quieted his hunger but given him a measure of new strength.

And, under the light of a streetlamp, he saw that a new index finger was beginning to sprout from the blackened stump between his thumb and middle finger.

Well, well, he thought. *Fancy that.*

CHAPTER **29**

Styx took Delacroix out to show him the city's past. With Grandpa Marc's pocket watch open in his hand like a dowsing rod, the zombie led the sapeur through the streets of Ostend.

The artists of a century ago, the colorful figures of beachcombers and shrimp fishers, the bourgeoisie who commanded the best seats in the theater and literally looked down on the ordinary citizens, wandered the streets around them.

But Delacroix saw none of it.

When Styx, still hidden behind the black woolen ski mask, peered through a café window, elbowed his young partner, and pointed out the painter James Ensor, there was no response. Even in the vicinity of the pocket watch, Delacroix was denied Styx's second sight. Where Styx saw the gay tumult of a gaslit evening among the elite of La Belle

Époque, all Delacroix, still imprisoned in the land of the living, saw—all he *could* see—was the dark loneliness of a modern-day bank's lobby.

"You don't see them?" insisted Styx.

"See who?"

"*Them.*"

"Who are you talking about? There's no one in there."

"Strange," said Styx, frowning. He wanted to laugh, but couldn't find the right sound.

Maybe the pocket watch only worked for him.

"You're serious about this?" Delacroix said skeptically.

"I see a completely different world," said Styx. "I can move around in it, interact with it. That door's probably locked for you, but I can open it and go inside."

Delacroix tugged on the bank's front door. Sure enough, it was locked tight. "Show me," he said.

Styx nodded slowly. "I don't think we stopped here just randomly. Every time this happens, there seems to be a reason."

"The Stuffer?"

"I think I'm getting closer." He looked through the plateglass window and found it almost unimaginable that Delacroix *couldn't* see what he saw.

On the other side of the window, the café was brightly lit and bustling with life. Cigarette and cigar smoke danced around the top-hats of the men who ringed the wooden tables playing cards. The walls were hung with posters and drawings in the style of Henri de Toulouse-Lautrec.

"Tell me what you see," Delacroix prompted.

"A young painter with a full beard and an odd feathered cap. I think it's Ensor." He turned from the window as if to apologize for seeing the invisible.

"I'm not sure I believe you," said Delacroix. "You could say Leopold the Second was in there, and how would I know any different?"

"No, I think he was at the train station. But you're right. What can I say to convince you? All you've got is my word."

Suddenly, Styx's tone changed. "It's funny. I always used to tell Victor he was spending too much time staring at screens—television, computer, phone, Xbox. I think I actually said once he was turning into a zombie." He remembered how to laugh. "Last night, I didn't just use my father-in-law's old computer to look up Paul Delvaux. I looked up my son too. He's on Facebook, Twitter, Instagram—whatever the hell that is. He's got his own YouTube channel. And *I* was the zombie sitting there for hours, staring at him."

"Styx, about your wife."

But Styx continued. "I thought if I spent enough time looking at all his online shit, it would be like I was back in his life. But that's not the way it works. We're a million miles apart, and the distance grows every minute. He's changing so much. In some ways, even faster than I am. You know what? He posted a—what do the kids call it?—a selfie on Facebook, and he's got a wisp of a mustache!"

"Styx, don't do this to yourself."

"I'm not doing anything to myself. It's just the truth. Maybe I can see into the past because that's all I have left." He turned back to the window and watched the people moving to and fro in what looked like a perfectly re-created film set. "I wish you could see it, Delacroix. You'd love it: the style, the clothes, the flair. That's when you should have been around. Me, if I could have picked a time to live, I'd've picked the Wild West."

"You should have been a writer," said Delacroix. "The way you describe it all."

"Maybe so. Who knows?"

Delacroix laid a gentle hand on Styx's shoulder and pulled him back to the present. "I have to tell you something," he said.

"What?"

"I didn't leave your note for Isabelle."

Styx nodded. "I figured."

"I couldn't do it. I'm sorry, but I just couldn't. I'm not even sure why. You said it yourself, it wasn't going to help her. Was I wrong?"

"I'm not sure what 'wrong' *means* anymore."

"Really, Styx, I—"

"Let me ask you something."

Delacroix took his hand from the zombie's shoulder.

"What do you think of her?" asked Styx.

"What do you mean?"

"You know what I mean. You ever look in a mirror, Delacroix? You're the opposite of me. A real gentleman. A *ladies'* man."

"Hey, you're the one who sent me over there."

"Yeah, but you're the one who went."

"Don't be ridiculous. I'm not—"

"I've seen the light in your eyes, these last couple days. It's her, isn't it?"

"I said don't—"

"You can't hide it, man." He turned away. "And I don't blame you. She deserves better than me. I had my chance, and I fucked it up."

"It's not what you think," said Delacroix.

"I think it is. You just don't know it yet."

In the café three women in bright-red dresses were on the small stage, high-kicking their ruffled skirts and petticoats in unison as, off to the side, a man in a striped shirt and sleeve garters banged on a piano. Someone spotted Styx looking in and came over to shut the heavy drapes.

"You think it over while I go in," he said. "When I come out, maybe we'll both be a little wiser—you about her, and me about the Stuffer."

Delacroix didn't argue. "What are you going to ask him?"

"Ensor?" Styx put a hand to the door. Where Delacroix had seen and felt a bank's modern metal handle, Styx saw and felt an old-fashioned glass knob. "That's the weird thing. I don't really need to ask him any-thing. The way it seems to work, he'll tell me what I need to know. They don't need any small talk. They just get straight to the point."

"Good luck," said Delacroix.

When Styx stepped into the café the scene came fully to life. He could hear the music from the out-of-tune piano now, an energetic can-can.

He looked around for the enigmatic James Ensor, but couldn't see him. Was he too late? Had the painter left during his conversation with Delacroix?

He felt himself drawn to the table closest to the little stage and saw a figure concealed behind a mask, a caricature of a creature out of Hieronymus Bosch: an inhumanly ugly bald man with a sharply pointed chin, bulbous nose, and huge ears. Styx stared into the eyes behind the mask. They reminded him of those eyes he'd seen once before, on a lonely beach beneath a yellow sou'wester. The eyes of the Stuffer.

"Mr. Ensor?"

A gloved hand pulled the mask away, revealing the condescend-ing face of James Ensor. His fame lay years in the future; at this time of his life, he was just on the verge of breaking through to success.

"I thought perhaps you recognized me, *cher ami*," said Ensor. "I saw you glancing my way from the street."

"I'm sorry to bother you, but—"

"No matter," said the painter, laying the mask beside him on the table. "You're a journalist, desirous of an interview? If so, you can find me every day in my salon above the shop of *ma maman*. No appointment necessary. I often receive visitors and friends who wish to consult with me."

"If you don't mind," said Styx, "I'd like to consult you here and now on an urgent matter."

"And who are you? A reporter, yes?"

"Something like that."

At that moment Styx understood why Delvaux and Marvin Gaye and all the others he'd encountered in the Ostends of the past had failed to be horrified by the goatish, noisome wreck he had become.

In a mirror behind the painter, Styx saw himself. There sat not Raphael Styx the zombie, but Raphael Styx the man. The old Styx, with his smooth, healthy skin, his strong chin, intelligent eyes, and human energy. The deathly pallor, the sloughing of the skin, the bloodstained fluid that leaked from his mouth and nostrils, all that was gone.

"Are you quite all right?" asked Ensor with concern. "You look like you've seen a ghost."

The irony of that remark struck home. Styx's first thought was that he'd seen the very opposite of a ghost, but then he realized that the healthy, normal face in the mirror *was* in fact the ghost of a man who now existed only in the past.

"I'm fine," he said, and turned his attention from the man in the mirror to the man across the table from him.

"Then what can I tell you, worthy sir?" Ensor snapped his fingers and murmured an order to the waiter who materialized by his side. "Beauty? Truth? The meaning of life?"

"I'm not interested in the meaning of life," he said. "I want to know about death."

"Interesting," said Ensor. "Today, coincidentally, I began work on a new canvas. It's rather promising, I think, inspired by that old master Bosch's crucifixion of Christ."

Two glasses of absinthe arrived. Ensor pushed one across the table toward Styx and took a sip of the other. "I'm thinking of calling it *Masks Mocking Death*," he continued. "An *hommage*, perhaps, to Poe's 'The Masque of the Red Death.' Have you read it?"

"No," Styx admitted.

"Or perhaps *Masks Confronting Death*. I haven't decided yet if the maskers or Death himself will play the principal role."

"What's your fascination with masks?" asked Styx, feeling that he was on the cusp of discovering something vital.

"Masks, my good man, are used for concealment. But I turn that convention on its head. I paint masks that reveal the hidden truths of those who wear them. The paradox appeals to me: my masks *un*mask the emotions that lie beneath our middle-class façades."

"But what does that have to do with death?"

"It is only when we look Death in the eye that our masks fall away. What is it, after all, that we hide ourselves *from*, if not the inevitability of collapse, dissolution, and decay? When the masks are gone, what remains is the ultimate truth, our terrified plunge into the Abyss."

"When we look Death in the eye," said Styx, "what exactly do we see?"

The painter laughed enigmatically. "We see ourselves," he said. "Death is a mirror, my friend. Oscar Wilde had it right in his *Picture of Dorian Gray*. Death cannot be cheated. Man wasn't made to be immortal. We age, we sicken, we die. We fight against it—think of the medical profession—but the battle has never, will never, can never be won." Ensor sipped again from his glass. He cocked his head and examined Styx thoughtfully. "But I have the impression that my answer has not satisfied you."

"I'd like to know more," said Styx. "I'm looking for—"

He searched for the right word, and the painter tried to help him: "Inspiration?"

"A man. He sees himself as an artist. Not a painter, but a sculptor who wears the mask of Death."

James Ensor stroked his beard. "Death, of course, is ineffable, but there *are* some who believe themselves capable of assisting Him in His work. They don the appearance of Death—but make no mistake, my friend, even Death's own appearance is just another mask."

"But who are they?"

"The only advice I can give you is to take nothing at face value. The ultimate truth lies behind all the masks, beneath the surface. Truth is figurative, not literal. It is in the way the facts are presented, not the facts themselves. Why is it that some cannibalistic peoples wear wooden masks when they cook their prey? Partly to frighten their prisoners, surely, but also to hide their own primal fears."

"So you're saying that those who do Death's work are scared?"

"Of course. And that explains why they mask themselves—as we all mask ourselves to conceal our terror. But you won't learn the true identity of the man you seek by tearing his mask from his face. You must see *through* the mask to the man who hides beneath it."

Styx was still unsatisfied. He took a small sip of absinthe, which was strong and tasted of black licorice. He could see the café window from where he sat, but Delacroix wasn't there. Delacroix waited a hundred years in the future.

"I'm sorry to harp on this," Styx said, "but the man I'm looking for *literally* wears a mask."

"If he veils himself from the world's eyes, then he clearly has something to hide. A fear, a regret, a memory—who can say?"

For the first time, Styx considered the possibility that the Stuffer might be operating not out of madness, but for some explainable reason. Perhaps the mask he'd chosen to wear was there to shroud some personal lack or weakness.

"I think I'm beginning to understand," he said, and he raised his glass in a toast. He was celebrating not only a step taken in the direction of the truth, but also a glimpse of the old Styx.

"Who is this person you wish to find?" asked Ensor.

"A man without a conscience, a sacrificer of innocent lives. He not only kills his victims, but he removes their organs and fills their bodies with sand or clay."

The painter considered this as if he thought he might try to capture such a scene on canvas.

"It sounds gruesome."

"It is."

"It makes me think of the ancient Egyptians, who buried their dead surrounded by their personal possessions. I have several Egyptian funeral masks in my studio. The high priests would wash a dead pharaoh's body and remove his organs—except for the heart, which would be needed in the afterlife. The body would be filled with herbs and spices, sawdust and salt, then sewn up and wrapped in linen for the journey to the Other Side."

"Yes, I've read those stories," said Styx.

"I hope you find your man," said Ensor.

Styx stood and tossed off the rest of his absinthe.

In an earlier life, it would have dulled the pain that even now still radiated from his hip.

"One final piece of advice," Ensor said. "Be careful. Watch your back. The next mask this man wears may so nearly resemble his true appearance that you won't even realize it *is* a mask."

Styx wasn't quite sure what that meant, but he knew it would become clear to him in time. He thanked the painter in the feathered cap and headed for the door. Before he left, he turned around for one last look and saw that Ensor's own mask was back in place.

He pushed open the door and stepped outside. When he clapped the pocket watch shut, he felt his hip break and his body gnarl and molder.

CHAPTER **30**

The next morning, it took Styx almost an hour to drag himself the mile from Marc Gerard's house southwest to the office of Dr. S. Vrancken, his orthopedist, in the Dorpstraat in Mariakerke, just across the street from the historic Our Lady of the Dunes Church.

Ever since his encounter with Gino Tersago the previous evening, Styx felt his physical condition improving. He wasn't exactly reborn, not that, but he certainly felt *better*. Except for his hip, which continued to plague him.

Could gnawing on Gino have had some kind of restorative effect on him? That seemed a logical explanation—if it wasn't absurd to use the word *logic* under these conditions.

But then what about his hip?

He hesitated before the security camera's electronic eye, asking himself for the third time in as many minutes if he could really go through with this.

Unlike some doctors, Dr. Vrancken didn't have open consulting hours; he was available by appointment only. Styx didn't have an appointment, but Vrancken would hopefully agree to see him without one. He chose his moment carefully, avoiding the doctor's usual hours.

Without some relief for his hip, he didn't see how he could possibly go on. Emergency surgery and an artificial hip were probably out of the question, but he remembered what Vrancken had told him the last time they'd met:

"With a little luck, you might be able to hold out for a couple of years. I can prescribe painkillers, if you need them, and, if it gets really bad, I can give you a shot of cortisone, which takes effect within a couple of days and can help reduce the irritability of the joint. But we'll have to follow up. I want you to get an X-ray, just to be sure."

Thanks to Gino Tersago, he now knew a handy home remedy for most of the thousand natural shocks that zombie flesh turns out to be heir to, but all the long pig in the world apparently wasn't going to mend a broken hip. This puzzled him.

Cortisone, he thought. *That's the ticket.*

It was worth a shot, anyway.

Shot. Cortisone. Ha.

He pulled off the ski mask, leaned close enough to the camera lens to blur the image, and rang the bell. If the doctor didn't faint at the sight of him, maybe he'd be willing to help. If not, he'd have to force him to cooperate.

How would that work, exactly? Would he be able to overpower him? He was about ten years younger than Vrancken, and the old Raphael Styx could have taken the doctor with one hand tied behind his back. But he wasn't sure how well the new Styx would fare in a fight.

"Can I help you?" a disembodied male voice said.

"Good morning," he said carefully. "I'd like to see the doctor."

"Do you have an appointment?"

"No, I don't, but it's an emergency."

He waited for what seemed like an unusually long time, and was about to give up and walk away when the door clicked open.

A moment later Styx found himself in Dr. Vrancken's small waiting room. Whenever he had visited in the past, there were always other patients on the sofa and in the row of wooden chairs, flipping half attentively through old issues of boring magazines, and a receptionist behind the desk's sliding glass windows, but today the waiting room was completely empty.

Styx took a seat on the couch. Soft Muzak trickled through speakers. A tall cactus stood in an earthenware pot on the marble floor. The fringe on the Persian throw rug was unraveling in spots. Three rectangles on the wall were darker than the wallpaper around them, suggesting that some redecoration was in progress.

Several minutes crawled by, and Styx amused himself thinking how the expression "time stood still" takes on new meaning when you're dead. What would he do, he wondered, if Vrancken decided to call the police? There weren't really all that many options open to him.

He decided to call the police himself, fished out his phone, and punched in Delacroix's number.

"Styx?"

"Yeah."

"What happened last night? I waited for you, but you never came out of the bank."

"The café. I wasn't in there that long."

"I waited for over an hour."

"Only seemed like a couple minutes to me. I guess time works differently in the past."

"Whatever. I finally gave up and went home," said Delacroix. "I hope you're not mad."

"Uh-uh. Want to know where I am now?"

"At Ensor's house?"

"I'm in my orthopedist's waiting room."

"Jesus Christ. What are you doing there?"

"Hoping he'll give me an injection for my hip. I can't take the pain anymore."

"What's wrong with your hip? It's in worse shape than the rest of you?"

"Gotta start somewhere. An ounce of prevention's worth—"

"Prevention?" scoffed Delacroix. "You're way past that point, Inspector. There's no cure for what you've got."

"What's your problem? Get out on the wrong side of bed?"

"I've been thinking about our little adventure last night. You painted a lovely picture of what you say you saw, but I didn't see a thing."

"I'm not lying, Delacroix."

"Maybe not. But that doesn't mean what you're saying is true. I saw you walk into a bank, and that's *all* I saw. Maybe you had a spare key?"

"You think I just imagined it?"

"I'm a cop. I need facts, not stories."

"How much help have the facts been in this investigation so far?"

"About as much as your cozy little chats with dead painters. You really think they're going to help us take down the Stuffer?"

"Ensor said some things that made sense," said Styx. "But I still haven't figured it all out. The key to the whole case is right in front of me. I just can't quite get a handle on it."

"You're letting all this romantic, melancholy shit from the past distract you. But I'm keeping my eyes on the here and now, Inspector.

I'm not dead. I have to go with my brains, not some spooky 'sixth sense.' Interrogations, alibis, motives, witnesses. That's the key to this case."

There was a confidence in Delacroix's voice that Styx hadn't heard before. "I'm getting back to actual police work today," said Delacroix. "We're bringing Paul Delvaux in for further questioning."

"Paul Delvaux's got nothing to do with it," Styx told him. "Not *your* Paul Delvaux."

"Don't be so sure. He's got no alibi for the Pignot murder. And he's on the board of trustees of the art school where she was killed, so he could have had easy access to the building."

"That doesn't mean anything."

"It's *something*. You've got nothing but a few *tableaux vivants* and some hallucinations."

"Listen to me," said Styx. "Ensor said something interesting last night about masks and a possible motive for the murders. We assumed the killer's just trying to give Death a hand, but he's not."

"So what *is* he doing, then?"

"The perp's interested in resurrection, in life after death, which might explain the sand sculptures. At least, that's what I understood from Ensor. He was talking about the ancient Egyptian high priests who mummified the dead kings, and how man's not immortal and even the doctors can't—"

"And this is all going to help us catch the bastard how?"

Styx heard a door close somewhere in the office suite. "Let me know about Delvaux," he said, and broke the connection.

A voice echoed faintly in the distance, as if Dr. Vrancken was talking on his own cell phone or saying good-bye to another patient.

Styx hadn't seen the orthopedist in quite a while—their last visit had been, in a very real way, a lifetime ago. All he could remember were the surgical scrubs: no lab coat, but a blindingly white short-sleeved shirt and drawstring trousers, as if Vrancken had been modeling the latest OR fashions for a magazine spread. Oh, and a white surgical mask that hung around his neck, like a general practitioner would wear a stethoscope.

Now *that* was a true professional.

Styx waited for the door leading back to the doctor's consulting room to open.

He waited and waited, but no one came.

Was this what purgatory was? A lonely wait in an empty room and piano music floating from the office stereo?

Again he heard a voice behind the door. He seemed to recognize it. It was the same voice that had responded to his ring at the front-door bell a few minutes ago, but he was sure he'd heard it somewhere else, not long ago.

He sat bolt upright on the sofa. No, that had to be a coincidence. Over a cheap electronic intercom system, all male voices sound pretty much the same.

He remembered looking into the camera lens in the lobby of the mysterious Spilliaert's apartment building in the Hofstraat, remembered the sound of the voice that had then responded to his ring. Could that voice and this voice possibly be the same?

He struggled up from the sofa. The longer he sat, the more pain radiated from his hip down through his leg to his foot. He stepped closer to the wall and examined the rectangles of unfaded wallpaper. He couldn't remember what exactly had hung there on his previous visits, but he had a vague recollection of colorful art prints. It was one of the things that had impressed him about S. Vrancken: the doctor, he remembered thinking, had taste.

But . . . ?

What had happened to the framed pictures?

He heard a soft cough from the other side of the door, which led from the waiting room to the back of the office suite. Could that be Dr. Vrancken or his nurse coming to usher him into the consulting room? He turned away from the missing pictures and looked back and forth between the two doors. One would take him deeper into Vrancken's territory, the other would return him to the street. Which way should he go?

He was frozen to the spot, unable to move in either direction.

Something was holding him fast, refusing to permit him either to advance or retreat.

What was it?

He knew the answer had something to do with those missing pictures—and then he had it.

The Surrealists!

He remembered the doctor's confident, comforting voice, and the white surgical mask he always wore around his neck. According to James Ensor, even the absence of a mask is just another mask.

"My God," he whispered.

Man wasn't made to be immortal. We age, we sicken, we die. We fight against it—think of the medical profession—but the battle has never, will never, can never be won.

What did doctors do if not fight against death? Could it be the Stuffer lurking behind Dr. Vrancken's waiting-room door?

Had the doctor recognized him on the surveillance cam's monitor, just as he'd recognized him in the lobby of the mysterious Spilliaert's apartment building in the Hofstraat and buzzed him in?

Did one of the missing frames here in the waiting room once hold a reproduction of a painting by Léon Spilliaert?

He couldn't remember. His brain was a sieve, and he could no longer tell the difference between his memories and pure hallucination.

Styx stumbled back a few steps. He'd come here for an injection, not to confront the Stuffer. He reached for his phone and was about to call Delacroix again when some faint sound or fainter instinct warned him that S. Vrancken was shuffling about his office.

What was he doing? Styx silently turned the knob and eased the waiting-room door open. At the end of the hall, the door to the doctor's office stood ajar. He could hear someone moving around in there. There was the rustle of papers, files, reports. How much longer before the doctor came for him?

Styx retreated back through the waiting room and out to the street. Moments later he had Delacroix on the line.

"I think I've got something," he said.

But Delacroix didn't let him finish. "Us too. Delvaux's gone. Packed his bags and put his penthouse up for sale."

"What?"

"You need me to spell out for you what this means?"

"But—"

"What have *you* got?"

Styx was at a loss for words. Was he wrong? Was he losing his mind? It had all seemed so logical. But now, speaking with Delacroix, it all seemed like mere superstition and coincidence.

"Chief Inspector?"

"Yeah."

"You still there?"

"Yes."

"Good," said Delacroix. "We've put an APB out on Paul Delvaux, and we've got every available man looking for him. But there's something else."

"What?"

There was a long pause, and then Delacroix said, "Your funeral."

"What?"

"You heard me. It's official. They've announced that you're dead."

"They haven't found a body!"

"It's going to be a sort of memorial service. Burial at sea. Isabelle says that's in your will—which she found. Under the woodpile next to the fireplace, right?"

Burial at sea, Styx thought. Yes, that's what he had wanted.

He'd even specified a recording he wanted played at the service, a catchy little rock song called "Come Sail Away."

I'm sailing away, set an open course for the virgin sea . . .

Kind of a no-brainer, really. He remembered his mother playing the record for him back in the late seventies, when he was just a kid, and telling him proudly that the musicians who wrote and sang it had created it just for him. They were an American band, Mama told him, and their name, like his, was Styx.

"It's tomorrow morning," Delacroix said. "You want to go?"

CHAPTER 31

The memorial service for Chief Inspector Raphael Styx took place in the Ostend harbor, on the little square where the Kapellestraat meets the Leopold III-laan. The mayor was in attendance, as were Commissioner John Crevits, most of Styx's colleagues on the force, friends, acquaintances, and even some of Styx's rivals and enemies.

The crowd was gathered around a long box draped in a white cloth. It looked more like an altar than a coffin. Victor and Isabelle, both completely emotionless, were the first to approach the altar. Each of them laid a single red rose on the cloth.

It's like a puppet show, thought Styx, who watched the proceedings from the balcony of Joachim Delacroix's apartment. Delacroix was wearing one of his most expensive suits for the occasion: a three-piece sea-blue Hugo Boss pinstripe set off by a matching pocket square and a gold tie clip. His Borsalino hat was cocked at a somber yet somehow rakish angle.

Styx leaned on Marc Gerard's old walking stick and watched through a pair of binoculars, like a crippled king observing a military parade. He wondered how the squad had managed to organize it all so quickly.

"What are they trying to prove?" he asked.

"They're not trying to prove anything," Delacroix said patiently. "They're burying you at sea."

"But I'm standing right here. What's in the box?"

"About two hundred pounds of rock. It was Crevits's idea. We had to do something. The Stuffer called him. He said he'd stop killing if we'd turn your body over to him. He said you'd be his coup de grâce."

"So Crevits set up this charade just to piss him off? Or does he think the bastard might actually turn up? To watch, or to try to stop the show?"

"What they *don't* want," Delacroix said, "is to let him think he's got the upper hand. Crevits made it absolutely clear: we don't make deals with serial killers. So we're mounting this performace to show him he can't have what he wants." He smiled. "We're doing a nice job, aren't we? The only thing missing's a choir."

"Are Isabelle and Victor in on it?"

Delacroix's smile disappeared. "They know you're not in the box," he said. "But they don't know *why* we're doing it. I think Isabelle assumes it's all for her benefit, to give her some sense of closure."

There were several police vehicles parked on the *Mercator* side of the Kapellestraat, but it wasn't clear if they were intended as a sort of honor guard or if they were there in case the Stuffer put in an appearance.

As six uniformed officers loaded the box onto a small boat tied up at quayside, the first notes of a song began to play through the speakers that had been set up for the event. Despite the specific instructions Styx had left, it wasn't "Come Sail Away." Instead, he heard the lilting wail of Van Morrison:

Beside the garden walls, / We walk in haunts of ancient peace.

Styx had to admit that the song fit the occasion well.

"Who picked the music?" he asked.

"Isabelle."

Her name floated away on the salt breeze.

"Where are they taking me?" Styx finally asked.

"Out there," Delacroix said, pointing north to the sea.

"Isn't that what they did with Osama bin Laden?"

"I don't think they made such a big show of it," Delacroix pointed out.

Through the field glasses, Styx watched John Crevits and a few of Isabelle's relatives step forward to offer comfort to his son and wife—his widow.

"Shit, this almost makes *me* want to cry," Styx said.

The boat pulled away from the dock as Van Morrison's voice faded. It swung out of sight around the sharp bend that would take it out into open water, and the crowd gradually dispersed.

Styx focused the binoculars on his son, standing there stoically with an arm around his mother's waist. He was proud of the boy's strength, yet he wished he could assure him that his father wasn't really gone, not entirely.

Styx swallowed uncomfortably. "You think he showed?" he croaked.

"Who?"

"Who the fuck do you think?"

"The Stuffer?"

"Yes, the goddamn Stuffer! He must have heard about it, right? I mean, that was Crevits's whole point?"

"Paul Delvaux is probably long gone, but maybe." Delacroix pulled off his Borsalino. "You think he'd have the balls?"

"Why not? We aren't even sure Paul's our guy. The Stuffer could be anyone."

"It'd make sense he'd want a front-row seat."

"I know one thing," Styx said. "If it were me, *I'd* be there."

A man stood on the deck of the Mercator, *the famous ship that had* brought the mortal remains of Father Damien, "the Apostle of the Lepers," back from Hawaii to Belgium. He had no interest in touring the ship. He'd bought an admission ticket only because it provided him with an almost perfect view of the policeman's funeral service. If it really *was* a funeral service.

He knew better than to show up at the quay, although he was confident that no one would recognize him. On the prow of the three-master, he felt safe enough to relax and enjoy the festivities: the eulogies, the poem read tonelessly by the tight-lipped little son, the oh-so-touching send-off ballad by that crabby Irishman Van Morrison.

What was going on here? What exactly were they up to?

The idea of consigning Raphael Styx's body to the sea simply made no sense. He had of course been following the case with intense scrutiny, and nowhere in the media—not in the papers, not on the radio or television, not on the internet—had there been any mention of the dead cop's body having been discovered.

There would *have* to be some sort of announcement if a missing person was found, wouldn't there? Dead or alive, it wouldn't matter, the news of such a find would be news indeed.

He didn't understand it.

And not understanding it made him angry.

Because he knew Raphael Styx wasn't dead. He'd seen him, still alive, with his own two eyes.

Delacroix said, "Crevits thinks the funeral will force the Stuffer back out in the open, whether or not he actually shows up for the ceremony."

"He won't be able to stand all the attention focused on something other than himself, you mean?"

"That's the idea."

They were sitting in one of the eight theaters in the Kinepolis multiplex. Every September, the Ensors—the Belgian Oscars—were held here, but this week the complex was hosting a retrospective of the films of Ken Russell. On the screen, Russell's 1986 *Gothic* was playing, and the poet Percy Shelley, his novelist-wife Mary, Lord Byron, and Byron's lover, Claire Clairmont, were gathered around a human skull before a roaring hearth in the huge main hall of an English castle.

Byron ripped open his shirt, so close to the fire that he was in danger of immolating himself. The flames cast menacing shadows of his body on the wall.

But Styx wasn't interested in the movie.

"I want you to do something for me," he whispered.

"Sure," said Delacroix.

"I want you to get a list of Dr. S. Vrancken's patients."

"Vrancken? Your orthopedic guy?"

"I want to check a few names."

"The man's a doctor, Styx. What's on your mind?"

"You ever heard of Dr. Jekyll and Mr. Hyde? I was at his office yesterday, like I told you, and I did a little research after I left."

"And?"

Styx began with some background. The rectangles on the waiting-room wall, the déjà vu similarity between the voices over the two intercoms. "And I found out," he went on, "that Vrancken lost his medical license not too long after he advised me to hold off on a hip replacement and right before the Stuffer's first killing. Officially, his practice is closed. That's why there were no other patients there yesterday, and no receptionist or nurse."

"Why'd they pull his license?"

"He was accused of malpractice. He's under investigation for negligence and medical errors."

"What sort of errors?"

On the screen, a Venetian mask was carefully fitted over the face of one of the women. Styx leaned closer to Delacroix. "Two of his surgical patients complained to the commission."

"Who? Don't tell me they were two of the Stuffer's victims?"

"No, but I'd really like to know if any of the dead women ever consulted the good doctor."

"What were the complaints?"

"I found an article that said he apparently left a medical instrument inside one patient's body. In the other case, there was severe internal hemorrhaging as a result of unsterile operating conditions."

Delacroix considered this. Finally, he turned away from the screen and said, "So?"

"So?"

"So what does that have to do with the Stuffer? Those cases prove the good doctor's a bad doctor, not a homicidal maniac."

Styx got up and walked out of the theater. Delacroix followed him.

"Look," Styx said, "you don't have to agree with me. Just get me the patient list."

"Those records are confidential. I—"

"He didn't just have a private practice, Delacroix. He was also on staff at the Damiaan Hospital."

"Which is important why?"

"Just listen to me. He saw some of his patients at his office—that was mostly people who could afford his private rates. His hospital patients were less well off. And the Stuffer's victims weren't exactly rolling in it."

"So you want the hospital list, not the private-practice list, I get it. But I still don't know how you expect me to *get* it."

"Don't play dumb. You know Isabelle works at Damiaan."

"Oh, come on, Inspector. She won't—"

"Then figure something else out. Go back and talk to the murdered women's families and friends. You're a cop, remember? Check their appointment books, their medical histories, their bank statements. I want to know if any of them ever saw Dr. Vrancken."

He turned away and hobbled off, then changed his mind and brought his dilapidated body to a halt.

"I want to rip off the fucking mask," he said.

CHAPTER 32

Although the memorial service had been tiring, and although Isabelle Gerard had been offered a week's compassionate leave by her supervisor, she went to the hospital that evening to work her usual overnight shift in the geriatric ward. There was no way she'd be able to sleep. She didn't like leaving Victor home alone, but he'd insisted he was fine to spend the evening by himself. They were so much alike in that regard—each of them respected the other's need to process the funeral in their own separate ways.

There was a fruit basket and a collection of sympathy cards in the fourth-floor canteen. From ten to ten thirty she was kept busy delivering cups of yogurt and glasses of water to her elderly patients. Then things began to settle down and by midnight the ward was quiet. The last medications had been administered, and the corridors were empty. Except for dealing with the one old codger with Alzheimer's who jabbed his call button every ten minutes to demand she put the dentures he'd just fished out of the glass of water on his side table back into the glass of water on his side table, there was really nothing to do.

In the lull between denture calls, she sat in the canteen and reread Victor's last two texts:

Tired, Mom. Going 2 sleep. Think I'm set 4 tomorrow. Night!

And then:

Oh, don't forget 2 wake me when U come home. Want to study a little more b4 school.

This was the first time Victor had texted her since his exams had begun. Until now, he'd sat up till three or four AM, cramming like a university student pulling an all-nighter, but the events of the day had turned him back into a thirteen-year-old who needed the assurance of his mother before he drifted off to sleep.

OK, she typed, hoping he was already dreaming, will do. Proud of you. Sleep tight. xoxoxo

She was still holding the phone in her hands when the light on the nurses' station call panel flashed. Someone was buzzing for her. Yawning, she checked the panel and saw that, for once, it wasn't Mr. Alzheimer's. This time the call had come from the room next to his, number fourteen.

Isabelle got up and started down the hall. At the far end, she saw Francine—another of the night nurses—transferring soiled bedsheets from a wheeled cart to the laundry chute. The fluorescent corridor lights were dimmed, and the weak illumination made the ward seem small and claustrophobic.

The door to room fourteen stood ajar. She eased it open noiselessly and slipped into the darkened room. The figure in the bed lay hidden beneath his top sheet. He'd probably peed himself and felt ashamed of his incontinence; that happened all the time.

She gently pulled back the sheet and saw, instead of a body, two pillows plumped into humanesque shape. She spun around, suddenly frightened.

Many times in her career as a nurse she'd found an empty bed where she'd expected a patient. Sometimes a disoriented elderly soul had simply gone for a nighttime constitutional, sometimes he was playing peekaboo behind the door. Once or twice the callboard had simply gone haywire, the wrong room's light had flashed, and the room she entered was empty, its previous occupant discharged or deceased.

But why the pillows? And why did she have the feeling that the room was not as empty as it seemed?

"Looking for me?" came a voice from the darkness.

Isabelle grabbed the bed's side rail. Someone was sitting in one of the two visitors' chairs, silhouetted against the curtained window.

"I'm sorry I startled you," said the man.

"Who are you?"

She wanted to reach for the nearest light switch, to give the stranger a face, but he stood up slowly, almost nonchalantly, and wagged a finger at her as if he'd read her thoughts. He took a step closer, and now she could make out the surgical mask that concealed his nose, mouth, and chin from sight.

What happened next happened without warning. In one sudden movement the man's right arm wrapped around her throat and cut off her breath. With his other hand, he clapped something to her mouth. Another mask?

The stink of chloroform filled her nostrils. She struggled against the drug, but resistance was futile.

"Shhh," the voice said. "You don't want to bother the others, do you?"

She felt consciousness drain from her body.

Her last thought was of Victor. Without her to wake him up, he would lose precious hours of study time.

"Sleep tight, Isabelle," the voice whispered. "Sweet dreams."

Transporting the unconscious Isabelle Gerard from the fourth floor of the Damiaan Hospital down to his waiting car was simple. It was the middle of the night, and all the Stuffer had to do was wait a few minutes for the other nurse, with her fake smile and her high voice, to get out of the way. He lay Isabelle on room fourteen's wheeled bed, covered her with the top sheet, rolled her down the corridor to the elevator, and pressed the button for the underground garage. Conveniently, it was Isabelle's job to keep an eye on the ward in case of after-hours trouble.

When he stretched her out on the backseat of the Santa Fe, snoring peacefully, and was on his way home—his *real* home, not the Hofstraat apartment he'd rented under Léon Spilliaert's name—he decided that Isabelle Gerard would have to be dealt with differently. It was pointless to kill her and stuff her, like the others. What purpose would that serve? No, she was a means to an end, not the end itself. He didn't like deviating from his original plan, but sometimes a creative artist has to take detours in order to reach his destination.

No, he wouldn't harm a hair on her pretty little head. All he had to do was lock her up and keep her where he put her.

An hour later, seated at his computer, he was still wearing the surgical mask. He no longer needed to conceal his identity, but in all the excitement, he'd simply forgotten to remove it.

He created a brand-new Gmail address—*s.t.u.ff.e.r@gmail.com*—then went to Facebook. When prompted to select a category for his new page, he studied the options on the drop-down menu and, chuckling, selected "News Personality."

The Stuffer, he typed, and hesitated, his fingers poised above the keyboard, searching for the right words to update his status.

> The Stuffer will present his fifth and most important sculpture, Isabelle Gerard, to the world within the next 24 hours unless the remains of Raphael Styx are turned over to him for his sole and exclusive use.

He read the paragraph three times. A nice little teaser, a preview of coming attractions. They'd certainly have to acknowledge that he was sticking to his principles.

He clicked Post.

*Styx sat alone in Marc Gerard's room. After watching a throng of peo*ple who, frankly, hadn't much liked him gather to wish him Godspeed on his journey to Valhalla, Styx wished he could sleep. The boring thing about being dead was that you didn't need to sleep. That had seemed like a blessing at first, but by now he was sick of it. There was nothing to distract him from his growing hunger.

Styx had always relished his dreams. Some people resented the idea of sleeping away a third of their lives, but he wasn't one of them. He missed the nightly opportunity to set aside the weight of the world and lose himself in another reality, a dreamworld in which he might be reunited with Isabelle and Victor and the fucking Stuffer had been stuffed into a prison cell once and for all. Or, better yet, a world in which the serial killer had never existed in the first place.

But now he'd settled in at Marc Gerard's old computer to see what the real world had to say about his memorial. Like a voyeur spying on his own existence, he visited Victor's Facebook page and read his son's latest status update:

Victor Styx
History is deathly boring!

The comment had already garnered ten Likes, mostly from classmates who were themselves wrestling with the ancient Greeks and Romans. For once he had to agree with his son: history *was* boring, as boring as death.

He clicked over to Isabelle's page and saw that she hadn't posted anything since his disappearance. Not surprising. Isabelle was a private person. She was always ready to help others through their trying times, but she believed in keeping her own miseries to herself. A typical nurse.

He was about to shut down the computer and pick up a book when a new message appeared on Isabelle's page.

It wasn't Isabelle doing the typing, though.

Her account had been hacked by the Stuffer.

And the words that unspooled across the screen were so horrifying that Styx thought at first he must have misread them.

The Stuffer's next masterpiece will be displayed under the title "Isabelle Gerard."

"No," Styx heard himself whisper. "Oh, Jesus, no."

He read it again and again, but the words didn't change.

He pushed away from the computer and grabbed his stick and headed painfully for the door.

An old, familiar sensation burned within him.

It wasn't hunger this time, but it would lead to the same result.

CHAPTER **33**

For the second time in thirty-six hours Styx turned into the Dorp-straat in Mariakerke and headed for S. Vrancken's office, right across the street from Our Lady of the Dunes Church, where James Ensor was buried.

It was a little after four AM, but this time he didn't hesitate to ring the bell. It echoed hollowly on the other side of the door, and Styx felt again that same sense of déjà vu, though this time he doubted the doctor was peering out at him through his security cam. As he waited for a response, his eye came to rest on the brass plaque mounted beside the door above a close-cropped boxwood hedge:

Dr. S. Vrancken, Orthopedics

Styx realized he had no idea what the S stood for. Simon? Sander?

In all the months he'd known the doctor, he'd never heard the man's first name mentioned.

Stefan? Samuel?

He must have seen it when he'd done his online research, but he couldn't for the life of him—shit, strike that. He couldn't remember what the hell it *was*.

He hadn't heard footsteps, but suddenly the door was thrown open.

The last few weeks had aged S. Vrancken. He was thinner, more sinewy, less kempt. The gray beard stubble failed to make him look distinguished. Instead, it gave him the air of a hobo. He looked at Styx and could not utter a word.

"Surprised to see me, are you?"

"It—it's impossible!"

"And yet it's true."

"My God, I never could have imagined this," Vrancken said. "Even if I'd dared to imagine it, I never could have believed it."

"And yet," said Styx.

"And yet, indeed. Is it really you, Chief Inspector?"

"In the rotting flesh."

"My God," the doctor breathed again.

"I'm not sure He had anything to do with it."

"But—how?"

"Not important," said Styx. "I'm here for answers, not questions."

He wanted to grab the man by the throat and choke Isabelle's whereabouts out of him, but he wasn't sure he was strong enough to prevail in a physical fight and figured his best chance of saving her was to outmaneuver Vrancken, rather than outman him.

"What happened the other day?" he asked. "I heard you back there, but you didn't come out."

"I couldn't," said the Stuffer.

"Why not?"

"I killed you, Styx. I shot you. You were *dead*. When I saw you through the videophone, I thought my mind must be playing tricks on me. You looked like something out of a horror film." He stared at the gruesome specter that faced him. "I must still be hallucinating."

" 'Fraid not."

"You're supposed to be dead."

"But here we are," said Styx.

"Indeed. You look awful."

"What can I say? Whatever I am, you made me, Doc."

"I don't under—"

"Cut the bullshit." Talking was taking too long. He might not be able to fight Vrancken, but he could surprise him. He found a well of untapped strength within himself and shoved Vrancken against the wall, and the putrescence that rose from his body swirled around them. "Where is she?"

"I haven't hurt her," said the doctor. "She's fine."

"Where is she!" Styx screamed. He clenched Marc Gerard's walking stick in his arborescent hands and pressed the wood deep into the flesh of Vrancken's neck, cutting off his air.

"I'm a doctor," Vrancken gasped. "I *help* people."

"Sure you do," Styx growled, putting all his weight onto the cane.

"Like I helped you . . ."

"Ask Reinhilde Debels and Elisa Wouters and Madeleine Bohy and Heloise Pignot what they thought of your help. You cut their throats and sawed off their heads and stabbed them to death and ripped out their organs and stuffed them full of sand. I bet they were thrilled to have your help."

"Or clay," Vrancken gagged, barely able to form the words. "I used clay for the last one."

As if he realized the absurdity of this remark, he looked at Styx again in hopeless silence. And as the horror sank in, he let out an inhuman scream, like an animal on its way to the slaughterhouse.

"Why?" Styx demanded. "What did any of them do to you? Were they patients? Were they filing more complaints against you?"

The doctor tried to respond, but the pressure on his neck made speech impossible. Styx backed off a fraction of an inch, and Vrancken coughed weakly. "They were on my list," he wheezed, "waiting for surgery. One of them needed spinal fusion, two needed knee replacements, and one a hip, just like you."

"And the model?"

"I was making a statement. I couldn't let that toad in the newspapers take my place."

"So what went wrong?"

"Wrong? Nothing. I never touched them. I couldn't—the medical board pulled my license. I was a surgeon for twenty-five years. I helped hundreds of people—and then I made two little mistakes, and those pompous bastards told me I couldn't help any more."

"So you killed them instead?"

"Their lives were over. Just like yours was over, Styx. Without me, all they had left to look forward to was pain. Pain, and the pity of others. I saved them from that. I *saved* them!"

"They could have found another doctor," Styx snarled.

But Vrancken didn't seem to hear him. "We've become a throwaway society," he explained hoarsely, earnestly, his hands fisted on the walking stick now, pushing back against Styx's pressure. "We build computers and cars and appliances *not* to last, so every five years you need the newest model. Even if they were healed, they would have died eventually. Five years from now, fifty years from now. It's all the same. Forgotten by society. But I gave them new life, I turned them into works of art this city will remember forever."

"You're insane," said Styx. "You're worse than me, you sick monster.

There are plenty of surgeons. Those people didn't have to die." And then he remembered. "*I* didn't have to die!"

"You did! You were . . ."

Styx looked at him. "What do you mean?"

"You didn't get my message on your voice mail?"

"The police have my phone."

"Then you don't know," Vrancken breathed. "You poor son of a bitch, you have no idea."

"What are you talking about?"

"Your X-rays. Your hip. The results weren't pretty."

"I don't—"

"It's not just arthritis, Styx. It's—"

"Stop it!"

"It's cancer. All over your bones and body."

And now Styx knew why his hip still hurt, even though the attack on Tersago had brought him such relief.

He'd suspected it all along.

"You were dead, Styx. Even *before* you died. Even before I did you the favor of killing you."

Styx remained silent.

"Don't you see? You were terminal, man! Ready to die! All I did was pull the trigger. I told you: I'm a doctor, not a murderer." S. Vrancken's brow furrowed, and the corners of his mouth turned up in a sheepish smile. "You weren't part of the plan," he admitted. "But look at the way it's worked out! Be honest: Would you really go back to your old life if you could? Aren't you better off like this?"

"Cut the shit, doctor. I'm asking you one more time: Where's Isabelle?" He threw all his weight against the stick, crushing it against Vrancken's windpipe.

"She's here!" he gasped. "I'll take you to her!"

Yet again, Styx let up.

"But do you really want her to see you like this?" the Stuffer panted. "Hasn't she been through enough? Do you actually think she'll want you back?"

The bastard. But it was a question that had to be answered.

"I'm not here to get her back," Styx said. "I'm here to set her free—from both of us."

"A noble sentiment," said Vrancken. "I'm telling you, Styx, I made you a better man than you were. I wish you'd—"

"Shut up," he commanded. "One more word and I'll—"

"You'll what? Believe me, Styx, without me you'll never find her." He made a last desperate gamble. "If I take you to her, will you let me go? I'll leave Ostend, you'll never hear from me again. Give me twenty-four hours, Styx."

A long minute passed.

And then Styx stepped back, and Vrancken sank to his knees, his hands massaging his damaged throat.

"Let's go," said Styx, tapping the metal fish at the grip end of his cane impatiently.

The doctor struggled to his feet. He opened the door that led back to his office, and Styx limped after him. Halfway down the hallway Vrancken stopped at another door. Behind it was a storage closet or a consulting room, and somewhere in there was his poor Isabelle. He dreaded the thought of her horrified reaction when she laid eyes on him. But once he'd gotten her away from the Stuffer, he would leave her to her future.

"It's dark in there," Vrancken said. "I'll have to get the light."

"Just do it," Styx spat.

The door creaked open, the doctor's hand slipped inside and felt around for the switch.

And came out holding a shotgun. He swung it into firing position, both barrels pointed straight at Styx's already bullet-riddled chest.

"I wasn't lying," the doctor said, as matter-of-factly as if he were offering a diagnosis to a new patient. "She's here, and she's unharmed. But I'm afraid you won't be seeing her. You and I have unfinished business to conclude."

Styx backed away. All he had to defend himself was his father-in-law's old stick.

"It's a shame about the buckshot," sighed Vrancken. "It'll do a *lot* of damage. But I suppose it'll just make the final statue even more surreal."

He welded his cheek to the stock and closed an eye.

There was nowhere for Styx to run, even if his hip would *let* him move any faster than an old man's hobble.

But what choice did he have? He'd taken three bullets already, but he wasn't sure he'd survive another one.

He turned and stumped back up the hallway, through the empty waiting room and out the door, expecting at any moment the blast that would blow his crumbling body to tatters.

Styx splashed through rain puddles and across the Dorpstraat and dodged around the side of the church. He could hear S. Vrancken behind him, but still the gun didn't fire.

The noise. Of course. If Vrancken pulled the trigger, the explosion would bring the neighbors—and the police.

Styx staggered through the sucking mud and pouring rain as fast as his limbs would carry him.

And the blackness of Our Lady of the Dunes' graveyard swallowed him whole.

CHAPTER 34

Styx didn't have a chance. He made what headway he could across the swampy ground, pursued by an even more horrible monster than he himself had become, but there was no escape.

His hip gave way, and the muddy grass wrapped him in a wet embrace. Flailing helplessly, he rolled onto a square of canvas staked out on the ground. It pulled loose beneath his weight, and he almost tumbled into an empty grave, just managing to stop himself at the edge of the open pit.

He drove Marc Gerard's stick into the ground and hauled himself erect, but the mud sucked at his feet and held him there, imprisoned, a scarecrow in the night. He couldn't even turn around to face the shotgun's blast when it finally came. In this downpour he knew the Stuffer would no longer hesitate to pull the trigger: the storm would swallow the double blast as easily as the wet dirt had swallowed his feet.

There was a rumble of thunder, and a bolt of lightning streaked across the sky.

In the few brief seconds of illumination it gave him Styx saw a brick catafalque supporting a concrete coffin, with bronze letters on the end closest to him reading

BARON JAMES ENSOR
1860–1949

"Styx!" The doctor's voice tore a hole in the night, and the moon came out from behind the clouds to reveal S. Vrancken standing over him in majestic silence, the shotgun pointed directly at his head.

"A perfect pose," the doctor smiled. "And the perfect location for my next exhibit."

Styx stood there next to the grave, frozen by the mud—and by fear.

"There are so many things I want to ask you," Vrancken said conversationally. "What's it like, there on the Other Side? Is it as terrible as they say—or as wonderful? How did it feel to be given a second chance at life these last few days?"

He set the gun's recoil pad against his shoulder, laid his cheek to the stock, and closed his left eye.

"Seems like old times, Chief Inspector. You remember our last encounter on the beach?"

"I remember," said Styx.

"You're awfully calm for a man staring eternity in the eye."

"Been there," Styx said simply. "Done that."

"I suppose we mortals can get used to anything. Even death."

The walking stick was hidden from Vrancken's view by the wall of the freshly dug grave. Styx tightened his grip on its copper head. The mud had shifted beneath his weight and there was a chance he might be able to work himself loose.

He wriggled his foot, felt the mud fight back but grudgingly release its hold. He took a painful half step forward.

And Dr. S. Vrancken, orthopedic surgeon, pulled the trigger.

The blast took Styx in the face, punched a dozen tiny holes in his throat, and ripped away half his jaw. Rotting flesh and bone fragments flew in all directions. But Raphael Styx stayed on his feet.

His left foot came free of the sucking mud, and he took another step. Vrancken's head snapped up in shock. He took fresh aim and unloosed the other barrel. This time the buckshot hit Styx full in the chest. He jerked back, then shook off the impact and staggered onward. There was no blood—all his blood had dried up long before.

Supported by Marc Gerard's cane Styx walked toward the doctor.

Vrancken fumbled in his pocket for fresh shells but dropped them. He fell to his hands and knees and scrabbled for them in the mud.

Lightning flashed again, and Vrancken looked up to see the monster he'd created towering above him. He turned frantically from side to side, searching for an escape route, but it was too late.

"No!" he screamed. "For God's sake, no!"

And with every remnant of his remaining strength, Styx swung the copper fish at the side of the Stuffer's head.

There was no need for a second blow.

The serial killer lay motionless at his feet. He was breathing, Styx saw, but it would be a good long while before he would return to consciousness.

Styx tipped his head back and let the rain wash his devastated face. A roll of thunder growled in the distance.

No, he realized, this time it wasn't thunder.

This time it was his stomach.

The animal hunger had returned.

He should get away now, before he could no longer resist the urge to feed. If he gave in, he knew his shattered jaw and the fresh wounds in his chest would quickly begin to heal.

But he also knew the old legends, knew that a zombie's bite would zombify the bitten one.

He had no idea if those stories were true, but could he take the chance of granting the Stuffer eternal life after death? Did the doctor deserve the same second chance Styx had received?

No, no, no.

Something deep inside him, deeper even than the ravening hunger, warned him not to open that door.

Half an hour later Styx plodded laboriously back across the church-yard's marshy terrain. He crossed the deserted Dorpstraat and let himself into S. Vrancken's office with the keys he'd taken from the unconscious doctor's pocket. He was drenched and sodden and steaming, but he didn't waste time trying to dry himself. He flung open every door he could find, till he came to the very last of them, at the far end of the hall. Painted on it in delicate script was the word *Lavatory*.

He stood there, still dripping, and stared at that final door. No sound came from behind it, but he knew she was in there. He could feel her presence. Vrancken had boasted that he would never find her, but that had been nothing but a bluff.

There was an old-fashioned keyhole set below the knob. All he had to do was turn the right key, and he could set her free.

Or would showing her what he had become only sentence her to a more permanent prison?

"Hello?"

The voice was so faint he thought at first he'd imagined it.

"Is somebody there?"

It was her voice.

She was alive.

"Please," she whimpered. "Let me out."

Styx swallowed painfully. The compulsion to throw open the door and gather her into his arms was almost overwhelming, stronger even than the hunger he'd felt in the graveyard.

But he fought against it just as hard.

He stood there, separated from her by an inch of wood and paint, and listened to her piteous crying.

He touched the golden key with a rotting finger.

How many times had he stood like this in their home, him on the outside of the bathroom door and her on the inside, weeping, avoiding him, protecting herself from him because he'd stumbled home drunk or high or both and she couldn't handle the sight of his pathetic, idiotic face?

"Can you hear me?" the voice behind the door pleaded. "Please help me. Let me out!"

How many times had he locked *himself* in their bathroom, with Isabelle on the outside pounding her fists against the door in frustrated fury, afraid to let her see what some gangster had done to him when he couldn't pay his gambling debts, his face streaked with tears and the residue of coke?

"I won't tell," Isabelle promised, more loudly now. "I swear it. I won't make any trouble for you."

Nor I for you, Styx decided.

He laid what was left of his head gently against the door. Eyes closed, he stood there and listened for one last moment to the sweet sound of her voice. He pressed his blackened lips to the door in a final kiss, and then he turned and went up the hall and through the waiting room and out of the building.

He took his cell phone from his pocket and pressed the speed-dial button he'd programmed.

"Who the fuck is *this*?" the person at the other end of the line shrieked, his voice clotted with a mélange of terror and fury.

"Who the fuck do you *think* it is?" said Styx calmly, despite the agony of having had half his jaw blown away.

"Styx? Is that you? You have to get me out of here!"

"Why?"

"It's—it's inhuman!"

"That sounds about right."

"You've got to get me out of here, Styx, before it's too late."

"It's already too late."

"Then why did you leave me my phone?"

"Call a friend," Styx suggested. "Call the cops."

"You know I can't do that. If they find me—"

"If they find you, they'll put you away for the rest of your life. It's too damn bad we don't have the death penalty, or they'd hang your sorry ass."

The silence between them stretched out for a very long time.

"Good-bye," Styx whispered at last.

But he didn't disconnect the call. He was in horrible pain, and the killer's helpless voice at the other end of the line was a bandage for his wounds. He closed his eyes and relished the memory of rolling the Stuffer's unconscious body into the open grave he himself had almost fallen into.

"Don't say good-bye," the Stuffer begged. "It's not too late. You can still save me."

"I'd save my breath, if I were you."

In his mind, Styx saw Vrancken stretched out in the open hole, his face exposed to the stars that peeked out from behind the storm clouds evaporating overhead.

It would have taken Styx five seconds to reload the shotgun, half a second to pull the trigger, and—death penalty or no death penalty—Ostend would be free of the Stuffer's depredations at last.

But he couldn't do it.

The old Raphael Styx had many times taken the law into his own hands. But, zombie or no zombie, the new Styx was just a cop, not a judge, not an executioner.

So he tossed the phone he'd found in Vrancken's pocket with his keys into the hole with him, draped the square of canvas over him to keep the dirt out of his mouth and eyes and provide him with a pocket of air, and began to fill in the hole.

He would rescue Isabelle, he decided, and Vrancken could decide his fate for himself. He could turn himself in or suffer worse consequences.

Now Vrancken's voice roused him from his reverie.

"At least I didn't bury them alive," he howled. "I showed them some compassion, you cocksucker! I didn't just abandon them to choke to death!"

"I bet your battery's almost dead. If you're gonna call the cops, Doc, now's the time."

"Fuck you, you bastard!"

He heard the doctor's light, rapid panting and wondered what it must feel like to be buried alive, not even in a coffin, nothing but a thin layer of canvas protecting you from your fate.

"Hey," Styx said, "I almost forgot. What does the S stand for?"

But there was no response.

He hung up and dialed Delacroix's number and told him where Isabelle was. He did *not* tell him about the Stuffer.

They'd find the body in a few hours, when the funeral party showed up at the churchyard and discovered that their loved one's grave was already in use.

CHAPTER **35**

It was not quite dawn. The man in the cap shambled along the side of the highway through a warm drizzle, supporting himself on an old walking stick with a grip in the shape of a fish.

There was little traffic at this hour. When he felt the headlights on his back and heard the crunch of tires slowing on the gravel shoulder, he turned into the glare.

The car stopped beside him, its motor still running. The window on the passenger's side slid down. Raindrops pattered on the roof.

Joachim Delacroix sat behind the wheel, dressed in Versace from head to foot. He leaned over and opened the passenger door. "Need a lift?"

Styx backed into the seat, used the walking stick as a lever to hoist first one leg, then the other from the ground. Delacroix watched him without comment. When Styx was settled, he released the hand brake and rolled back out onto the road.

"Where is he?" Delacroix said.

"Who?"

"Jesus, you know who."

"You'll find him," Styx said. "Soon, I think. Probably within the next couple of hours. He won't give you any trouble."

"So it *was* Vrancken, then?"

"What difference does it make? You'll find out when the time comes."

"You don't want to know how she's doing?" asked Delacroix.

Styx didn't answer.

"Except for the shock," the rookie said, "she's fine."

"What did you find in Vrancken's office?"

"I have no idea. They were turning it upside down when I left to take Isabelle home."

"It doesn't matter," said Styx. "The case is closed. There won't be any more killings."

They drove on.

"So why did Paul Delvaux put his penthouse up for sale and take off?" Styx asked.

"If he ever comes back, I'll ask him."

"You're not still looking for him?"

"Why should we? He's a weirdo, but as far as we know he hasn't actually done anything *wrong*. You want my opinion, Ostend's better off without him." Delacroix smiled. "Maybe *that's* why he ran off. Ostend's changed. Maybe he's gone off in search of the Ostend of a hundred years ago."

A comfortable silence filled the space between them.

"So what now?" asked Delacroix at last.

"Just drive."

"Where do you want to go?"

"Away," Styx said. "Out of Ostend. That's all I know right now."

Delacroix drove on. The only sound in the car was the rhythmic swish of the wipers.

After a while, Styx spoke. "That Lord Byron guy?"

"The sapeur of the Romantics? What about him?"

"He spent his whole adult life on the run, moving from country to country, running away from his debts, from the women he betrayed. I think that might be *my* future, too."

Delacroix turned inland, away from the sea and the faded glory of Ostend.

Raphael Styx sat beside him, staring straight ahead but not at the rain or the highway lights that flickered by. He was looking beyond an invisible wall to a new world he couldn't quite see, let alone understand.

Delacroix glanced at Styx.

He saw the shattered jaw, the pellet holes in the throat, the gaping chest wound. The liquefied eyes, the purge fluid leaking from nose and ears and mouth, the sloughing of the skin, the misshapen hands clasping and unclasping the handle of the battered old cane. He saw the sad, discolored face, a face that had seen things no one else had ever seen, things no one else should ever have to see.

When the silence grew impossible to stand, Delacroix switched on the car radio. Massive Attack's "Unfinished Sympathy" was playing, and it provided a soundtrack for the two men's completely different lines of thought.

Joachim Delacroix thought of Isabelle, while Raphael Styx could think of nothing but the terrible hunger that gnawed at his gut.

He tried to distract himself. Was Victor finished with his exams? How would Isabelle remember him? Would the old Rafe Styx ever have changed his ways, if he'd been given the chance?

But the hunger could not be denied. It grew more insistent with every passing mile. He could smell fresh meat beneath Delacroix's aftershave and deodorant, and feel his deepest, most inhuman instincts well up within him. He fought desperately to contain them, clenching his rotten teeth, almost biting his own tongue.

He turned away, saw his face reflected in the side-view mirror, lit briefly each time they passed beneath a lamppost.

It was a long and lonely ride on the highway. The rain intensified, hell's floodgates opening wide.

Delacroix asked him something, but Styx had just cranked up the stereo and couldn't hear the question beneath Massive Attack's hypnotic percussion and Shara Nelson's soulful vocals:

. . . a soul without a mind,
In a body without a heart,
I'm missing every part . . .

AUTHORS' NOTE

Styx is a work of fiction, and the characters and incidents are the products of the authors' imaginations.

Paul Delvaux, James Ensor, René Magritte, and Léon Spilliaert were all real people, and all of them lived and worked in Ostend at various periods of their lives. Marvin Gaye was a real person, too, and he spent about a year in Ostend in the early 1980s.